The Soultrapper

Stanislava Buevich

A gift from Kelly Lacey

Enjoy your book! Please use invite collab with the handles in our kit for your book mail posts. Have a great tour! From Kelly Lacey

Gift note included with **The Soultrapper**: a virtual reality escape room mystery for teenagers

Copyright © 2024 by Stanislava Buevich

All rights reserved.

No portion of this book may be reproduced in any form without written permission from the publisher or author.

Contents

Dedication	1
1. One	3
2. Two	17
3. Three	26
4. Four	41
5. Five	56
6. Six	65
7. Seven	75
8. Eight	85
9. Nine	96
10. Ten	104
11. Eleven	111
12. Twelve	119
13. Thirteen	132
14. Fourteen	139

15.	Fifteen	148
16.	Sixteen	158
17.	Seventeen	170
18.	Eighteen	183
19.	Nineteen	189
20.	Twenty	197
21.	Twenty-One	210
22.	Twenty-Two	217
23.	Twenty-Three	230
24.	Twenty-Four	239
25.	Twenty-Five	249
26.	Twenty-Six	257
27.	Twenty-Seven	267
28.	Twenty-Eight	275
29.	Twenty-Nine	285
30.	Epilogue	299
	Acknowledgements	305
	About the author	306

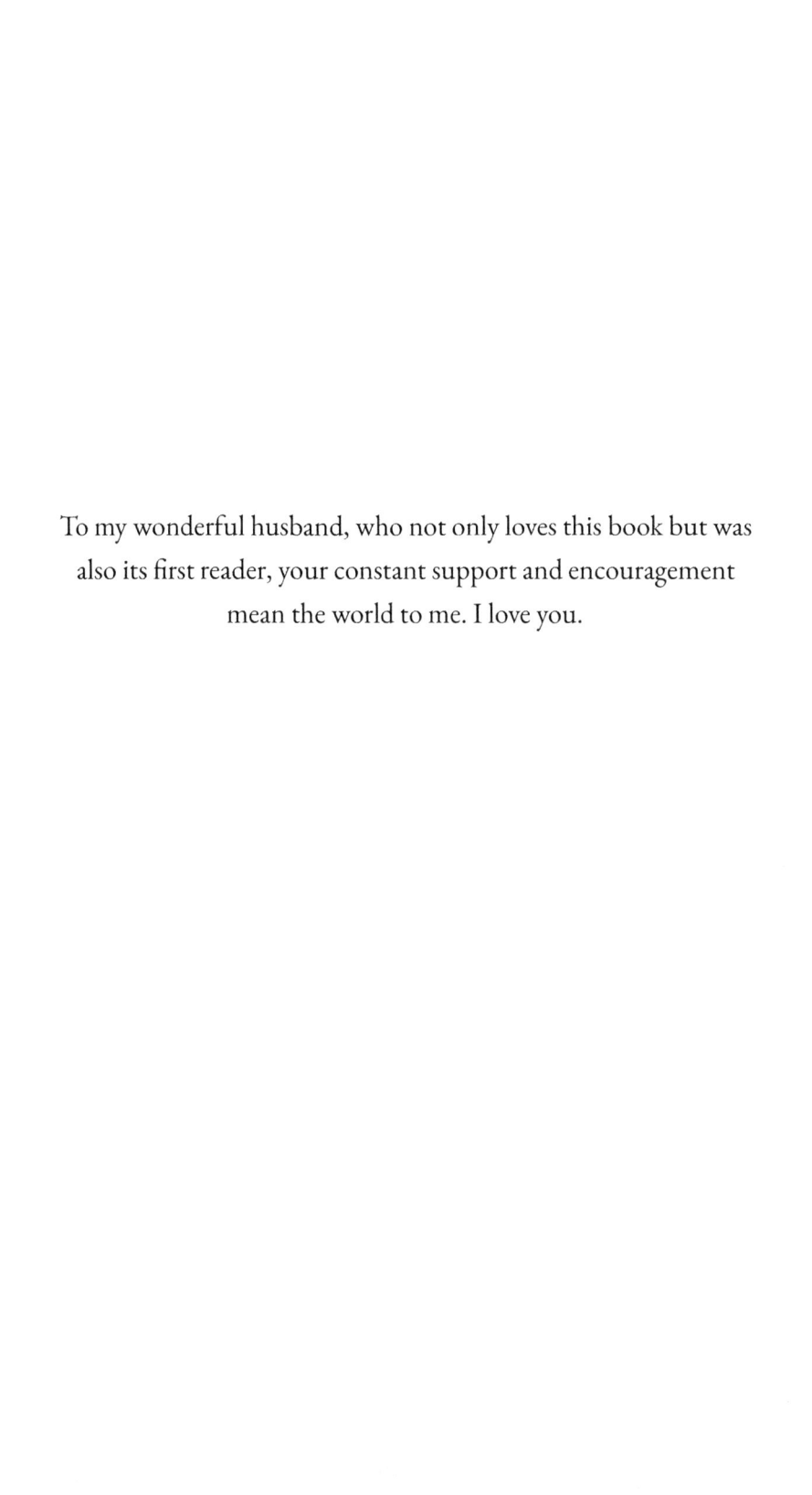

To my wonderful husband, who not only loves this book but was also its first reader, your constant support and encouragement mean the world to me. I love you.

One

"Miss O'Shea, would you like to share your thoughts?" Mr Arche stared at Stef without blinking.

"Umm..." was the only response she could manage.

For a moment, Stef had completely forgotten where or who she was, and now, she couldn't wait to leave. Of course, the more eager you are for something to be over, the longer it seems to take. A forty-five-minute lesson on Earth and Space stretched further than a trip to the nearby moon, or so it seemed to Stef. It's not that she didn't enjoy learning or wasn't interested in outer space; she did, and she was. It's just that today, she and Paul were finally going to finish The Depths of Atlantis by Riddle Corp, an EPIC third-person adventure game they'd started over two months ago, and she could hardly contain her excitement.

"Umm..." Stef repeated, biting her cheek.

"I see. Could I have a quick word with you after class?"

Stef's heart sank. Mr Arche's 'quick word' could easily stretch into a half-hour monologue about upcoming exams and how fortunate she was to study at Granger Academy. Honestly, if Stef had a pound for every time someone told her how lucky she was to be here, she would probably be able to afford the exorbitant school fees that her mother didn't have to pay because she worked at the Academy as a tennis instructor. And she'd only been going there a few months.

"Mr Arche, could you please repeat the question?" Stef cleared her throat.

"A quick word after class?"

"No, sorry. I mean the one before that."

"Alright then." Mr. Arche folded his arms across his chest. "We were discussing what humans might evolve to look like on Mars if we were to colonise it."

"Ah, of course. Well, I think humans could become taller initially because Mars' gravitational pull is significantly lower than Earth's. Lower gravity would weaken our bones and muscles, expanding our vertebrae and making us taller. But then, as our bones become weaker and smaller, humans born on Mars would become smaller, too. We could potentially develop orange skin, as carotenoids offer a certain amount of protection against harmful UV rays, and on Mars, radiation is significantly higher. It would be highly beneficial from the evolutionary perspective to have orange skin. Ultimately, though, human Martians are likely to mutate so much due to radiation and trying to adapt to the radically different environment, that they might not even be human anymore but another species altogether. I think."

This is precisely what happened in Missions to Mars: The Final Frontier, another absolute firecracker from Riddle Corp.

The teacher's eyes were fixed on Stef the entire time, peeking over the rims of his round glasses, his beard unavoidably brushing his chest. More or less successfully, he managed to keep a smile from growing too wide.

"I would still like a quick word, please. After the lesson."

Stef huffed, unable to hide her disappointment.

"Is there anywhere more important you have to be after school, Miss O'Shea?" He raised his eyebrows.

"No, sir. Of course not."

"Very well, then."

***

Chitter-chatter filled the halls on the other side of the door of a now-empty classroom. Stef waited for whatever punishment Mr Arche might come up with, fiddling with the oversized pin of her purple uniform kilt, which she found utterly ridiculous. Mr Arche eased himself into a swivel chair.

"You weren't paying attention in class," he said, twirling gently from side to side.

Determined to get this over with as quickly as possible, Stef remained silent, casting her eyes down in a show of repentance and remorse. Mr Arche exhaled.

"I noticed that you haven't signed up for any after-school activities. I think it could be helpful. Is there anything you enjoy? Music? Dance? Coding?"

Stef lifted her eyes instinctively.

"Ah. So there is something. Coding it is. It's every Thursday after school. You can start today."

"I can't," Stef said.

"You can't?" Creases multiplied on the teacher's broad forehead.

"No, sorry. I can't today; my friend is waiting. I am not sure about next Thursday either. I'm usually quite busy on Thursdays."

And Fridays, and Tuesdays, and Wednesdays, and occasionally Mondays, which, since she was five years old, were reserved for Paul and playing puzzle-based computer games at his house.

"Alright, Miss O'Shea. I strongly recommend that you sort out your Thursdays. It would be good for you." He didn't blink and continued staring at Stef for much longer than she was comfortable with, as if she were an exhibit at a museum. Then, he finally exhaled.

"Fine. You may leave." He rubbed the bridge of his nose.

Stef's smile grew wider.

***

Paul waited for her by the gate. He was dressed in a forest-green suit with a St. Francis of Assisi School emblem machine-stitched on his jacket pocket in black thread, bits of which stuck out in all directions.

Stef spotted him from the top of the school steps, an imposing, white marble tongue that rolled down from the red brick beast's mouth. The school building looked alien in East London. If it weren't for a prominent golden plaque that read Granger Academy, the school could have easily been mistaken for a town hall, perhaps in Westminster. It was as if someone had excised a

West London mini-palace and transplanted it here, along with its extra-green lawn in the middle of the barren, dirty-brick landscape of Barbican City. It was an elegant swan surrounded by concrete, graffiti, and cars from the 1980s, which made it perpetually smell of exhaust fumes. Of course, it needed a tall steel fence with pickets stuck out of the ground like spears; it seemed only natural.

Paul looked unusually nervous, pacing back and forth along the sidewalk. His shirt was untucked, and his tie was undone, as Stef expected. The school guard, as always, was up on his feet, keeping a watchful eye on Paul, his hands on his belt as if he were a cowboy in the Wild West. Stef bounced past him, dispensing a stern glance. Since she had changed schools, Paul had been at the gate every Thursday when he had a half day, but still, the guard made it his mission to make himself visible.

"I'm sorry about that," Stef muttered.

"What? No. I told you before, it's nothing."

They walked to the bus station, passing a shop called Kidz Castle. It sold toys, books, games, and all sorts of things that Stef found tremendously exciting. She couldn't help but stare at the window displays every single day. And every day, without fail, a man with grey hair which mushroomed over his head like ragweed stood at the shopfront holding the same old beaten sign that said: GIVE ME THE BODY!

It didn't make much sense to Stef because he already had a body, unless he somehow thought he was just a floating head with arms. Plus, she wasn't exactly sure who the man thought had taken his body in the first place. Stef had heard others call him the Barbican Nutter. It seemed fitting but gave her a sinking feeling in the pit of her stomach regardless.

"Stef, listen." Paul scratched the back of his head.

But Stef's glance caught sight of their game in the shop window, and her eyes lit up. Instantly, everything else, everything not related to Atlantis, became a white noise in her ears.

"I am so excited. I couldn't concentrate at all today. It was hopeless. I think I have finally figured it out, though. It's in the runes. I mean, think about it."

"Yeah, Stef. That makes sense," Paul said.

"Are you okay? You seem... weird." She glanced at him curiously.

"Weird? No. I'm alright." He forced a brief smile.

"Aren't you excited? You'd better be! We are finally going down to Atlantis itself. This is it! I can feel it. This is it, Paora." Stef's eyes sparkled. She bit her lip and studied her friend's reaction, waiting hungrily for a response.

"Paora? Where's that one from?" he asked without interest or conviction.

"You're not going to venture a guess?"

"Nah. Sorry, Stef. I don't have a clue." Paul looked down at the ground, avoiding eye contact at all costs.

"It's Maori. Isn't it great?" Stef beamed with pride, nudging him a little on the elbow.

When they were about eight, Paul had a homestay language student from Spain living under their roof for over a month. His name was Pablo, which he explained was the same as Paul. Since then, Stef had been calling Paul all the different variations of his name she could find. Sometimes he was Pablo, sometimes Paolo, sometimes Pavel, Pavlos, or Pal. Once every couple of months, she would throw in a new one, a curveball, and see if Paul could guess where it came from. Usually, Paul was just as thrilled about it as she was, but today, he seemed completely indifferent, broody, and nervous. His hands were in his pockets, his shoulders were slumped, and he didn't look at her once.

"Are you sure you're alright?" Stef asked.

"Yeah, totally. Maori. Wicked."

***

They lived on Eastcastle Lane, just off the motorway that eventually ended in London, on a narrow street which, contrary to common sense, managed to fit not one, but two rows of multicoloured cars parked on either side. They lived in fun-sized dusty-white houses made of brick and cracked drywall, all squashed together like conjoined siblings. Each just a little bit different from the other – a little bit wonky, a little bit crooked. They came with compact back gardens, little front porches, miniature gnomes peeking from toy-like bushes, tiny flower beds – both real and plastic – and neighbours who'd known them since they were babies.

By half past five, they arrived at the front door, embellished with a large silver banner that read: Congratulations On Your New Job!

"It's today? I completely forgot!" Stef said, squeezing Paul's bicep with both hands.

"Yeah. Mum went all out. She baked a cake."

Paul seemed annoyed by all this, if anything. The house keys rattled between his fingers.

"It's just a job," he said.

"Just a job? JUST a job? Are you kidding me? It's only the best job in the whole universe!" Stef shrieked.

"Yeah, yeah," Paul grumbled and unlocked the front door.

He wasn't kidding. Inside, many more banners with long shiny fringes hung down from the ceiling like beaded curtains. Silver balloons completely invaded their living room space. They came alive when Stef stepped in, bouncing against each other, floating through their habitat. The house was unrecognisable but for the faint lingering smell of veggie patties, coconut, and vanilla. It made Stef's mouth water every time she was here. She couldn't help it. It was Pavlovian. There was genuinely nothing in the world she loved more than Cynthia Thomas's patties.

The cake stood tall and proud in the middle of the table, ready to greet whoever crossed the threshold. It was completely white, like a giant snowball. Stef figured it was covered in desiccated coconut. A sparkly silver cake topper read, 'We Are So Proud'.

"Where is your mum, anyway?" Stef said.

"She went to meet him. Like, pick him up from work. Seriously. The man is twenty-four years old."

"It's sweet." Stef's lips curled into a smile.

"It's unnecessary." Paul clenched his jaw. "Right. Anyway. Shall we get it over with?"

***

Paul's unfashionably chubby computer was making the most desperate of sounds, resembling a wailing seal, trying to turn itself on. They waited in silence. Stef's eyes were fixed on Paul, trying to crack him like a code. He didn't dare look at her. She bit her nails anxiously while he tapped his foot on the carpet.

"Listen," Paul finally exhaled.

"I knew it!" Stef held her breath.

"Fine. You knew it. You always know everything, Steffi!" He threw his arms into the air.

Stef gasped. She couldn't believe he'd called her that. She hated that name; she hated it with all her heart, and he knew it. He, of all people, knew it better than anyone. Her neck, face, and arms erupted in misshapen red blotches, her omnipresent freckles seemed more pronounced, and her ginger hair looked even more fiery. Paul smacked the computer on the side to hurry it along.

Stef's name was, in fact, Steffi. It was her first name, and Graf was her middle name, meaning her full name was Steffi Graf O'Shea. When someone made fun of celebrities giving their children strange names, she secretly longed to be named Waterfall or Periwinkle – anything seemed better than Steffi Graf O'Shea. Stef had nothing against the tennis legend herself. In fact, she held her in high regard. But that didn't mean she wanted to have her exact name plus O'Shea at the end. When people called her Stephanie, assuming it was her full name, she didn't correct them. She planned to change her name as soon as she turned eighteen to just that – Stephanie. Just Stephanie. Well, okay, Stephanie O'Shea.

"So, what is it?" Stef's chin trembled, red blotches spreading down to her arms.

"I don't think I can play computer games with you every day like this anymore," Paul said without looking at her.

"What? Why?" Stef's shoulders dropped. She didn't know what he was going to say, but she hadn't expected that.

"I... I got a girlfriend now, and she wants to do stuff, like go to the movies and..."

"Are you serious? A girlfriend? Who is it?" Stef's nostrils flared slightly.

"Does it matter?" Paul cast his gaze even further down, angling his face away from his friend.

"Nadia?" Stef whispered.

"Stef." He touched his forehead.

"Blanca?" she said a little louder.

"Please."

"Alex?" Stef almost shrieked.

Paul didn't respond, and the room fell quiet but for the electric wails of a struggling computer.

"So, it *is* Alex." Stef crossed her arms on her chest. "A girlfriend. You're just fifteen."

"Sixteen almost, and I hate to break it to you, but it's high time you started dating. Yeah, most blokes in my class have already pulled a girl or... more. And I'm sitting here every day wasting my time with you!"

When Stef was seven, she fell off a bicycle and broke her arm. It was an open fracture, with a piece of bone ripping right through her skin, and there was blood everywhere. It hurt, it hurt badly, but this, this was on another level. Her eyes widened, and her nose began to itch, anticipating a flood of tears. Stef fought as hard as she could to keep them at bay, but her eyes became blurry, and she knew she was losing the battle.

Stef jumped up and rushed to the toilet as quickly as possible, locking the door behind her and turning on both taps. She felt the tears flow down her cheeks as fast as the tap water, merging into one big sea of pain inside the basin, twisting into a vortex and disappearing down the deep black hole.

There was a hesitant knock on the door. "Stef?"

She squinted at it as if that would help her see through it, or maybe she could shoot laser beams out of her eyes and knock Paul unconscious.

"I'm sorry, alright? I didn't mean it like that. You know I didn't. Let's just finish the game, okay?" he said.

Stef looked at herself in the mirror and splashed her face with cold water. No amount of splashing or wiping could conceal the fact that she'd been crying. Her face and neck looked like a red and white atlas; her nose and eyes were ruby and seemed to have expanded about three hundred per cent. For a moment, she genuinely thought about either spending the night in Paul's toilet or escaping through the vent just so that he didn't get to see her like this. However, neither of the plans was remotely feasible, so she had no choice but to abandon the idea.

Stef opened the door and looked straight at an apologetic Paul, holding her head high.

"I have allergies," she said and marched past him, enjoying the fact that she was still quite a bit taller than him.

Keys rattled in the lock downstairs. Paul's mum and brother were back. Stef could hear a forced, "Wow. It's... a lot... of shiny things."

She hurried down the stairs. "Ringo! You have to tell me all about it. You have to tell me. Everything, everything. Was it amazing? Was it incredible? Hello, Mrs Thomas."

Stef waded through the balloons on the ground, making the floor come alive.

"Are you alright, my dear?" Cynthia Thomas asked, glowering at her youngest son who remained at the top of the stairs. She gently pulled Stef towards her, cupped her chin, and stroked her cheek with her thumb. For a moment, Stef relaxed into the familiar touch of the calloused fingers.

"What happened, my dear. Was that boy rude?" Whenever Cynthia was mad at either of her sons, she didn't dare use their names. It was 'that boy' or 'this boy' or just 'boy'.

"No, Mrs Thomas. I have allergies," Stef said.

Cynthia pursed her lips and raised one eyebrow. "Uh-huh. Are you staying for supper?"

"I promised my mum to be back by seven," Stef lied.

Cynthia scowled at her youngest boy, who hadn't moved an inch, her eyes narrowed. The only thing in the world Paul was afraid of was his mother.

Ringo cleared his throat, trying to diffuse the situation. "There's enough time for my present then."

Paul's older brother looked almost identical to him, only his shirt was ironed and tucked. He wore glasses, not because he couldn't see properly, but because he thought it made him look more respectable.

Stef beamed, her freckles sparkling like spilt glitter. "From Riddle Corp?"

"Yup." Ringo gave Stef a quick wink.

"You didn't!" Stef covered her mouth with both her hands.

"I did. But wait, you don't even know what it is yet. I mean, it's cool, but..."

Ringo wriggled out of his navy backpack and pulled on the zipper. Stef's feet pattered against the linoleum. The open bag revealed two white, shiny cubes. Stef snatched one and gasped.

"A VR headset? No way!"

Ringo also produced a pair of long gloves made from white plastic inserts and flexible black fabric.

"Woah!"

Stef placed the headset on the table and reached for a glove, slipping her entire arm inside. She gaped at her hand as if it wasn't hers but something precious, something magical.

"Can you actually feel what you touch in there, do you think? Is that what the gloves are for?"

"I guess." Ringo shrugged. "I haven't tried it myself."

"And they just gave all this to you?" his mum interrogated.

"A bloke who works there did. I think it was on the way to the dumpsters. They discontinued the game for whatever reason. I don't think it ever made it to the market."

"Why was it discontinued?" Paul's mocking tone echoed down from the top of the stairs. Everyone turned their heads towards him.

"I don't know. Maybe it's got a few glitches. Maybe they are working on a new version. Maybe it's not that great, okay? It's my first day; give me a break. Still a VR."

"Oh, great. Thanks then," Paul scoffed.

"I think it's brilliant," Stef said, carefully examining the headset. "It's an actual VR. Like Virtual Reality, Paulo. You must be at least a little curious. Is there a disk or chip or something?"

"It's all inside. You just pop it on."

"The whole VR set with just one game? Who'd want to pay money for that?" Paul smirked.

"There you go, mystery solved. They probably made this one as a prototype, but it wasn't cost-effective. Anyway, try it out. Let me know how it goes."

Ringo ruffled Stef's hair in a tender, brotherly way, then wrapped his arm around his mother and planted a kiss on her temple.

"I gotta do some work first, okay? Then I'll have cake."

"I'll start the supper," Cynthia said, pursing her lips.

Stef looked up at Paul with puppy-dog eyes, cradling the VR set in her arms. She forgot all about Atlantis, the girlfriend, and how insensitive he'd been, and that she was still really terribly mad at him.

"Fine. Okay. Let's do it," Paul said.

Two

Stef watched as Paul grumbled and slipped on the VR headset. He was already wearing the gloves and clearly didn't like them, just as expected. At least he was doing it. Stef grinned and followed suit. Everything went dark.

"What do we do now?" she said, her heart beginning to race. Stef felt completely cramped in the total darkness. It was oddly unsettling. She'd never thought she had an issue with darkness or tight spaces before.

"Is there like an ON button or something?" Paul wondered aloud.

"Didn't see one." Stef felt for the buttons around the headset, resisting an overwhelming urge to rip the thing right off.

"Maybe voice commands?"

"Let's try. TURN ON THE DEVICE?" Stef said, forming her lips into a tight 'O' and slowly letting the air out. The headset started to glow, and darkness receded. Colours began to appear at the edges of Stef's vision, starting with red and then progressing through orange, yellow, green, blue, navy and finally, purple –

the whole rainbow. Then, there was a bright flash, and she was surrounded by light.

This new world lacked corners or edges – an endless, bright vacuum. Stef could still feel a solid surface beneath her feet, but she couldn't see it. It made her stomach lurch and she tried to focus on something visible. She could see Paul, or at least she assumed it was him, as he looked nothing like his usual self, rather a standard white male avatar of average height, build, and light-brown hair. Stef couldn't help but giggle.

"What's so funny?" The avatar spoke in Paul's voice.

Stef chuckled even harder. "Oh, please change. It looks terrible."

"You don't look much better."

Stef examined her arms. The freckles were gone, and her chest seemed enormous, as though someone had stuffed her blouse with two overinflated balloons. She couldn't stand it. Blond hair, resembling seaweed, cascaded down her shoulders. She ran her fingers through the silky alien threads.

"I can actually feel it. Like it's real. It's so weird."

"Alright, how do we change what we look like?" Paul exhaled.

"Well, if voice commands work..."

"CHANGE AVATAR?"

"Hello and welcome." The voice echoed around them in a soft, female timbre.

Stef flinched, feeling it reverberate deep inside her head, as if the sound bypassed her ears entirely.

"Did you... feel that?" Stef exclaimed with wonder.

"I've heard about this technology where the sound is beamed directly into your head, but I didn't think it existed like... commercially. Odd, right?"

"My name is Ariadne," the voice interrupted. "I am your virtual assistant. Welcome to The Disappearance of Eden Rose. May I take your names?" Ariadne spoke in a melodic tone, and Stef thought she sounded eager, as if Ariadne was just as excited to play the game as Stef was.

"Stephanie," Stef said. "My name is Stephanie."

Paul tried to suppress an eye-roll, but not entirely successfully.

"Paul," he said.

"Nice to meet you, Stephanie and Paul. Would you like to change your avatar?"

"Yes, please," Stef replied with relief.

"Permission to scan your features?"

"Permission granted," Paul said, faking an RP accent.

"Initiating scan."

Stef's skin tingled, and as she looked down at her arms, freckles dissolved across her skin, smattering through like stars in the night. Her hair returned to its familiar shade of ginger. She glanced at Paul. He almost looked like himself again: brown eyes, brown skin, short curly hair. Only he seemed older and considerably more put together. He looked like Ringo.

"This is crazy," Stef said. "I had no idea Riddle Corp had something this advanced. Ringo was sure they were going to destroy it, right?"

"Doesn't make sense, does it?"

"Are you satisfied with your avatars?" Ariadne politely inquired.

"How are we supposed to know?" Just as Paul uttered the words, a mirror appeared before Paul, floating in mid-air before he even had a chance to scoff.

There was a mirror in front of Stef too. Her insides curdled when she saw her reflection. It was as if she'd been through a time machine and emerged ten years older. Her lips were covered in bright red lipstick, her eyelids had a darker, smoky appearance, and her eyelashes were curled and clunky with thick mascara. Stef rubbed her eyes instinctively, trying to rid herself of the makeup.

"What's wrong now?" Paul asked.

"Lipstick is what's wrong. And eye shadow."

"Well, some girls at school wear makeup," Paul mumbled.

"I'm sure Alex does," Stef muttered under her breath.

"What?"

"Nothing."

"Are you satisfied with your avatars?" Ariadne repeated.

"No!" Stef exclaimed.

"How can I assist you, then?" Ariadne sounded almost offended.

"I don't want makeup on my face, and I want to look my age," Stef replied, rubbing her face.

"How old would you like to be?" Ariadne inquired.

"Fifteen years old. I am fifteen," Stef said.

"No problem," the voice responded cheerfully, and like magic, the makeup vanished. Stef's complexion softened, and her cheeks puffed up like dumplings. Relieved, she turned to Paul. Much to her delight, he also looked like his normal self again.

"Alright. Whatever," Paul huffed. "How do we play?"

"Would you like to initiate your tutorial?" Ariadne continued.

"Do we have to?" Paul put his hands behind his head, and Stef couldn't tell whether he was bored, annoyed, or frustrated. It hurt Stef. It physically hurt her.

"Of course, Paul. We don't have a clue how this works." Stef tutted. "Ariadne?"

"Yes?"

"We would like a tutorial, please," Stef said, glancing at Paul. His eyes were closed, and he was shaking his head.

"Excellent! And to answer your previous question, Paul, yes. You have to have a tutorial. It is part of the game. So, initiating the tutorial."

As if struck by lightning, Stef's insides tensed into one big ball of nerves, and a tingling electric current rushed through her whole body. For a moment, she couldn't breathe. Her ears started to buzz, and her mind became fuzzy, making her feel like she was about to faint. A wave of coldness surged through her veins before all the tension retreated. Stef gasped, trying to catch her breath, clawing at her neck in panic. She wasn't inside the vacuum any longer but in a small room with light grey walls and a tiled floor. A wooden desk stood at the centre with a vase of multicoloured flowers on top. On the left was a metal cupboard with a large padlock holding it shut. Stef did a slow 360-degree turn. There was nothing else inside the room – nothing at all – except for a bright red door with a cerulean-blue 'V' painted on it. Paul stood precisely where he was before, but with a slightly uncertain posture, as if he couldn't quite find his balance. He pressed his hand to his stomach, bending forward. Stef thought he looked a little queasy, a little green in the face.

"Are you okay?" she asked.

"Yeah," he said. "This felt... real."

"I know!" Stef exclaimed, her face glowing with wonder.

"Welcome to your tutorial, Stephanie and Paul." Ariadne's voice beamed into their skulls.

Stef flinched and pressed her hand to her temple. The voice echoed through the deepest of crevices inside her mind.

"The Disappearance of Eden Rose is a first-person virtual reality escape adventure experience in which you will be required to solve mini-puzzles and open locks to unravel a mystery. In this tutorial, you are trapped inside a room. You must find a way to escape. As the red door opens, your game will begin."

"Like an escape room?" Paul scratched his head.

"The Disappearance of Eden Rose is a virtual reality puzzle-based escape adventure," Ariadne insisted.

"Okay. Okay. Don't get your knickers in a twist," Paul said.

"Pardon?"

"Nothing. Ignore me."

"So, we can, like... look around?" Stef asked.

"Please do have a look around. You can touch everything, and you can use whatever you find. Please be aware that you can only take things that are small enough to carry with you. But you won't need anything from this room."

"That's too cool," Stef said, smitten with awe.

"Are you ready to begin?" Ariadne asked cheerfully.

"Frankly, I can't wait." Stef smiled and rubbed her hands together.

"If you need me, just say my name, and I will be able to assist you."

"Great," Stef said, rushing to the padlocked cupboard and cupping the metal lock. "Wicked. It's so heavy. I can actually feel that it is heavy."

"Door's locked." Paul was by the red door, tugging on the handle, as if it would be that easy.

"It's all locked. Surprise, surprise. First, we need a four-digit code for the padlock. I assume the key for that door is inside. Paolo, you see any numbers?"

"Well," Paul began, "the V on the door could be a 5. If we're talking Roman numerals."

"Of course," Stef shrieked. "What else?"

Paul scratched the back of his head, while Stef bounced over to the desk and pored over its surface, scouring for a clue. There were no tangible objects on top other than a round glass vase with four roses, identical in shape but different in colour. They were red, blue, orange and purple. Stef lifted the vase and peeked inside, running her fingers along its shape – she couldn't see anything unusual. She grabbed the roses in a bunch, water dripping from their stems onto the desk. Stef dabbed her fingertips into the puddle.

"Wow! I can feel that it's wet. How did they do this?"

Paul dipped his whole hand inside the vase.

"It must be like, I don't know, your brain telling you that it's water, so it must be wet, right? It's a brain trick."

"It must be," Stef said, studying the flowers. There was nothing remarkable about them other than their colours. Stef had a hunch that they were important, that they meant something, but she couldn't quite put her finger on it. She stuck them back inside the vase, inadvertently rearranging the bouquet. Suddenly, the flowers started to move, gently floating inside the water. Stef held her breath and grabbed Paul's arm instinctively. The flowers organised themselves back into their original order and settled down.

"I knew it. Red, blue, orange and purple. That's the correct order. That V is a 5, and it is blue," Stef said.

"Five must be the second number of the code for that padlock." Paul's expression was turning more serious and engaged by the second, as he hunted for more clues. Stef could almost feel his heartbeat quicken, her own heart matching his rhythm. Warmth spread through her body; her friend seemed like himself again.

"Look here." Paul pointed to the side of the desk, tracing numbers with his finger. "One, two, three, and so on."

Stef squatted down for a better look, noticing small orange circles etched along the edge of the desk.

"Eight," she counted in a flash. "The orange rose is third, so the third number is eight."

Paul hurried to the padlock, confidently setting the second and third numbers to 5 and 8. Stef continued to inspect every inch of the room, but nothing stood out.

"Can we move something, do you think?" she wondered aloud.

Without hesitation, Paul gave the cupboard a firm push on its side. It glided effortlessly along the wall, as if on ice, revealing hidden tally marks behind it – one complete set of five and two singles. They were purple.

"Seven," Paul declared. Stef promptly changed the last number on the padlock to 7.

"Ha!" she cheered, feeling victorious.

"Just one left," Paul said, eyes scanning the space around him.

"That's just it, Paolito!" Stef grinned with triumph.

"What?"

"One! The first number is one. Besides that red rose, what else in this room is the exact same shade of red?"

"The door." Paul's lips couldn't help but curl into a smile.

"The door and the plank above it," Stef added, her eyes bright with excitement. "Look at its shape."

With the top and bottom planks framing the red door, the entire structure resembled the Roman numeral for one.

Stef swiftly turned to the padlock and entered the last number. The lock clicked open, dropping into her waiting hands. Overjoyed, she felt a rush of adrenaline coursing through her, leaving her slightly dizzy. She flung open the cupboard doors, revealing a silver key hanging on a peg. She tossed it to Paul, who stood ready by the red door. He pushed the key into the silver lock. It rattled and twisted on its own as though by magic, and the door swung open, instantly flooding the room with an unbearably bright light which made them both squint and shield their eyes.

"Congratulations, Stephanie and Paul. Your best time is fifteen minutes and twenty-three seconds. Welcome to the game."

Three

Nothing could've prepared Stef for what happened next. The light burst inside the tutorial room, behaving more like a substance than light itself. It surged upwards like an enormous ocean wave and swallowed them whole in one gulp.

Stef's insides clenched tightly, like a squash ball, and then, with a quick release, she found her back pressed against Paul's, feeling his nervous breathing. The sliver of ground beneath her feet was barely sufficient to accommodate the both of them. They were marooned on a minuscule oasis in the middle of what seemed like a bustling motorway in a buzzing, sprawling metropolis of the future.

Vehicles zoomed past with warp-like speeds, or at least Stef assumed they were vehicles. It was difficult to tell for certain amidst the blur of silver, black, white, green, and yellow. Lights streaked before her eyes, amid the high-pitched roar of traffic. Abrupt gusts of wind ruffled her hair and clothes every time an unidentified object zipped by. Each time, she flinched and held her breath, fearing that she would be swept off her feet. It was as if they were stranded in the middle of a Formula 1 racetrack on an alien planet.

Stef clutched Paul's hands just a bit harder and pressed her back more firmly against his, afraid to stray an inch away from his body, or else be consumed by the city.

Past the motorway, Stef noticed an array of skyscrapers stretching up towards the sky, their tops lost in the thick canopy of clouds. The buildings, all silver and shiny like mirrors, infinitely reflected one another – a glass jungle.

"What do we do now?" Stef yelled, having to shout to out-scream the motorway.

"It's only a game. We can't get hurt."

"Are you trying to convince me or yourself?"

"Both?" Paul closed his eyes, then screamed into the wind, "Hello, Ariadne? Ariadne?" There was no response. "Great. Thanks, Ariadne. Cheers, mate! Didn't she say to call her name if we needed help?"

"Yes, she did. Maybe she can't hear." Stef attempted a joke.

"What?!"

"Never mind!"

"Okay, Stef. Look around. How do we get out of here? Talk to me. What do you see?"

"Same things you do, I assume. Flying cars or whatever those are."

"And those tall buildings...?"

"And..." Stef's wrist began to itch, distracting her from the urgent matter of devising an escape plan. Focused on the irritating sensation and feeling annoyed, she found the courage to move her hand and scratch the bothersome area. That's when she felt something unusual – something springy, rubbery, and new. Stef glanced down at her trembling hand.

"Paul? Are you wearing a watch?"

"What?"

"A watch! Are you wearing a watch?"

"No. Actually, wait. I am?"

The watch was black and square, with a strap made of soft rubber. A countdown timer glimmered in bright red against the dark screen – 58:25 – with the last set of numbers rapidly decreasing – 24, 23, 22...

"Is yours counting down too?" Stef's stomach twisted, as if she were staring at a timer on a bomb.

"Yeah." Paul swallowed and tapped his watch nervously. Light burst from its screen, projecting jumbo 3D letters above them like gold foil balloons, displaying three numbers, each followed by a choice of action.

CALL FOOD DELIVERY

CALL A TAXI

CALL THE POLICE

"Call a taxi!" Stef hollered.

An instant later, one of the vehicles abruptly halted, hovering before them. It was indeed a flying car – a black platform that curved at the front with the distinctive grille and round headlights of a London black cab. The rest of the vehicle was made of glass, with a transparent dome encasing its interior like an extravagant dessert. The cabin featured two rows of four cushioned seats adorned in a green and gold jacquard fabric with Eastern patterns of elephants and paisley. There seemed to be no steering wheel, pedals, or driver. The car emitted a slight huff, lowered itself to the ground, and opened like a locket. Two steps unfolded from its side, inviting the passengers in.

"Should we go?" Stef asked, not entirely convinced.

"We don't want to be stuck here forever, do we?" Paul said, climbing inside. He bounced lightly on top of the cushions. "It's comfortable."

Stef exhaled for courage and followed, settling into the seat beside him. The dome closed as soon they were both seated, making Stef feel like a fish in a bowl. Tilting and swaying side-to-side, the car lifted itself clumsily into the air. Stef thought she was inside a 'Ball in the Hole' game and instinctively dug her fingers into the cushion.

"Where to, love?" A male cabbie's voice with an East End accent croaked out of thin air.

Paul turned to Stef, unsure of their destination. Stef's eyes flickered, and she bit her cheek.

"Imagine we were in an unfamiliar place in the real world. Where would we go?"

"Town centre," Paul said with a confident nod.

"Town centre!" Stef repeated louder.

The car jerked forward and swayed like a ship in a storm. Paul leaned sharply into Stef, who almost slid off her seat. She pressed her feet hard against the floor, preventing herself from tipping over.

"Town centre it is!" the invisible cabbie cheerfully replied as the car finally found its balance. It zoomed into the motorway traffic like a spaceship, going from zero to fifty thousand in half a second, or so it seemed to Stef. Her head slammed into the headrest, and she clutched Paul's hand, screaming as her stomach filled with insufferable butterflies.

Mere seconds later, they were hovering above a peaceful market square – a respite from the frenzy – although still entirely surrounded by the mirrored skyscrapers. The cab gently descended to the ground, and Stef breathed a sigh of relief. She caught a glimpse of her reflection in one of the nearby buildings and noticed how pale her face had become. Her wrist vibrated with urgency, and she glanced at the watch. The timer had reset to 60:00, standing still this time. She couldn't help but feel both a sense of relief and foreboding at once.

Around the square, market sellers had arranged themselves in a triangular formation under red canopies. Due to the lack of other customers, everyone eagerly stared at the new arrivals. The cab came to a complete stop, huffing gently as the glass dome opened up like a blooming flower. Stef stumbled out of its confines, groggy, dizzy, and clutching her abdomen with both hands.

"I don't want to do this again. Ever."

Paul exhaled with relief. "It was very... realistic."

Stef straightened herself back up but still looked queasy. "What do you think is happening to our bodies right now?"

Paul looked puzzled. "Like... What do you mean?"

"I mean, I feel as if I am here. As in, actually here. But that can't be true, can it?"

"No, of course not," Paul said, trying to maintain his composure.

"So we are..."

"We're in my bedroom, Stef." Paul let out a chuckle – a strange combination of sarcasm and cluelessness which, judging by the embarrassed look on his face, he, too, was acutely aware of.

"And when we were in the cab just now, flying through the air like on a mad roller coaster, we were still inside your room, right?"

"Y-y-yeah, of course, Stef."

"And we didn't fall. We just managed to find someplace to sit. Blindfolded. I am pretty sure I was sitting down, as in actually sitting down."

"Yeah. I mean, no. It's all part of the illusion, Stef. Virtual reality. That's how it works," Paul said, trying to sound confident, but Stef wasn't at all convinced that he was.

She considered his response for a moment, then raised her hands slowly to her temples, feeling for the VR headset.

"If I wanted to stop playing, I could just take the headset off, right?"

"Right," Paul said, a crinkle flashing between his eyebrows.

Stef pressed her hands to her head – all she could feel was her skin and bones. Before she could panic, a young boy on a vintage pink bicycle zoomed past, nearly knocking her off balance. He rang his bike bell three times and shouted.

"Today's paper! Londelhi Daily! Extra! Extra! Robbery of the century!"

The bell chimed as he tossed the newspaper at Stef and Paul, landing it right between their feet. Stef turned to look at the messenger, but he had already vanished into the maze of market stalls or the skyscraper forest. Stef peered into the dark gaps between the buildings, as if they were supermassive black holes that would gladly swallow them whole if given the chance.

Paul bent down for the paper. The headline sprawled over the front page in bold, red letters read, 'EXTRA! EXTRA! EDEN ROSE STOLEN! Page 13'. Paul raised his eyebrows and unpeeled the pages, revealing that there were no page numbers except for the one marked 13.

"That's odd," he commented.

"It probably means that all the other pages don't matter to the gameplay," Stef said.

Paul cleared his throat and began reading the article aloud. "This morning, Eden Rose, one of the largest diamonds in existence, was reported missing by Sandeep Bigwig, billionaire and entrepreneur. The 300-carat pink beauty was taken from Mr Bigwig's estate on Connaught Marg. The diamond is rumoured to have been gifted to Marilyn Star, a famous actress and Mr Bigwig's longtime girlfriend. Police are looking for clues and asking anyone with information to come forward. I guess, that's the mystery we have to solve."

"I thought Eden Rose was a person," Stef said.

"So did I, Stef. So did I." Paul closed the newspaper, gaping at Stef. "Now what? Any ideas?"

Stef pivoted on the spot slowly, examining their surroundings. There was nothing remarkable about the town centre other than the market.

"The market?" Stef shrugged.

"Let's do it."

***

It was a fruit and vegetable market, and each seller only offered one type of food. There were bananas, carrots, broccoli, red bell peppers, aubergines, pumpkins, blueberries, cherries, and nectarines.

All the produce looked unnaturally perfect, like something out of a TV ad, and emitted a rather strong scent, but they didn't smell like real fruits and vegetables, but rather like car fresheners.

"There are a lot of people here, and they are all looking at us," Stef said, forcing a perfunctory smile.

They strolled cautiously through the stalls, as dozens of sellers held out their fruit, offering it to Stef and Paul, their faces painted with unnatural smiles which gave Stef chills. Their postures and faces were frozen, like living statues. Only their eyes moved, all fixed on Stef and Paul.

One stall stood out from the rest, piled high with hundreds of scissors, forming a giant scissor-filled ant hill.

"Look at that one." Stef pointed at the strange stall.

"Odd one out. Gotta mean something," Paul said and started towards it.

"Would you like to buy an apple?" A voice behind stopped them in their tracks.

A woman dressed in a purple and gold sari was minding an apple stall. She looked different from everyone else – more vibrant, more real. She had long brown hair and mischievous, striking green eyes. She held out one big, juicy red apple between her well-manicured fingers, her nail polish perfectly matching the fruit.

Stef's mouth watered at the sight of the luscious apple. She hadn't eaten a crumb since lunch, which had been hours ago, and she had barely managed to eat anything with all the students staring at her, judging, whispering, snickering. Or so she imagined.

"How much is it?" Stef asked.

"Normally, it's four Rupees. But for you, it's free. If you play me for it," the woman said, flashing a secret smile.

"Play you for it?" Stef asked curiously.

"Heads or tails?" The woman opened her palm, revealing a large bronze coin.

"Okay, tails."

The woman's eyes sparkled as she tossed the coin up. She caught it on the back of her hand, trapping it under her other palm. She smiled and peeked inside, not showing it to Stef.

"Your lucky day," she said. "Besides, I don't like to see children go hungry." She batted her long eyelashes, extending her arm towards Stef, who grabbed the apple with a grateful smile.

"Do you think I'll taste it?" Stef turned to Paul.

He raised one eyebrow. "That would be like crazy wicked."

Clutching the fruit tightly, Steph moistened her lips and drew it closer, opening her mouth in anticipation. She was about to sink her teeth into its juicy flesh when someone snatched the apple right out of her hands.

"Hey!" she yelled at the thief on a bicycle, darting towards the dark, narrow gaps between the skyscrapers. Without hesitation, Paul and Stef charged after him, straight into the mirrored forest.

***

Stef instinctively held her breath, as she found herself inside a mirror maze. A shadow darted in the corner of her vision, and she dashed after it, only to crash into her own reflection. She stared at herself, her chest rising and falling. She was out of breath. She turned to the left – there she was again, but she didn't even know if it was a copy of her or a copy of a copy. Her effigies stretched infinitely in all directions, crowding her way. Confusion clouded her mind; she was here, there, and everywhere. Her head started to spin.

"Paul? Where are you?"

"I'm here!"

Stef snapped around, following the sound, but it bounced off the walls and ricocheted in random directions. The endless copies of herself started to seem alien, like a word losing its meaning when repeated over and over again. Stef took another step and almost stumbled. Stretching out her arms, she felt for the obstacles. Paul groaned from somewhere behind her; he must have bumped into the glass again. She wished she could see him – her point of compass. The sound echoed through the narrow passages, multiplying by a hundred. Stef tried to walk straight, follow a path, but the path curved and twisted back onto itself, coming to an abrupt halt, and she was confronted with her reflection again. She looked into her own eyes, or at least she thought they were her own. The pupils narrowed into tiny dots, resembling full stops after a long sentence. They looked frightened.

"Stef, are you okay?" Paul's voice enveloped her in its soft, familiar timbre, and she felt his breath on the back of her neck. She had to blink twice to recognise his face in the mirror. He was right behind her. She spun around and threw her arms around his neck.

"Oh, thank goodness. Let's just go back."

"Do you know the way back?" Paul asked.

Just then, a shadow darted past. It was him – the thief – here, there, and everywhere, ad infinitum.

"He's here," Stef whispered. Paul ripped himself out of Stef's embrace, launching into pursuit, but instead he crashed into a mirror, which rippled from the impact like mercury.

"Woah," Paul said, mesmerised. "That's new."

"Stop! Wait!" Stef yelled at the thief with an apple.

To her surprise, he listened. Out of breath and panting, he stopped and slowly pivoted, his eyes glaring at Stef with a mixture of curiosity and apprehension. Stef extended her hand towards him, silently asking him to stay put. The teen flinched slightly, his gaze shifting between Stef and Paul's reflections. His shirt was messy and untucked, and he wore dated green breeches that instantly reminded Stef of her old school uniform, Paul's uniform. Clutched in his hand was the blood-red apple which he lifted high above his head. He scrunched up his entire face and smashed the fruit onto the ground with all his might. The apple splintered into a red numeric code upon impact and vanished forever. Paul took a cautious step towards the guy.

"Don't move," the thief barked.

Paul froze and raised his hands in the air. "We're not gonna hurt you."

"You can't eat anything in here," the guy said.

"Is that a rule of the game?" Paul asked.

"No. And yes. If you eat something in the game, he has you. You lose, do you understand? Why are you even here? And how?" The thief's eyebrows furrowed.

Paul took another step forward, hands still in the air. The thief instinctively pulled backwards.

"Stay where you are," he shouted.

"We are not going to hurt you. We just want to talk. We need to find out what happened to that diamond, I guess, right?" Paul said.

"Diamond? Ha ha ha ha." The thief blinked continuously, his mouth stretching into a grin. "Now that's funny."

"Why is it funny?" Stef said.

Suddenly, he wasn't laughing any more. His face turned deadly sombre, sending goosebumps down the back of Stef's neck.

"Just leave," the guy continued. "For your own good. Leave and never come back."

Just then, the world grew darker as a shadow swept across their light source. All colour drained from the thief's face as if he had just seen a ghost. He steadied his breath and slinked backwards until his path branched to the left. It was his chance and he grabbed it, bolting away, swerving between the buildings like a skilled ninja, leaving Stef and Paul with no chance to follow.

Suddenly, something dark reflected in the mirrors. Stef had to squint to discern a shadowy figure dressed in a hooded cape in the distance. It resembled a faceless Grim Reaper or perhaps Darth Vader. The backlighting made his contour glow ominously. Stef held her breath, her body tensing, ready to react to whatever might happen next. But the shadow jerked to the side and vanished without a trace.

Stef felt a warm glow on her skin, painting a shard of sun along her face. She could see the way out of the glass jungle. She exhaled, allowing her body to relax, but only for a brief moment.

"That was weird," Paul said.

"That was all part of the game, right?"

"Of course," Paul replied, though he didn't seem convinced, not in the slightest.

"You don't think that teenager... and everything here is just a bit too real?"

"It's a very advanced game, Stef. I'm thinking Ringo could be in trouble," Paul said with an uncomfortable chuckle.

"We should tell him."

"We should definitely tell him. But I'm thinking, like... we should go. Like now. That was enough excitement for one day, don't you think?" Paul's voice wavered, and he raised his hands to his temples where the headset should be. He glanced at Stef, panic flashing in his eyes.

"Hey, Ariadne!" Steph yelled as loudly as she could.

Nothing.

"Maybe if we go back?" She tugged Paul's arm, her eyes fixed on the beacon of light. "Maybe there is a way out."

Stef followed the path towards the light, and finally, they were out of the maze. She exhaled with relief as her ears filled with the familiar buzz of the market.

"Now what?" Paul asked.

"Ariadne?" Stef repeated, her tone laced with both hope and desperation.

"Hello, Stephanie. Hello, Paul." Ariadne's voice reverberated inside their heads as before. Paul raised a fist in the air and cheered.

"Ariadne? Where were you, mate?" Paul laughed with relief.

"Whatever do you mean, Paul?"

"I called for you. I screamed, 'Hello, Ariadne' when we were stuck out there on that motorway thing."

"Oh, but you told me to ignore you. I was simply following your instructions. Previously, you told me not to get my knickers in a twist and then to ignore you."

"Great, a passive-aggressive computer program," Paul sniggered.

"And just now, inside that... whatever it is?" Stef pointed at the skyscraper forest. "I called for you too."

"Oh, I think you must've been inside a periphery. I must inform you that you were off-limits, and to continue with the game, you must always return to one of the gaming locations. From there, a taxi will take you anywhere you want to go. But the taxi wouldn't work in the periphery. All the elements of the game don't function in the periphery, including myself. The peripheral area is to keep you from wandering astray and should be avoided for safety reasons."

"Safety reasons?" Paul scratched the back of his head.

"Safety reasons," Ariadne repeated.

"What kind of safety reasons, if you don't mind me asking?" Stef inquired.

"Safety reasons."

"Okay. Well, that was helpful," Paul mumbled.

"Anyway, we just want to quit and save, Ariadne. Would that be okay?" Stef said.

"Certainly. I will save your progress. Next time, you will start at your last gaming location, which is here, in the town centre. Are you sure you want to quit and save?"

"Yes. Please," Paul replied without a moment of hesitation.

In an instant, they were back in total darkness, and Stef was loudly aware of the headset pressing on her cheekbones and tugging at her hair. Yanking the gloves off first, she freed her head from the device. Her eyesight was blurred, but she could make out Paul's shape. He was in the exact same spot as he had been before they started playing. Stef blinked repeatedly and rubbed her eyes to restore her vision.

"Wow. That was..." Paul started, pulling the headset off. His forehead was marked with deep lines from where the device had been most uncomfortable.

"Weird?" Stef finished his sentence.

"Yeah. Pretty awesome, though, too, I must admit."

"Paul?"

"Yeah?"

"You know what was really weird?"

"What?"

"Ariadne said that gaming elements don't work in the periphery, or whatever. You know, that maze, but..."

Paul knew exactly what Stef meant. His eyebrows furrowed, and his mouth opened slightly.

"The thief," he said.

"The thief."

Four

"So it was..." Paul tossed the VR goggles onto his bed, and they bounced lightly.

"A glitch?" Stef didn't sound entirely convinced.

"I guess."

"Hey, where were you, guys?" Ringo's head popped up in the doorframe, startling Stef.

"Ring! You scared us," Paul exclaimed in relief.

"Where did you guys go?" Ringo asked, scanning the room curiously.

"What do you mean?" Paul said, his brows drawing together.

An uncomfortable expression stretched across Ringo's face. "Um. Okay. I didn't mean to intrude."

"We were just playing the game, Ring. It's... incredible, actually. You gotta try. But... are you sure... are you absolutely positive that you were allowed to just take it?"

"A guy who works at the junkyard said they were about to destroy it, so he gave it to me."

"The junkyard?" Stef's eyes widened in shock.

"Yeah, it's like a big room where they keep all the old games, consoles, unwanted memorabilia."

"This," Paul said, lifting the headset, "is not old, bruv. It's like, so not old."

"Okay, well, you want it or not?" Ringo said.

"Oh, we want it," Stef insisted. "Right, Paul?"

Paul's expression changed, doubt etched on his face.

"Yeah. Sure," he said, lowering his gaze. "We want it. Just…"

Ringo glanced at his brother, then at Stef, then back again. Neither wanted to make eye contact with him or the other. Catching a whiff of a very smelly elephant that was obviously in the room, Ringo raised his index finger and wagged it in the air.

"I'm just gonna…" he said, and disappeared from view.

Stef's gaze was fixed on her feet. Her pink socks with little bunnies in purple bonnets had always made her smile. But not this time. This time, she was embarrassed – embarrassed for the socks, the bunnies, and their silly little bonnets. She clenched her teeth, her fingers forming a fist.

"Stef?" Paul mumbled, scratching the top of his head with increased vigour.

"It's okay," Stef said. "You want to spend time with your girlfriend."

"We're supposed to go to the movies tomorrow. I'll text you after, okay? Maybe like… we could play this weekend, sometime, or something?" Paul forced an uncomfortable smile.

"I have something tomorrow anyway," Stef lied, flipping her long hair. "I have a life, too, you know."

"Okay. Cool."

"Okay! Cool!"

***

"Okay. Cool," Stef replied to her mother, Claire, who stared at her with such intensity that it disrupted the safe passage of cornflakes through Stef's throat. A flake got stuck in the middle somewhere, causing her to cough forcefully to dislodge the offending particle.

"Do you promise?" Claire O'Shea wasn't about to back down.

"I promise. I'll sign up for the club, okay? If it makes you all get off my back."

Claire gasped, and Jason O'Shea, Stef's father, put down his *Daily Mirror*, folded his hands, and raised his eyebrows higher than Stef had ever seen them go.

"Language, young lady," Jason said in a calm, restrained, and gentle manner. Everything Jason did was in a very calm, restrained, and gentle manner, which was not something one would typically expect from a six-foot, fourteen-stone PE teacher by day and personal trainer by night.

"Sorry," Stef grumbled.

"You need to try harder, Stef," Claire said.

"I *am* trying."

"I am not so sure that you are," Claire said, taking a bite of her toast.

"I am. But nobody likes me."

"Nonsense. Why wouldn't they like you?" Jason poured himself more coffee from a silver pot.

"Because, you know, I'm new, and I'm a teacher's daughter."

"Steffi."

"Don't call me…"

"They're just kids. You're new. They're curious about you. Wouldn't you be? But they mean well, I am sure," Jason said, taking a sip from his World's Best Dad mug.

"Fine."

"Look, Mr Arche says you're very clever. You just need a bit of… guidance." Claire touched her husband's hand gently.

Stef could barely suppress an eye-roll.

"Fine, I'll try harder," she said, not looking directly into either of her parents' eyes.

Then she released her spoon, which clanged against the bowl, and launched herself up from the chair, causing it to screech sharply against the floor. Stef dropped the half-empty bowl of cereal into the kitchen sink, grabbed her backpack, and headed towards the front door.

"I'll wait for you in the car," she said, slamming the door behind her. The noise made Claire bounce in her seat. She rested her hand on her chest and looked at her husband.

"Kids these days," said Jason O'Shea, returning to the *Daily Mirror*.

***

Stef tried desperately not to fixate on the round wall clock above Mr Arche's head, but her eyes seemed to have a will of their own. She was powerless to resist their insistent drift towards it. Even though there was nothing to look forward to after school anymore, she still wanted to be out there as soon as possible.

Mr Arche kept a vigilant eye on Stef throughout the entire lesson. Whenever he spoke, he fixed his gaze on her and awaited acknowledgement, forcing her to nod along as though she were a bobblehead. This made the situation even more challenging for Stef, particularly when her eyes inevitably wandered to the clock again.

Between checking the time and making sure to nod, some of what Mr Arche said managed to penetrate her eardrums. She genuinely tried to pay some attention. After all, she had promised Mum, and as far as she was concerned, she had fulfilled that promise. She had even signed up for the coding club. Luckily, it wasn't until next Thursday, and she still had a week to come up with a plausible excuse not to attend.

But then Mr Arche dropped a bombshell.

"And before we finish, I have some bad news," he announced, and the classroom erupted in boos, forcing Stef's wandering mind to snap back to the present.

"Alright, settle down, everyone. Tomorrow, you will submit a 3000-word essay on the potential consequences of colonising Mars. End of discussion."

Further disgruntled cries filled the air, causing Mr Arche to raise his voice.

"We've discussed this topic enough. It shouldn't be too difficult, right, Miss O'Shea?"

Stef huddled deeper into her seat, casting a sidelong glance at the rest of the class. All eyes were fixed on her. She didn't like the attention; it only made her feel smaller.

"Nothing to worry about, Miss O'Shea. Judging from your comments yesterday, you are well-versed on the subject," Mr Arche declared.

Stef didn't raise her gaze. Instead, she silently gathered her stationary, waiting for the school bell to mercifully signal the end of the lesson.

***

"Are you heading to the library?" a small voice quivered behind Stef. If it hadn't been for a gentle tap on her shoulder, she might not have realised the question was directed at her.

One of her classmates, Jihae Lee, stood with her arms wrapped tightly around a big, fat biology book. Beyond her name, Stef knew absolutely nothing about the girl.

"Maybe next time," Stef replied. "I have to be somewhere". Just as she blurted out the lie, she realised it was the most she'd ever said to a Granger student.

"I noticed you've joined the Coding Club?" It seemed as though Jihae wasn't going to give up so easily.

"Yeah," Stef muttered, her eyes flickering longingly towards the exit before returning to her classmate. Jihae stood frozen, her lips curved into a smile, clearly awaiting further discussion. Stef despised small talk with every fibre of her being, but she had promised her mother.

"So, like... are you in it or something?" Stef would definitely mention this interaction to her mother.

"I am the president," Jihae said. Then her cheeks blushed, and her eyes expanded. "I didn't mean it like... I am THE PRESIDENT. You know? I'm just... I guess I'm quite good at... computers." Her alabaster cheeks were about as red now as two ripe tomatoes.

"No. It's great." Stef took a wildly exaggerated step towards the exit and froze in a halfway position with her legs spread out like a Yoga Warrior. She didn't think the move through. Keeping constant eye contact with Jihae, she fully expected her to get the hint and leave her alone. But she didn't.

"I'll see you next week?" Stef's nostrils flared. She was growing increasingly aware of the awkwardness of her current pose, but moving back would mean accepting defeat and engaging in more small talk, and moving forward would bring her face-to-face with Jihae, which held even more potential for a physical comedy disaster.

Much to Stef's dismay, Jihae didn't move an inch. She stood still as a statue. An increasingly red statue. Then she shifted slightly in her spot, and Stef held a hopeful breath.

"Yeah. Next week. Cool," Jihae said, utterly oblivious. "I'm going to the library now. It's great – the library. The internet is really fast. They have lots of books. And... magazines of sorts. And also some periodicals..." Jihae tilted her head to the other side but still refused to move.

"Aren't those just magazines?"

"I don't know. Is there a difference? Anyway, they've got both, and scientific papers too." Now, she was the bobblehead. "Maybe you'd like to join me? We could work on the paper together."

"Um." Stef considered the proposal for a moment. "I have somewhere to be. Unfortunately. So, yeah. No. I mean. I can't."

"Sorry. I didn't mean to... you know. Um. Take up your time or anything." Jihae lowered her gaze and tucked a strand of hair behind her ear.

"That's okay," Stef said, her front leg really starting to burn.

"Yeah. Okay. Maybe next time?"

"Great."

"Yeah. Great. Sorry. Bye." Jihae flashed a quick smile and, with a coy wave of her hand, finally cleared Stef's path. Stef exhaled with relief, completing the step. Jihae scurried in the direction of the library. Stef rubbed her sore thighs, then made her way towards the exit.

Jihae Lee was right about one thing: The Granger Academy Library was a sight to behold. Stef had only been once, during a mandatory tour of the campus. It was a grand old building, grander even than the Academy itself. It was spotlessly white with tall columns supporting part of its roof – an East London Parthenon. Everything inside was carved out of dark maple and smelled of money. At that moment, there wasn't a place in the world where Stef wanted to go less, but the promise of a good internet connection was tempting, considering the assignment. Stef bit her cheek and pursed her lips to the side. She could, of course, go home and try her luck with the good old Dial-Up or...

***

"Hello, Miss Wilson," Stef said with an open smile.

"Stef? What are you doing here?" Miss Wilson, a young and pretty librarian at Stef's old school with blond curls and painted red lips, seemed genuinely surprised. She opened her arms for a hug, which took Stef aback. She couldn't recall ever hugging Miss Wilson before, and the unexpected gesture made the situation awkward for both of them. Stef stood still like a tree while Miss Wilson wrapped her arms around her, holding the embrace for what felt like an eternity.

"Is it alright if I study here?" Stef finally asked.

Miss Wilson blinked erratically as her eyes widened in surprise.

"It's closer to home," Stef explained.

Suddenly, Miss Wilson shimmied, as if she were about to dance, and replied in a higher-pitched voice than usual, "But of course! No problem. Take a seat."

"Do you think my old password works? For the computers?"

"Take mine!" Miss Wilson shrieked, still in her heightened state of excitement, as she wiggled her fingers while scanning her desk.

"A-ha!"

She found a pen, scribbled her login details in a notebook, tore out the page, and handed it to Stef with a courteous smile.

"Thanks, Miss Wilson."

The library looked exactly as Stef remembered it – littered with light wooden desks, haphazardly placed, professions of young love scribbled over them with neon markers and naughty words scratched out with sharp objects. Mismatched chairs of different shapes, sizes and colours were scattered around. The far wall was lined with a single row of grey desktop computers with thick, curved screens. Simple bookcases held far too many vacant spaces, with books arranged by the first letters of their titles, rather than the last names of their authors. It was empty. It was always empty.

Stef brushed her hand gently against one of the desks, its bumpy surface threatening to splinter and lodge into her skin. She exhaled. Everything looked the same, everything except Stef herself. She caught a glimpse of her reflection in one of the thin wall mirrors strategically hung around the library to make it seem more spacious. Her deep purple uniform looked almost offensive, and it made her cringe. She looked like an aubergine, a ginger aubergine, and in Stef's opinion, ginger certainly didn't go with purple. She shrugged off her blazer, draped it over the back of a wobbly chair, and installed herself in front of a computer.

Drumming her fingers on the table, Stef stared blankly at the screen. She didn't quite know where to start, but she vaguely remembered Paul mentioning a website called Wikipedia, an online encyclopaedia of sorts. Paul was great with those things, always up to date with the latest technological advances. Stef, on the other hand, wasn't as computer-savvy, but she was smart, loved challenging puzzles, and was exceptionally good at maths. Perhaps joining the Coding Club wasn't such a bad idea. Maybe she could actually learn something useful.

She typed MARS into the Wikipedia search box. The assignment was about that, so reading everything she could about the planet seemed like a good starting point.

Mars is the fourth planet from the Sun and the second-smallest planet in the Solar System, larger only than Mercury; in English, Mars carries the name of the Roman God of War and is often referred to as the 'Red Planet'.

Stef exhaled and raised her eyebrows. Maybe she could just write down what she had already articulated in class, but she wasn't sure how to expand that into 3000 words. Here she was, stuck on the third planet from the Sun, in front of a computer screen, trying to load her brain, which relentlessly refused to be switched on.

Stef heard a musical giggle coming from the back of the library, and the room filled with a blend of pungent perfumes. Stef snapped around, surprised that someone in Assisi was aware that the library existed. To her chagrin, it was none other than Alex and her posse, consisting of her three BFFs: Nadia, Blanca, and Harriet.

The posse gathered around a square table, with Alex perched on top, towering above her loyal subjects. Her gaze briefly met Stef's. Visibly taken aback by the unexpected encounter, Alex frowned, then forced a lightning-brief smile before returning to her conversation.

Stef couldn't help but notice that their faces were heavily made up, as if Van Gogh himself had applied their cosmetics. Alex's eyelids were smeared with blue and green eyeshadows, and her lips were blush-pink, as if trying to pretend it was their natural colour. Everyone had impossibly curly and impossibly long lashes that batted heavily over their eyes like peacock's tails. Stef imagined that those four had read a book at some point titled something like How to Be a Girl, and they followed it to the letter. Was she supposed to look like this too? Did Paul want her to look like this?

A strange sour feeling welled up in Stef's stomach. Something she hadn't felt before; something completely alien. She forced herself back to the computer, muttering the words from the Wikipedia page as if saying them aloud would help her concentrate. It didn't. Her eyes kept drifting towards Alex's reflection on her computer screen. Alex had a date with Paul later that evening. Her Paul. The library walls seemed to vibrate with that girl's voice, with her laughter. What could possibly be so funny? Were they talking about Paul? Were they talking about her? About the hideous purple jacket that slouched conspicuously over her chair?

The computer switched into screensaver mode, snapping Stef back to the present. She grabbed the mouse and was about to click when something caught her eye. The screensaver displayed a picture montage of the school's history. It started in the 1980s when it was founded by a Catholic priest, whose name Stef couldn't remember.

The pictures transitioned smoothly from one to the next, diffusing into each other with a cool special effect. The old photographs were interspersed with the new, some in black and white, some in colour. Stef even recognised a few from her old yearbooks.

There were pictures of the old church, which looked more than half the size of the new one. Stef remembered that the new church was built ten years ago or so and was donated to the school by a generous benefactor. Her dad told her he had started working at the school around the same time. It was the only building in Assisi that could rival Granger. Tall, lanky, and elegant like the spire of a French Cathedral, it boasted the most intricate wooden carvings of Jesus, Mary, and all the Apostles. It was the most impressive building in the whole suburb, and the students were rarely allowed inside.

Stef's eyebrows furrowed at the photograph from 1995. It was a typical picture of the graduating class, all neatly arranged in their uniforms. There wasn't anyone she recognised. However, the photo made her uncomfortable, like an itch she couldn't scratch. She pored over it, her nose almost touching the screen. There was something about that image... But before she could figure it out, the picture diffused into another more recent image from a football practice with Paul and his mates. Stef smiled instinctively, then clicked the mouse and returned to the Wikipedia page. But the memory of that earlier photograph refused to let go, making it impossible to concentrate on her assignment. Curiosity continued to prickle from within; she had to do something about it.

Stef got up from her seat and walked through the room towards the librarian's desk, passing Alex and co on her way. Stef smiled courteously and managed a barely audible "Hi". They all looked at her, and for once, they stopped laughing.

"Hi," Alex replied, glancing Stef up and down like some sort of alien. No doubt she hated Stef's kilt and that ludicrously gigantic pin that did nothing for the skirt except hang there.

The librarian's eyes sparkled as Stef approached her desk, anticipating a question.

"That screensaver..." Stef began, her mind still busy formulating precisely what she wanted from Miss Wilson.

"Ah, yes. They made it for the school's 20th anniversary," the librarian pre-emptively replied.

"There is a picture of the class of 1995. Is there any way I could look at it up close?" Stef asked.

Miss Wilson blinked continuously, scanning her desk again.

"Um. Actually," she clicked her tongue and patted the side of her face, then exclaimed, "Ah! Yes, of course. All the pictures were scanned from the yearbooks. They are all in there under Y for

Yearbook. We have one for every year since they've started making them."

She pointed towards the bookshelves.

"Thank you, Miss Wilson," Stef said, heading to the shelves labelled W – Z in bold black letters.

The yearbooks were printed with forest-green hardcovers, matching the uniform, with black lettering announcing the year at the bottom of their spines. All of the books looked identical except for one. The 1993 edition was bound in black, with the year and the school logo etched in silver lettering. Stef pursed her lips and reached for the 1995 one.

Flipping through the pages, she found the picture she was looking for – the one from the screensaver. It still made her gut curdle, but she couldn't understand why. Stef narrowed her eyes, scrutinising the faces, postures, and surroundings, determined to uncover the photograph's secret. Still, she couldn't understand it. Stef let out a long exhale, about to give up when it finally hit her with the speed of a bullet train.

"The uniform!" Stef shrieked.

In 1995, the school uniforms were vastly different from their current style. The boys sported green breeches, crisp white shirts, and matching green blazers – the exact outfit of the mysterious teen from the Disappearance of Eden Rose. The only difference was that the thief was missing the blazer. Stef's heart raced with excitement – she couldn't wait to share her discovery with Paul. Finding the boy himself in the yearbook would have been the cherry on top, though it seemed a bit far-fetched. Still, Stef flipped through the pages, scanning for his face. Then, she noticed that her hands were starting to tremble. As always, her intuition raced ahead of the logical side of her brain, and she struggled to catch up. Her gaze drifted to the black yearbook. It seemed even blacker now than a mere moment ago; it was tar-black, carbon-black. She reached for it, her hand shaking, and opened the first page.

Big, bold black letters on stark white glossy paper read: 'In loving memory of Ollie James, Annabel Harley and Gemma Madison'.

Stef's mouth dropped open, and she hastily flipped to the next page. Suddenly, Stef's arms felt like jelly, and the book seemed to weigh over a hundred tons. It slipped through her fingers and fell onto the floor with a heavy thud, stirring up dust on the yellow carpet. Her ears buzzed, her vision grew hazy, and her knees threatened to buckle.

Staring at her from the pages of the 1993 Yearbook was the photograph of Ollie James, his smile stretching from ear to ear. Ollie James R.I.P. The very same Ollie James who had snatched her apple just yesterday in *The Disappearance of Eden Rose*.

Five

"What happened to those kids?" Stef slammed the yearbook into the desk before the perplexed librarian, whose eyes blinked continuously as she chanted, "Umm," as if it were a Buddhist mantra. Her chant morphed into a drawn-out, "Iiiiiiiii don't know. It was way before my time here."

"Three kids died," Stef said, her gaze fixed on Miss Wilson.

It was one thing if a character in the game was based on a living, breathing person, but quite another if he'd been deceased. A ghost! A ghoul! This boy was dead. And not just him, but three others as well. They all died at the same time, on the same day, 24.02.93. There must have been an accident, a terrible one. Bizarrely, there was no mention of it in the yearbook. There was nothing but the three short paragraphs in their individual obituaries: 'Beloved son', 'devoted daughter', 'a maths wizard'.

Maths, in fact, was the only common thread among these three, aside from the school they attended. All three were members of the Maths Club at St Francis of Assisi Catholic.

"I can see that," the librarian finally replied, raising her palms like a barrier, as if the black book could somehow curse her.

"You see, I am playing a computer game with a character based on that boy. He looks just the same, even the uniform," Stef said as she tapped her index finger against the boy's smiling photograph.

"Okay." The librarian's lashes fluttered like butterfly wings.

"It's weird, right? The game was discontinued, and as far as I know, we have the last copy. But that boy... It's like his memory lives in that game or something. I thought... I don't know..." Stef's posture shrank. She didn't really know what she thought or what she could do. She just wanted to do something.

The librarian's smile seemed too wide, as if an invisible puppeteer held her lips open with strings. Her heart wasn't in it.

"Maybe that boy's parents would want to see him again? Even if it's just in a game," Stef mused aloud, her eyes darting around in their sockets. Her back straightened, and she seemed to have grown taller. The librarian started nodding continuously without letting her smile drop even a millimetre.

"Sure, that sounds like a splendid idea. Still, it's before my time. You can try Sister Christina, but I think she's out for the day. Come back tomorrow? The library is about to close." She tapped her wrist as if it had a watch around it. It didn't.

"Can I take the book with me? Just until tomorrow!"

The librarian's nods organically turned into shakes. "I can't let you do that, I'm afraid. Sorry. It's school property, and you don't even go here anymore."

Stef bit her cheek and frowned, before an idea struck her.

"Wait! Could I take a picture? With my phone?"

"I-I-I don't see why not." The librarian was still shaking her head, making her answer difficult to decipher. Stef decided to take it as a 'yes'. She rushed to her jacket, still slumped over a chair, clutching the black book in a tight embrace. She pulled her phone out of a purple pocket and snapped a picture of the boy. Now, all she had to do was show the picture to Paul, and together, they would surely think of something.

***

Paul didn't reply. Stef texted 'SOS', their code for something urgent, but received no response. It was likely that Paul wasn't allowed to use his phone. He must have been trapped in a dimly lit cinema, subjected to one of those tedious, cookie-cutter romantic comedies on a dizzying screen, munching on popcorn that reeked of burned butter and tasted painfully salty.

Alternatively, perhaps he had completely forgotten about his phone. One of his arms was probably snuggled around Alex's shoulders while the other reached for the Pic-n-mix they shared. They would be smiling and laughing, and he'd nervously shake his leg, just as he always did, contemplating when to kiss her. Stef shuddered at the thought. Either way, he was indisposed.

"Earth to Steffi!" Jason O'Shea stared at his daughter from behind an array of silver takeaway containers that separated them. He leaned into the back of his chair, his left ankle on top of his right knee, looking very debonair.

"Sorry, what?" Stef asked with a start.

"Steffi, dear, we haven't seen you all day. Could you please grace us with your presence?" Claire O'Shea said.

"What? What was the question?"

"How was school, pet?" her dad said, taking a sip of beer.

"Oh, good. Very good." Stef picked up her fork and knife and cut into the chicken on her plate.

"Did you make any friends?" her mum asked.

"Um, uh-huh. Yeah, I did. I made a friend."

"Really?" Claire's face lit up.

"Uh-huh. Jihae Lee."

"Really?" Claire's eyebrows drew together, forming a deep vertical wrinkle between them.

"Yes. Why?"

"Well, it's just that Jihae is one of my students. I would've thought she'd mention something to me."

"She didn't?" Stef exaggerated surprise.

"Not really, no. She did say you were busy after school, though. How's Paul?"

Stef's whole diaphragm contracted in a spasm. Her shoulders drooped, and her face sank. She looked down at her plate, lazily poking her fork into her sad chicken.

"I... didn't see him today."

Both of Stef's parents' eyes and mouths widened in apparent shock.

"Really?" They exclaimed in unison.

"I had to study," Stef grumbled.

Claire blinked repeatedly, staring at her child with a mix of shock and disbelief. "Well, that's... good."

Stef stabbed the fork into the chicken, imagining it was Alex or maybe Paul. She so wanted to tell Paul about Ollie James. Just then, a sudden realisation struck her like lightning.

"Dad!" she exclaimed, gaping at her father.

"Is everything okay, pet?"

"Dad! You started at Assisi ten years ago, right?"

"I did." Jason put his beer down.

"I was at their library today?"

"You what?" Claire exclaimed, and Jason gently placed his hand on hers.

"Dad! I found an old yearbook. A black one. Some kids died. Do you remember that?"

"Steffi, for goodness sake!" Red blotches began to develop on Claire's face, not dissimilar to Stef's own. "Jason!"

Jason squeezed his wife's hand a little tighter. His eyes remained fixed on his daughter.

"Yes, I remember. Why do you ask?"

"I'm just curious. I've never heard about this. Someone died? At school?"

"Not at school, no. There was an accident. At the Barbican tunnel. A school bus crashed. Well, not a school bus, but a bus with schoolchildren. Three of them were ours. Terrible, terrible tragedy. They were clever kids; they'd won something, some sort of a maths competition. And... a trip to central London, a day visit. But on their way back..." He raised his eyebrows and let out a deep sigh.

"I don't remember that." Claire frowned.

"It was before you joined the faculty, darling."

"Sure, but a tragedy like that... You'd think someone would've mentioned something," Claire said.

"Well, we were told not to. The principle was quite adamant. There was a vigil and a black yearbook. A new church. And then life went on as normal."

"A new church?" Stef asked.

"I think it distracted from the tragedy. It gave us something else to concentrate on, for better or worse."

"Worse, Dad. For worse." Stef's hands tightened into fists.

"Well, I'm not so sure. Strange rumours were going around. It was better to move on." Jason took another sip of his beer and licked his lips.

"What sort of rumours?" Stef's eyes narrowed.

"I don't think it's appropriate to discuss this over dinner, pet," Jason said.

"I agree," Claire added.

"But Dad!"

"Eat your chicken."

***

Stef stared at her phone, wishing she could will Paul to text with the power of her mind – telekinesis. She sat cross-legged on her narrow single bed, alone in her room, surrounded by pastel pink walls with candy-coloured bunnies frolicking throughout. Her back leaned against the wall she shared with Paul. She wore pink unicorn pyjamas and cradled the Nokia in her lap like a little kitten. Apart from two or three pieces of furniture, the room hadn't changed since Stef was in utero. She loved it.

Suddenly, the screen lit up. PING. A new message. Stef held her breath, grabbing the phone ravenously. He'd answered. Paul had finally answered. She clicked on her messages, fingers trembling with excitement. '5 mins' the message read. Stef's shoulders dropped, heavy with disappointment. She tossed the phone to her feet, and it bounced like a pebble on water. She wasn't exactly sure what she expected Paul to say, but it definitely wasn't that. What if something had happened? What if she was hurt? An SOS text warranted more than '5 mins', surely. Stef scoffed, feeling anger starting to sizzle.

Just then, there was a knock on the wall behind her. It was the secret knock they'd used since they were six. It was supposed to spell out CHAT in Morse code – long knock, short knock, long, short, pause, short, short, short, short, pause, short, long, pause, long. It was highly impractical, difficult to remember, and way too long. Stef loved it. She couldn't hide her smile even if she tried.

The CHAT signal could only mean one thing. Stef leapt off the bed and rushed to the window. Twisting the metal latch open, she lifted the bottom pane, and flakes of old paint drizzled on top of her ginger hair. Then she grabbed hold of the plastic pink cup dangling on a piece of string and stuck her head outside. There he was, Paul, poking his head out of his window, holding his end of the string phone. Paul covered his mouth with his blue cup. Stef pulled the string taut and placed her pink cup over her ear.

"Hey. You alright?" Paul said, his voice awkward and somewhat hesitant.

Stef nodded in response.

Truth be told, their windows were close enough to hear each other if they spoke just a bit louder than usual. And if they wanted to ensure the neighbours didn't overhear, they had mobiles and landlines as backup. However, they never resorted to any of those options. A string phone always seemed far more exciting and adventurous.

"I found something in the library," Stef began, her eyes gleaming. Paul placed the blue cup over his mouth. It was Stef's turn to listen.

"Yeah, I heard. What were you doing in the old library, Stef? Alex mentioned she saw you," Paul said.

Stef frowned and gave Paul a stern look, as if to convey that he was missing the point entirely. She gestured for him to pay attention with a vigorous wave of her hand. He huffed loud enough for Stef to hear, clearly annoyed, but obeyed her command.

Stef took a deep breath.

"The boy from the game, the VR game, is real." She spoke slowly, carefully selecting her words and nodding at precisely the right moments. Paul's eyebrows furrowed, and he opened his mouth to speak, but Stef silenced him with a hard stare. She wasn't finished.

"I saw him in the yearbook, okay. He is dead." She widened her eyes to emphasise the word 'dead'. "There was a picture of him. His name was Ollie James, and he's dead. He died in 1993. I took a picture with my phone. Dead." Stef felt funny about using the word 'dead' so frequently, but she believed the situation warranted it. She continued to glare at Paul with her eyes wide open, tears forming because of the wind and her stubborn refusal to blink. Paul tilted his head and side-glanced Stef, looking somewhat perplexed.

"Okay. Hold on a second," he called from his window and disappeared into his room. Stef hurried to her bed, snatched her phone, and prepared the picture. ☐

She scurried down the stairs, her footsteps thumping loudly against the wooden surface. She glided towards the front door, her socks allowing her to slide like an ice skater. A knock. She flung the door wide open and thrust the phone out, nearly shoving it into Paul's face.

"Dead!" she exclaimed. Paul leaned back and inspected the photo, his eyebrows rising higher and higher. Then he drew a deep breath and held it for a moment.

"Okay. This *is* weird." Finally, he exhaled.

Six

Poring over Paul's convex computer screen, Stef typed 'Bus Crash Barbican Tunnel 1993' into the Google search bar. Paul decisively hit Enter with his index finger. The search produced 63,000 results. Stef huffed and threw her arms in the air.

"We can't go through all of these."

"Let's see," Paul said.

The top five pages were dedicated to the Barbican Centre, its recent exhibitions, screenings, and events – all unrelated to any sort of a car crash. Paul scrolled down, his face twisted into a frown. There was something about a traffic accident in America, general information about the Barbican Tunnel and its history, a Wikipedia page about the Moorgate Tube Crash of 1975, and more unrelated information. Paul continued to press his finger into the keyboard, switching to the next page and the one after. There was nothing. Absolutely nothing.

"Stef, are you sure about this?"

"That's what my dad said. There was a bus crash inside the Barbican Tunnel that killed three Assisi students, among others. You saw their pictures."

Paul huffed, shaking his head. "It's just that... something like this would have info about it online. Old news articles... something." His eyebrows furrowed briefly, then shot up, almost reaching his hairline. "Unless..."

"Unless someone was trying to hide the truth." Stef finished his thought, and a shiver ran down her spine.

"Someone very powerful," Paul whispered, as if afraid to utter the words aloud. "Because how do you hide the truth from the press?"

"You don't. You can't. But you can pay them a lot of money to keep quiet." Stef bit her cheek.

"How do you keep everyone quiet? You can't buy everyone, can you?" Paul said.

"Keep looking." She flicked her eyes towards the computer.

"There are thousands of results," Paul said.

"Do you have somewhere else you need to be at this hour?"

"No." Paul rolled his eyes slightly, just enough for Stef to notice. He clicked the mouse again, reached page 12, and scrolled through the results, slowly letting go of his tired breath. Page 13. Scroll. Scroll. Scroll.

"Wait, can you go back?" Stef pressed her finger against the screen. "Up, up."

Paul complied, rubbing his eyes with his mouse-free hand.

"There!" She pointed. "Look."

The page header read, 'Barbican Children: A Cover-Up of a Tragedy'. Paul clicked on the link. Everything went blank. They kept staring. Nothing. A little circle inside the address bar spun round and round. Loading. It was like watching an endless washing machine cycle.

"Slow internet is the worst," Paul grunted, slamming the mouse a few times against its pad. Then he gave the computer a firm side-slap for good measure. The web address changed from google.com to conspiracymorpheus.com.

"See. It works. All it needed was a nudge of encouragement," he said with a smile.

They gaped at the screen, their expressions identical – open mouths and wide eyes. Paul read aloud.

"Hello, my truth-seeking friends. If you find yourselves on this page, then you are well on your way to opening your small minds, tightly controlled by the state media. If you find yourselves here, it means that, like me, you refuse to be a sheep, a cog in the propaganda machine. You refuse to be lied to. You refuse to be used. You refuse to slave away day in and day out for the fat cats. If you are reading this, you chose the red pill. Don't you think that we are all entitled to the truth in the age of information? The truth about Area 5 and The Kennedy Assassination, among many other unspeakable government conspiracies?"

Paul paused, hovering the cursor over the highlighted words. The usual arrow turned into a little hand, indicating that you could click those words for further information.

"Okay, yes, this guy sounds a little nuts," Stef said, biting her cheek.

"Or girl," Paul added with a smile.

Stef couldn't contain a chuckle. She nudged Paul with her elbow and took over reading.

"So… Kennedy Assassination… I, for one, refuse to be lied to!" Stef exaggerated a frown, squeezed her hand in a fist, and punched it dramatically up in the air. "I refuse to be a tool in a never-ending machine of lies!" she continued, adopting the mannerisms of a fascist dictator.

Paul laughed, and Stef carried on.

"The story I have for you today is straight out of the textbook of lies. It takes place in London, United Kingdom of Great Britain and Northern Ireland. In the land of top hats, bangers, mash, and the Queen. Paulito, is he serious?" Stef highlighted her flaring nostrils with an exaggerated tut. "On the day of the 24th of February, 1993... Oh, there we go, that's when they died, 24th of February, 1993. So... A bus carrying thirteen school children crashed inside the Barbican Tunnel on the eastern side of the capital city. All thirteen children were declared dead at the scene. At the time, local news channels reported the story briefly, as if the deceased were stray neighbourhood cats. In fact, this horrific tragedy received almost no coverage. No public vigils, no sympathies from the royals, no montages on BBC, CNN, or Fox News. Just quiet funerals, with only family members in attendance. Imagine that! Think for a moment! Thirteen children died, and yet, no one seemed to care. It's almost as if they were trying to hide something. But what was it? The answer is... I don't know, but as always, I have my theories. My research into the matter has yielded limited results. Only very few people connected with the tragedy agreed to an interview, but I did uncover some pieces of this very peculiar puzzle. A. The victims were all winners of a maths and science competition run by Riddle Corps, a UK-based gaming giant. It was to inspire children from the outskirts of London to pursue careers in STEM (which is what they call Science, Technology, Engineering, and Mathematics across the pond)." Stef gasped in disbelief, "Riddle Corps? No way."

"It actually makes sense. Someone in the programming department knew of this and wanted to honour those kids in their next game. Hence, they designed the Ollie character. It makes perfect sense. Keep reading."

"B. The bus was returning from a private tour of Riddle Corps headquarters in the City of London when the driver lost control of the vehicle and crashed into a wall. Now, this raises all sorts of red flags. Why did the driver lose control? The medical experts blamed a stroke, but this brings us to the next point. C. The driver is the only survivor of the tragedy. A stroke victim is the sole survivor of a deadly crash? Unlikely. D. Some parents agreed to talk to me, and guess what? They never saw their children's bodies. When the bodies were released to them, they had already been cremated. And finally, E. There is evidence of large sums of money transferred to the victims' families in exchange for keeping quiet. Large sums of money had also been donated to the victims' schools, as well as the sole survivor – the bus driver – who, from what I've heard, is now living the big life in St. Lucia. Now, if this doesn't sound like a cover-up, what does? Did Riddle Corps kill thirteen children, or was there someone else involved? Government? The royals? Perhaps. Or maybe, for a moment, we may speculate of an alien involvement, and in this case, the picture looks far more complex."

"This is completely bonkers. Aliens? I mean, this guy is mental," Paul interrupted.

"Or girl," Stef added.

Paul smiled, let go of the mouse, leaned back into his chair, and crossed his hands on the back of his head.

"This person..." he continued, "has absolutely no evidence about anything at all. No reasonable theories. No remotely plausible guesses. Aliens? Really? If anything, it seems Riddle Corps have been really generous in compensating the families."

"So, why isn't there more information about it online?"

"It was a long time ago, pre-mainstream internet. And yeah, maybe Riddle Corps didn't want its name associated with a horrific tragedy. I get that. But aliens? Come on!"

"There's just a bit left. Here... alien laboratory. Okay... questions remain. What happened to the Barbican children? If you have any relevant information, don't hesitate to get in touch via Contact Form. As always, I am here for you. I am your eyes and ears, your brain and your common sense. Always yours, Morpheus."

"This... person has watched *The Matrix* a few too many times," Paul suggested.

"Morpheus. It *is* a man, I reckon. And there's no such thing as watching *The Matrix* too many times." Stef tutted, making Paul chuckle.

Hovering the cursor over *Barbican children*, Stef clicked on the mouse.

"Look. It's got all their names. See? And their pictures. There are so many pictures."

Stef scrolled through a digital photo album filled with smiling faces, and an inescapable dread gripped her whole being.

"Alright, Stef. What's next?" Paul was visibly uncomfortable. He twisted himself away from the computer and towards Stef. His face was so close. Stef wanted to smile. Not because Paul was smiling at her – he wasn't – but because he looked like himself again. She knew his face better than anyone else's in the whole world. This face. The face of a boy with kind eyes and gentle features, one that would shine like a sunbeam when he was truly himself. Stef was never more comfortable in her skin or more at home than when she saw her reflection in Paul's eyes. She didn't speak for a while. She just looked at him, her smile escaping, her face dissolving into it fully.

Then he coughed uncomfortably, and that wonderful face of his contorted into something foreign, something new. His chin was up, and one of his eyebrows towered over the other, as though he was trying to project that he didn't care about any of this. It shattered Stef's heart into a million pieces.

"Should we contact him?" she asked.

"And say what?"

Stef shrugged. "We have information. It says here to contact him if we have any relevant information."

"We don't really know anything."

"We know about the game." Stef pushed Paul out of the way, carefully but firmly, regaining control of the mouse. Click. The contact form looked simple enough. All she had to do was fill in the blanks. Her email, she did just that, and the information. She went with: "Have some info. Get in touch." Click. Sent.

"Alright then," Paul sighed, "that's it?"

He still looked aloof, and Stef hated it.

"If you don't mind, I'd like to borrow the VR set. I can play before bed. On my own," she said, clenching her teeth.

"You want to play on your own?" Paul's expression was of surprise mixed with a smidge of jealousy. Stef could still read him all too well. He wanted to play. She smirked a little.

"Yeah. I mean, you can join if you want, but... like... whatever."

Stef felt those blotches developing on her face like images on a Polaroid picture. She closed her eyes, trying to will them away, but the more she thought about them, the more eager they were to erupt. She pushed her hand out.

"So, can I have it?"

Paul took a deep breath, scratched his cheek, and scanned the room.

"Ah, yeah," he muttered as if he suddenly remembered, and pulled the top desk drawer open. Sure enough, it contained the VR sets, neatly stacked, gloves folded.

"I'll go and find Ollie. On my own," Stef said. "I'm sure you've got other plans." Her face was red, and her neck itched violently, like from a nasty rash, but she stood tall and proud, like a giraffe. Paul pulled the headset out of the drawer and handed it over- just the one headset and one pair of gloves.

"Thanks," Stef said, swallowing the tears away and stomping out the room.

***

"Welcome back, Stephanie. I've been expecting you," Ariadne's voice chimed as if singing along to an inaudible melody.

"You have?" Stef felt a strange twinge inside her core.

"You quit and saved *The Disappearance of Eden Rose*. Would you like to continue?" At that moment, Ariadne's voice sounded particularly saccharine to Stef, eliciting an involuntary cringe.

"Yes, I would. I would like to continue, please. Where we… where I left off." Stef tapped her foot impatiently.

"I am afraid that's impossible, Stephanie," Ariadne said. "You would have to start a new game. Beginning with the tutorial."

"What? Why?"

"You have quit and saved…"

"Yes, yes, I know that."

"… A two-player first-person virtual reality escape adventure experience – The Disappearance of Eden Rose – cannot be completed by one person."

"Um. And I can't, um… switch?"

"I'm afraid you would have to start over. Beginning with the tutorial."

"I don't need a tutorial. I remember how it works."

Silence filled the impossibly white space around Stef for a little too long; it was a little too uncomfortable.

"Ariadne?"

"You will have to begin with the tutorial." Stef couldn't see Ariadne, but she imagined a vast smile plastered across her face, a generic white female face, so vast that it was painful to hold in place.

"I guess I'll have to go back to…"

"Wait. I'm here," a soft voice echoed from far away across the whole world. Stef jerked her neck and saw a tiny black speck growing bigger and bigger in the distance. The whole place seemed even whiter somehow. It was starting to hurt her eyes, and she had to squint.

"Stef?" It was Paul. She could now make out his silhouette. He picked up the pace with ease, as if strolling along a moving walkway.

"I see Paul has joined the adventure. Excellent news!"

"Is it?" Stef frowned, taken aback by Ariadne's enthusiasm.

"Would you now like to continue the virtual reality escape adventure experience that you have quit and saved?"

"Paul? What are you doing here?" Stef asked. Paul was already close, gliding in front of Stef like a spectre.

"You can't continue a two-player game with one person, Stef. It's obvious. I don't have any other plans tonight, other than going to bed, so... I thought I'd lend you a hand," Paul said, trying hard to sound as cool as ice.

"So, would you like to resume the game?" Ariadne repeated, sounding a tad impatient.

"Sure," Stef said, attempting to sound like she didn't care too much, but a slight smile flickered on her increasingly flushed face.

Seven

Stef gasped for air as if waking up from a nightmare. They were back in the Londelhi town centre. Paul held a wide-open newspaper that concealed his face from Stef, yet she never doubted it was him behind it.

At first, Stef didn't realise that her body was completely paralysed. When she did, a cold wave shot through her veins – panic.

"I can't move," she managed to utter through barely moving lips. Her face, her whole body, were frozen, as though every drop of her blood had turned to ice.

"I can't either. Maybe it's loading or something," Paul mumbled, as if speaking with his mouth full. Then his shoulder joints made a sharp cracking sound, and the newspaper lowered, finally revealing his face. The sight of it made everything seem just a little bit better, much like the sun in London when it deigns to emerge.

"It's just a game, Stef. Breathe," Paul said. "It's like when the browser freezes. Maybe." As Paul spoke, his lips gradually loosened, as if the ice inside was melting.

He cracked his neck with a loud pop and shook out his arms. Stef felt her own muscles soften, much to her relief. Throwing her head back, she spread her arms wide and took a deep, satisfying breath, until a familiar quiver on her wrist reminded her of the watch.

"Damn. I forgot all about the timer," Stef muttered, staring at the bright red 60:00 glowing across her wrist.

"Should I press it?" Paul asked.

Without waiting for a reply, he tapped the screen, releasing the golden projection. It radiated above them, making them tilt their heads back.

CALL FOOD DELIVERY

CALL TAXI

CALL THE POLICE

"You know, it's funny." Stef bit her cheek.

"Something is funny?"

"The first option is to call food delivery, and yet that guy Ollie… he said we shouldn't eat anything in here," Stef said.

"Must be all like… part of the game. It'll probably become clearer as we go along."

A brief smile flashed across Stef's face. 'Go along'. Paul wanted to continue; he wanted to carry on playing. With her.

"Yeah, you're probably right," she said, trying to sound nonchalant. "Anyway, what's next?"

"Next, we play." Paul winked, then returned his attention to the newspaper, swatting through its unruly sheets. "Maybe there's a clue."

Stef gently rested her chin on his shoulder, glancing through the paper with him. Aside from the story about the diamond on page 13, there were no numbered pages. However, it was brimming with numerous articles about imaginary locals and their strange stories. There was a piece about a man in America who found a potato chip that looked like Jesus. There was a story about a German Shepherd who wandered onto a football pitch during a League One match and scored a goal. There was one about a housewife who'd swallowed a toad. The toad was successfully extracted alive and now lived with the woman as her pet.

"I remember that one," Stef said. "I've read about that in real life."

"Whoever designed this game had a sense of humour."

"This guy." Stef tapped her finger into the newspaper, which rustled under her touch.

There was a story about a man named Zach, no surname Zach, who became the first person in the world to win a Nobel Prize for programming a computer game. A black-and-white picture accompanied the article, depicting a man with long, blond, dishevelled hair.

"For sure," Paul smiled. "He couldn't resist."

"Maybe there is a picture of Ollie James too."

"Who?"

"Paolito!" Stef slapped Paul's shoulder, ready to crack a joke. But feeling suddenly self-conscious, she cleared her throat instead and smoothed her clothes. "That boy who died," she said in a low, hushed voice.

"Oh, yeah. Let's see." Paul continued to wrestle with the newspaper, searching for Ollie. He shook his head at each page and punctuated the lack of findings with "Nope".

"Nope," he repeated, reaching the very last page. "Oh, wait."

"You found him?" Stef stretched her neck to see.

"Not him. But look... the last page has a number. It must be important."

"Page 26."

On the very back of the paper, there was a map. The Londelhi map didn't look like a regular map, but rather a sketch outlining all the main neighbourhoods in Londelhi. There was, of course, the town centre, beneath which it read "YOU ARE HERE". Stef also spotted the Westminster Police Station, the Taj Mahal Hotel and Casino, the Kitty Kat Club, and the Bigwig Estate. The entire layout formed a ten-by-ten square enclosed by a dotted line, with a pair of scissors drawn next to it.

"Scissors, hey." Stef smiled. "I know just where to find those."

***

The purpose of the lonely scissor stall among the dunes of fruits and vegetables finally became apparent. Stef and Paul watched the vendor - a tall, broad-shouldered figure – move in a programmed loop. He appeared realistic for about thirty seconds, but prolonged observation revealed his limitations. He swayed side-to-side, flashed a smile, waved at a neighbouring stall, wiped the sweat off his forehead, and then picked up a pair of scissors to inspect the blade. Afterwards, he placed them back down, and the loop restarted. He paid no attention to Stef and Paul.

"Some of the characters are more convincing than others," Stef said, ogling the robotic vendor.

"Yeah, like Ollie James and that dude in a cape."

"And that apple merchant." Stef turned to observe the woman in a purple sari standing behind her stall with her fists resting on the wooden table. Her poison-green eyes remained fixed on

Stef, while perfect red apples glistened before her. Stef offered the woman a nervous smile, which the woman returned.

"She gives me the creeps," Stef whispered.

"She's just a bot."

"She's a bit more sophisticated compared to this one." Stef wrinkled her nose at the scissor salesman, who was currently examining his product. He placed the scissors back down. Loop over.

"I'm gonna try talking to him," Paul said, puffing out his chest. "Excuse... excuse me." Paul cleared his throat.

The bot adjusted itself in a mechanical manner, resembling an automaton on a Disneyland ride, and turned towards Paul.

"May I help you, sir?" He blinked, only once, for an unnaturally long time.

"I'd like to purchase a pair of scissors, please," Paul enunciated as if addressing someone with a limited grasp of English.

"That will be four rupees, sir." Another unhurried blink.

Paul turned to Stef, a hint of embarrassment creeping into his voice. "We don't have any money."

Stef let out a sharp exhale. "Let me try."

"Sir?" she began. "Could we borrow your scissors for a moment?"

She picked up a pair, looping her fingers through to demonstrate their use. Snip. Snip. Snip. There was a pause. Suddenly, the bot snapped his head at Stef. She flinched. The salesman blinked again, just once, then straightened himself and stretched his long arm, pointing directly at Stef, yelling, "Thief! Thief! Thief!"

"No. No. No. I didn't..." Stef hurriedly returned the scissors to the pile and raised her hands above her head. But it was too late. Sirens blared in the distance, drowning out the commotion and gasps that filled the air. The bot kept screaming and pointing, as if malfunctioning.

"Okay, you know what?" Paul snatched the scissors, cut out the square from the paper, and folded the map into his back pocket. "Thanks for that." He flashed a smile at the screaming bot, grabbed Stef by the hand, and pulled her away. The bot continued to shout and point at an empty space.

They ran as fast as they could towards the labyrinth of mirrors, thinking they would be safe in the periphery – but they were late again. In an instant, the entire square was cordoned off with yellow tape. They were surrounded. Armed police, clad in padded vests, helmets, earpiece wires, masks, and dark goggles which covered their faces, closed in on Stef and Paul from all angles. The teenagers froze, raising their hands in surrender.

The police advanced like a pack of black roaches, moving in perfect unison as if they were one entity. They drew their guns, knelt, and took aim. The menacing clicks and clacks of the oversized weaponry made Stef's heart flutter. Sirens screamed, assaulting her ears. Helicopter blades chuffed overhead, but she couldn't see them. The unbearable flashing of the blue and red lights made it difficult to see much at all. The noise and the light overwhelmed her, and Stef desperately wanted to cover her ears but didn't dare move.

"This is part of the game, this is part of the game, this is part of the game," she recited over and over.

Then the lights stopped flashing, and through the narrow slits in her eyelids, Stef could make out a rotund black silhouette separating from the crowd, moving closer and closer. Red lights illuminated his contour from behind, making him look like some sort of a demon.

"What have we here?" the demon boomed. Stef opened her eyes a little wider and saw his face. She didn't expect it – his face was pleasant and jolly. He looked like a mall Santa Claus who had shaved off his beard and joined the police force. His hands rested on his belt, which squeezed his big, bouncy belly in two.

"A pair of common tieves, I see." He had an Irish accent and pronounced 'thieves' with a hard T.

"We are not thieves!" Paul shouted back.

"That's what a tief would say." The policeman chuckled, sending ripples down his body that made him jiggle like jelly.

"We didn't steal anything!" Stef stomped her foot hard into the ground.

"Well, that would be fur me to decide. Take 'em away." He smiled wide enough for Stef to see all of his teeth, and then it happened again. Stef tried to move her foot, but it wouldn't budge. Cold spread through her legs, moving up and up, taking over her entire body, rendering her completely immobile. She closed her eyes and clenched her teeth, feeling her ears buzz and her head grow unbearably light as the cold flooded her bloodstream.

With a start, she gasped and opened her eyes. She found herself inside a room that was unmistakably a holding cell in a police station. Through the black metal bars, she could see a wooden table and a green plastic chair. A window on the side wall was wide open, letting in a gentle breeze that caressed thin lace curtains, making them flutter. Stef could feel the air puffing tenderly against her skin.

Above the table, a silver-framed sign read: 'You can only do your best. That's all that you can do.' To the other side of the table, Stef could just make out the contour of a door. It was as white as the wall around it, but discernible upon closer inspection.

The room was filled with inexplicable sounds of indistinct chatter and telephones insistently ringing, as one would expect in a busy police station. However, the room was empty, save for Paul, who was perched on a crooked metal bench inside the cell, scratching the back of his head.

"There's a padlock," he muttered, nodding towards the barred door. Stef spun around and approached the lock, cupping it in her hand. She could feel its weight and the cold of the metal so vividly that it caught her breath. She wondered if she would ever get used to how real this game felt.

Catching a glimpse of the watch on her wrist, Stef saw the crimson 59:34:35, monotonously ticking away. Her stomach curdled again.

"The countdown has started," she said.

"I noticed."

The padlock was a standard square brass variety adorned with the Riddle Corps logo and a four-digit code. As Stef's hand released its grip, the hidden door swung open with a bang, letting the jolly policeman in. His face beamed with delight, two perfect rosy circles gracing each cheek as if painted on with rouge. He waddled across the checkered linoleum floor up to the bars, a litter of keys clanging joyfully on his leather belt with each step. The keys were threaded through a wide silver circle, a fixture every prison guard in every movie Stef had ever seen had hanging on their belt. Stef found it perplexing that this particular policeman would need so many keys, considering they were locked in with a code and the white door had no discernible keyhole. It was, perhaps, to hammer in the point that this man was in charge, and they were his prisoners.

As the fog of adrenaline dispersed, Stef noticed that, apart from the constricting belt, the policeman wore a fitted navy jacket with round silver buttons, matching trousers, and a cap with a silver Londelhi Police emblem beaming proudly at its core.

"Well, well, well," boomed the sumptuous man. The whole room seemed to pulsate with his timbre. "Once a tief, always a tief."

"What's that supposed to mean?" Paul protested from the back, not bothering to get up from the bench.

"You two. You stole the Eden Rose, didn'tcha?"

"What?" Paul wrinkled his face in a grimace. Stef's mouth opened slightly in surprise.

"I am Superintendent O'Shady of the Londelhi police force, and you shall address me with respect, young man. If you didn't steal the diamond, then prove it." He chuckled.

"Well, actually, it's up to you to prove we're guilty. It's innocent until proven otherwise, is it not?" Stef narrowed her eyes and straightened her back. Taking a step forward, she clenched the bars tightly with both hands.

"You're free to search us, mate. We don't have the diamond," Paul added.

"And we didn't steal the scissors either. We just borrowed them for a split second." Stef put her hands on her hips.

"A-ha. But ya do know about the diamond, don't ya?" the policeman winked, as if he'd just caught them in a lie.

"Um... It was in the papers. The theft of the century," Paul said.

The superintendent narrowed his eyes, angled his face to the side, and studied them both carefully.

"Who are ya?" he said.

"We're... We're... just playing..." Stef said, but as she uttered the truth aloud, she realised that she wasn't sure it was actually true.

The superintendent's face relaxed into his usual smile. Circles on his cheeks seemed even rosier than before.

"Playing?" he cackled. "I see. Adventurers. So you claim you are The Puzzle Masters, do ya?"

"Yes. The Puzzle Masters. That's us." Paul rose from the bench, joining Stef. He squeezed her arms gently from behind. Stef caught her breath. She closed her eyes briefly and dabbed her burning cheek with an icy hand to keep herself from turning tomato-red.

"Well, well, well. If you are indeed The Puzzle Masters, then it shouldn't be difficult for ya to prove it." Superintendent O'Shady gave out a hearty laugh, patting his big round belly. "I think it's time for tea."

Tipping his hat, as if he were Charlie Chaplin himself, he disappeared through the barely-visible door, and the room fell quiet, but for the ambient hubbub of the telephones and the wonted office jibber-jabber.

"I guess we need to figure out that code," Stef said, flicking her eyes at the glistening gold padlock.

Eight

"Any more ideas?" Paul said, his head lolling back against the brick wall.

The padlock felt heavy in Stef's hands.

"It's not colour-coded like before. Even if there were numbers in this room, how would we know which one goes where?" She bit her cheek.

The glowing red watch dial inexplicably flashed 23:15. Had it really been that long? Stef's hands trembled, and her stomach swarmed with butterflies ready to burst out of her windpipe. She couldn't help it, even though she knew it was just a game. 'What's the worst that could happen?' she thought.

"What do you think happens at zero?" Stef's voice quivered.

"Game over?"

"What happens when it's game over?"

"Stef, it's just a game. A very, very advanced game, that's all."

"That doesn't answer my question." Stef turned to Paul, her eyes pleading for an answer. He remained silent. Stef exhaled and tightened her grip on the lock.

"It's just a game. Just a silly little game," she muttered under her breath, but the butterflies refused to settle.

Paul rose from the bench and approached Stef, placing his hands on her shoulders.

"Stef, we can do this," he said, kneading her tense muscles with his strong fingers. "We've cracked all sorts of puzzles, right? Like that crazy hard one. That human-to-merman periodic table formula thing."

"Pablo, we had to look that one up," Stef replied, releasing the padlock with a clang. It dangled mockingly in its original position. She turned to face Paul, the corners of her lips drooping.

"Just the periodic table. And now you know it by heart," he said, his thumb resting gently in the centre of her chin. Stef raised her gaze, oblivious to the tender gesture; the cogs in her brain were too busy turning.

"Nothing in this room could be a number, except for the bars," she said, taking a step back. "And there are fourteen of them. We need four digits." Stef rubbed the bridge of her nose and took a deep breath. "Okay. Let's start over." She straightened her spine and stretched her neck taut, attempting to regain control of her anxious breathing. Then, stepping into the middle of the prison cell, she rotated slowly, scanning the surroundings with heightened attention to detail.

"What am I missing?" she whispered, her eyes narrowing at the window and the fluttering curtain, the brick wall, the nearly invisible door, the desk. Whatever it was she was meant to see – she didn't see it. A profound sense of hopelessness washed over her. The puzzle made no sense. None of it made any sense. Tears threatened to spill from the corners of her eyes. She fought hard to contain them.

"Letters, too, I guess," Paul said, gesturing towards the silver-framed sign hanging above the desk.

"You can only do your best. That's all that you can do," Stef read aloud. "You're right. There are forty letters."

"Wow, that's quick counting! Doesn't help though, does it?" Paul exhaled, letting his lips trill.

"It's two sentences. Maybe 20 and 20?" Stef's anticipation tingled through her skin. "Worth a try?"

"Definitely worth a try."

Stef's fingers raced across the lock, punching in 2-0-2-0. She held her breath.

"Rats," she muttered.

Paul groaned in disappointment. "I thought we had it."

"This sign stands out, doesn't it?" Stef said, turning her attention back to the words on the wall.

"You can only do your best. That's all that you can do," Paul repeated, furrowing his brows. "What do you think it means?"

Stef's gaze remained fixed on the strange words that meant so much and yet so little with an unwavering concentration. Her pupils dilated. A glint grew in her eyes that only Paul could discern. He knew that when the glint appeared, Stef was on the brink of a breakthrough.

"Oh!" Stef gasped, blinking rapidly.

"You've got it, haven't you?" Paul smiled, studying her face.

"Our best. We can only do our best. Do you remember what she said?" Stef beamed at Paul, her eyes radiating joy.

"Who said what, Stef?"

"Ariadne," she exclaimed, then tensed up momentarily, expecting to hear Ariadne's voice. There was nothing but silence. "Strange," Stef muttered, conflicting thoughts streaming through her head like motorway traffic. It took her a moment to sort them into orderly compartments. Then her wrist vibrated – a ten-minute warning.

"Stef, can you clue me in?"

Stef grabbed Paul by his arms, squeezing his biceps. "Remember Ariadne mentioned the game begins as the red door opens?"

"During the tutorial?" Paul's forehead creased.

"Yes. Do you remember what she said right after the door was already open? Meaning it was already part of the game."

Paul's eyes widened as comprehension dawned. "She said, 'Congratulations. Your best time is...' something I don't actually remember."

"She said your best time is fifteen minutes and twenty-three seconds. Your best time. You can only do your best." Stef beamed, her pulse racing.

"One, five, two, three," Paul repeated, and his cheeks dimpled. "You and your insane memory."

Stef dashed for the lock, her fingers dancing nimbly across the keypad: 1, 5, 2, 3. The lock released with a satisfying click and dropped to the ground with a clatter.

"You did it." Paul let out a laugh.

"Well, well, well," chuckled the superintendent.

Stef gasped, startled.

The policeman was leaning against the wall, arms crossed. Stef had no clue how he appeared there. He seemed to have materialised out of thin air, but there he was on the other side of the now wide-open cell.

"You two must be the puzzle masters indeed," he chuffed. "Aren't I lucky? In that case, you two must assist the Londelhi police department in solving the crime of the century. Are ya up for the challenge?"

"Um..." Paul screwed up his face.

"We are. Of course, we are," Stef said.

"Eggcelent." The policeman lovingly rubbed his big belly. "I am Detective Superintendent O'Shady. I am always at the station if ya need me. You can visit or call anytime. I will give you these badges..."

He held out two star-shaped pins, which he gave to Stef. She studied them in the palms of her hands – brass stars with Puzzle Master etched in the centre. She squeezed one tight and handed the other to Paul.

"So," O'Shady continued, "as long as you have these badges, you can question anyone in Londelhi, and they will know that you are here on official business. Eden Rose is the largest pink diamond in existence. Yesterday, it was stolen from a private residence. A mansion belonging to Sandeep Bigwig. He lives there with his famous girlfriend. You may have heard of her. Marilyn Star's the name."

"Sure." Paul's forehead creased.

"If you are going to work the case, I must share all the information I have with ya, Puzzle Masters. There are eight suspects. No more and no less." He chuckled, his belly wriggling like jelly. Then, he proceeded to count on his fingers, starting with his thumb. "Number one: Mr Crawley, the croupier at The Taj Mahal Hotel and Casino. Marilyn is a regular client of theirs. Two: A local Mafia boss, Don Rigatoni. He owns the casino and the club. I've heard he and Bigwig had a disagreement of sorts. Three: Boris, the bouncer at the Kitty Kat Club. Rumour has it he has a thing for Marilyn and has it in for Bigwig. Four: Katya, the dancer at the Kitty Kat Club. She has a thing for Bigwig and has it in for Marilyn. Five: The Frenchman who arrived mysteriously just a day before the diamond was reported missing. He claims he's here on business. But you know what I always say? Never trust the French. He's staying at the hotel. Six is, of course, Marilyn herself. Because you know what I always say? Never trust a woman. Seven is Bigwig. There was quite an insurance on that diamond, you know. And last, but not least, is me. Because you never know if you're speaking to a corrupt copper." With those words, he narrowed his eyes into thin ribbons and leaned a little closer. Then, in a sudden shift, he burst into hearty laughter and resumed his usual cheerful tone. "Anyway. Myself and the entire Londelhi police force would greatly appreciate your assistance in solving this case. Best of luck. And I shall leave you to it." With that, he turned abruptly and strode towards the barely visible door.

"Wait," Stef called after him, but he ignored her.

The door slid open, and he stepped through it. Stef lurched after him, but the door slammed shut just in front of her nose. There was no handle, no knob, nothing.

"Did you get any of it?" Paul sighed.

"You know I did. But... how do we get out of here? That's what I was going to ask him." Stef tried pushing the door, but it wouldn't budge. In fact, it seemed to have turned into a solid wall, with no hint of its frame remaining.

"Um…" Paul scratched his chin and wrinkled his nose.

Stef remembered her watch. She gave it a light, uncertain tap. Once again, the big letters loomed over her head.

CALL FOOD DELIVERY

CALL TAXI

CALL THE POLICE

"We can't call a taxi here, can we?" Paul said.

"Worth a try?" Stef shrugged and exclaimed, "Call a taxi, please."

Just then, a gust of wind rushed into the room through the window, making Stef hold her breath and close her eyes. When she reopened them, the small window wasn't that small anymore, nearly doubling in size and still growing. It stretched wider, spanning the entire wall, then extended from floor to ceiling. With each expansion, the wind grew stronger, whipping Stef's hair. The window continued to grow until it ceased to exist, leaving behind an open wall – or perhaps, the big, fat absence of a wall altogether.

"Are you seeing this?" Stef shrieked.

Paul stood close beside her, his warm breath stiffening against the back of her neck. She understood why; she knew he was terrified of heights. It didn't affect her the same way; in fact, quite the opposite, it exhilarated her.

Stef approached the edge and peered down. Beneath her feet, flying cars zoomed by. They must've been incredibly high up because the ground was obscured by a blanket of clouds. Stef could only see the cars, like fish swimming in the hazy waters.

She imagined herself standing on the ledge of a skyscraper. She wondered what would happen if she jumped. Would she float in the clouds like a bird, or would she plummet to the ground, and the game would be over? Would she feel that she was falling?

"Stef, what are you doing?" Paul's voice quivered.

He dared not venture anywhere near the edge, his complexion paling with queasiness. Stef shuffled even closer to the precipice, her toes hanging over the abyss. Balancing on her heels, she raised her arms as if preparing to take flight. The wind enveloped her, teasing the possibility of lifting her up into the air. She had never felt so free.

"Stef, please." Paul swallowed.

Then, with a sudden gust and a familiar whoosh, a Londelhi taxi appeared before them – the very same one that had taken them to the market. It hovered in mid-air in front of Stef. She stepped back, allowing space for the dome to open and the steps to unfold.

"Welcome back, love," the cheerful voice of an invisible cabbie exclaimed. "Where to this time?"

Stef glanced at Paul over her shoulder. He furrowed his brow momentarily before retrieving a crinkled map from the back pocket of his jeans.

"Bigwig Estate?" He tapped his finger at the location.

"Sounds like a plan." Stef winked and stepped into the levitating vehicle. "To Bigwig Estate, please."

"No problem, love."

The dome closed with a huff, cocooning them inside. Stef's stomach clenched in anticipation of the acceleration. What she hadn't anticipated was a hand slithering onto her shoulder from behind. She let out a startled shriek and catapulted out of her seat just as the cab launched into the air. Stef tumbled backwards and saw him. Crouching behind the silk taxi seats was Ollie James, his hands raised in surrender.

"I'm sorry. I didn't mean to startle you."

"What? How?" Paul said.

"There's only one real car in here. It was only a matter of time. I had a feeling you might come back. Plus, it's a good place to hide."

"Wait? What?" Paul blinked repeatedly.

"Hide from who? The person who stole the diamond? That man in a black cape?" Stef dug her hands and feet into the floor like a spider.

Ollie James lowered his arms, his eyes bulging. Then, suddenly, he let out a dry laugh – the driest laugh Stef's ever heard.

"Ha. Ha. Ha."

"What's so funny?" Paul glanced at Stef. She shrugged.

The laughter stopped abruptly, as if someone had snipped Ollie's vocal cords with garden shears.

"You really don't get it, do you? It's not about the diamond. It is not about the game. The person in the cape? That was the Soultrapper," he said.

"The Soultrapper?" Stef echoed.

Ollie James brushed loose strands of hair away from his face and slowly reached for his back pocket. A pair of scissors gleamed in his hand – the same ones from the market stall. Ollie spread the blades apart and clutched the scissors like a shiv.

"Woah," Paul said, just as the taxi jerked to a stop. The dome opened, letting the fresh air in, and before they knew it, Ollie James grabbed Paul's hand, scratched the blade across his palm and leapt out of the taxi like a springbok, running as fast as he could towards the periphery.

"That hurt!" Paul screamed, launching himself into pursuit. But Ollie was too nimble and fast for Paul, who quickly halted, doubling over to catch his breath.

Stef stepped out of the taxi. The dome immediately closed with a huff, and the car lifted and swooshed away.

Approaching Paul, Stef examined his hand. It was slashed from thumb to pinkie, blood seeping through in small round globules.

"It's not deep," Stef said.

"It's not real," Paul countered. "But it sure hurts. What is his problem?"

"I don't know. Just when I thought the game was straightforward – solve puzzles, talk to people, find the diamond." Stef pursed her lips and blew gently over Paul's wound.

"I know. What's a soultrapper anyway?"

"Someone who traps souls?" Stef chuckled. "It's crazy, right?"

"Like real souls? Yeah, it's mad. It's a game, Stef."

"I know, I know. It's just a game," she repeated, though a flicker of doubt lingered in her eyes.

"But..." Paul hesitated, "It's gotta be late now. Is it alright if we call it a day? I'm knackered."

"Yeah. Of course. We can carry on tomorrow or... some other time... when you're free." Stef cast her eyes down, a faint smile masking her unease. She knew her cheeks were turning bright pink.

"Hello, Ariadne?" Paul called out.

"How can I help?" Ariadne's singsong voice immediately replied.

"Now she's here," Stef muttered under her breath.

"Hey, Ariadne, mate. Can we leave it for now?" Paul scratched the back of his head, momentarily forgetting about his injury. It stung, and he winced in pain.

"Are you alright, Paul?" Ariadne crooned with faux concern.

"Totally fine. Don't worry about it."

"Would you like to quit and save?" she said.

"Yes, please," Stef replied,

"Very well then."

Stef's breath tightened, and her skin buzzed and tingled as her mind diffused into something inexplicable. It was as if she had entirely vanished from existence, but only for an instant.

With a sharp inhale, Stef eagerly freed her sweaty head from the heavy helmet. She was back in her room, or at least she assumed it was her room; Stef was enveloped in darkness. Her phone lit up quietly, confirming her location. There was a message from Paul.

"SOS. Your front door in 2."

Stef's brows furrowed. SOS meant something serious. Without giving it much thought, she sprinted out of her room and scampered down the stairs to the front door. Hastily, she pulled it open. Paul was already on her porch, looking entirely bewildered and panting heavily. He extended his hand. A slash ran from his thumb to his pinkie finger; dried blood crusted its outline.

"Alright, Stef. Maybe it's not just a game."

Nine

Mr Arche's mouth moved, which is how Stef knew that he was indeed speaking. Hearing what he actually had to say was an impossibility on par with telekinesis. Stef's mind screamed louder than anything on the outside of her cranium, its deafening pitch overpowering everything. It was too much. It was all too much. The teacher gaped directly at her, not looking too pleased. Uh-oh.

"Miss O'Shea?" Mr Arche's glasses slipped to the tip of his nose.

"Huh?" Stef wondered whether the enormity of the situation had reduced her to only being able to communicate in monosyllabic grunts.

Mr Arche continued speaking, but despite Stef's best efforts, she couldn't understand him. His words sounded muffled, like static. Stef had an idea what the topic of his speech was, of course. She was supposed to submit 3000 words on the subject of colonisation of Mars. Understandably, she had forgotten all about it. And while it was understandable to Stef, she doubted Mr Arche would be able to understand it at all. What was she supposed to say? Admit that she had been stuck inside a game which is quite possibly an alternate reality controlled by someone or something called the Soultrapper? For a moment, she considered telling the truth. Even if he didn't believe her, it was a big step up from the 'dog ate my homework' excuse. Stef opened her mouth.

"Um," she managed to utter.

Mortified, she shut her eyes and, after a few moments, felt a warm pat on the back of her hand – Mr Arche's warm, soft fingers.

"Miss O'Shea? Miss O'Shea? Miss O'Shea?!" The last 'ay' sound echoed its way into Stef's skull, and she snapped back to reality.

Stef could hear her teacher let out a slow, disappointed breath. On top of that, he looked concerned. Very concerned.

"I am sorry," escaped Stef's trembling lips.

"Miss O'Shea. I believe it is time I had a word with your mother – 4 p.m. tomorrow, after school. I will be expecting both of you in my office." He leaned closer, ensuring that their conversation remained private. Stef was grateful for that.

The school bell rang so suddenly that it made Stef's shoulder spasm. At least the school day was over. Stef was grateful for that too. Sure, a parent-teacher grilling session loomed on the horizon, but Stef was determined not to let it bother her today. Today, she had far more pressing matters to attend to.

***

"Paul," Stef gasped, her gaze fixed on his hunched frame beyond the school gates. Skipping down the school steps, she was aware of a smile creeping over her face; her lips tingled, and her heart began to flutter. Not wanting Paul to notice, she decided to be as nonchalant about the unexpected visit as possible.

As always, the school guard stood watch. Stef dispensed a scoff in his general direction before turning her attention to Paul.

"Didn't expect you here today. Don't you have plans with Alex or something?"

Stef puffed her chest out just a bit too far, making her look like a turkey.

"Please don't," Paul said, throwing his head back.

"Whatever do you mean?" Stef batted her eyelashes.

"I mean, it's quite obvious we've got a far more important issue to deal with," Paul said.

"If you say so." Stef flipped her hair – a manoeuvre she had never attempted before in her life. She could immediately feel her face and neck turning bright red.

"Look, I got us in. Well, Ringo did. To be honest, I don't know what we can find there, but it's worth a try."

"Wait, what? In? In where?" Stef's eyes widened, as realisation dawned, her attempt at casual indifference failing completely. Did he really mean…?

"Riddle Corps," Paul confirmed.

Stef's jaw dropped, her entire face lighting up like Christmas lights. "Are you serious? When?"

"Today, actually. In fifteen minutes."

Stef glanced at her phone. "Tight."

"Yeah, we better hurry."

***

Riddle Corps headquarters were famously located in the City of London, not far from the Barbican. It was wise to take the Tube instead of risking a traffic jam on the bus, but Stef hated the Tube. She found the whole experience utterly dreadful.

Busses were easy. Buses were all the same - blank faces staring out of the windows, into the void, or at other commuters; a young mother hoisting a cumbersome baby stroller; someone coughing; someone talking loudly in a foreign language; girls giggling; children crying. It was a familiar experience, cosy in its predictability.

But the Tube was different. The commuters on it seemed transformed, as if gliding two hundred feet underground turned regular humans into mole people.

It was eerily quiet, but for the rumbling of the train, like a starving gut. The vacant faces of the commuters were hypnotised by their mobile screens, clutched tightly between their fingers. The phones uplit their faces, which made them all look like maniacs in horror films. Stef's spine tingled. She tried to focus on Paul's face instead, but even he looked alien underground. She could hardly wait for their stop. When the voice finally announced it, she sprang to her feet and leapt out of the train carriage as fast as she could.

"You're claustrophobic, you know." Paul dropped the unsolicited comment.

It wasn't helpful. But Stef felt instant release once the sun's rays hit her skin, and she thought that perhaps Paul had a point.

The City was a bizarre mixture of glass and brick, the ultra-modern and the traditional. People scurried every which way, involuntarily clad in their dark suit uniforms, hands clasped around their oat milk cappuccinos, matcha lattes, and chai teas; their eyes cast down at the pavement, lest they invariably see someone they worked with or used to work with and be forced into a stop-and-chat.

The Riddle Corps building was even more impressive than Stef had imagined. She knew it was designed by a renowned modern architect, and she had seen pictures of it in the papers. She'd heard that it had won awards and was famous the world over. But looking up at it from below made it look all the more spectacular.

The building had a peculiar shape, resembling a ball of crumpled paper, hence its nickname, The Crumple. Each crinkle was formed by the strategic placement of glass panels, of which there seemed to be millions. Every panel was entirely reflective, camouflaging the building so seamlessly into its surroundings that it became almost invisible, yet always moving, always evolving, always breathing in sync with the city.

"It's..." Stef struggled to find the words.

"It's nice," Paul said.

"The Big Ben is nice. This is... astounding."

"Whatever," Paul huffed and started towards the revolving door.

Ringo was already there, chatting with a receptionist in the lobby – a pretty blond with thick curls. Stef noticed her cheeks blush slightly when she laughed. Ringo must've said something funny.

"Ring," Paul called out, and Ringo immediately turned towards him. His mind lagged behind somewhere in the riveting conversation, and it took him a second or two to register that his visitors had arrived.

"There you are. I've been waiting." He flashed a quick wink at the receptionist, who coiled a strand of hair around her index finger.

Ringo put his hands on both his guests' shoulders as if they were one composite person.

"So, this is it. This is where I work," he said with much pride and satisfaction.

"It's..." Stef began.

"It's nice," Paul finished.

"It's insane!" Stef corrected.

"So, what do you want to see first? Actually, there is a certain degree of secrecy here, so I can't take you just anywhere."

"Your office?" Stef suggested.

"Desk. And no. Sorry." Ringo sucked in air through clenched teeth.

"Maybe where they test out the new stuff?" Paul said.

"Can't do that either."

"Okay, so where can you take us?" Stef's forehead wrinkled.

"Here, the museum, and the gift shop."

"There's a museum?" Stef asked.

"And a gift shop," Ringo said.

"Alright. Let's go to the museum." Paul lifted his arms and let them fall, slapping his thighs.

"Follow me."

***

The 'museum' was a small gallery, a stark white 50-square-metre room with pictures on its walls and old consoles displayed in glass cubes atop white pedestals. A miniature of the entire building was proudly exhibited in the centre. There wasn't another visitor in sight.

The exhibition took you from the 1960s, when the first Riddle Corps computer game was created, to a section called 'Riddle Corps and the Future', where they announced games currently in development. There wasn't any mention of VR, and nothing remotely resembled the Eden Rose headset. The last exhibit featured a mobile phone, which was just one big screen with no buttons.

"We are moving into mobile gaming and the development of mobile phones themselves. We think it's the future. This one is completely touch screen. Isn't it cool? We're launching it this year," Ringo explained with an air of self-importance.

"We?" Paul smirked. Stef nudged him in the midriff.

"No VR?" Stef asked.

"No. It wasn't popular. I told you... junkyard. How is it going, by the way?"

"Oh, it's going," Paul said.

Stef circled the room slowly, uncertain of what she wanted to find. Her eyes curiously scanned plaques describing Riddle Corps' prizes and achievements, the names of designers and developers who worked there, and every CEO the company had ever had. She noticed screenshots from *Depths of Atlantis* and *Mission to Mars*, among many other games she'd played and loved. But one game stood out from the rest, mainly because she'd never heard of it: *Detective Dark*. Stef was convinced she'd played all the games Riddle Corps had ever released.

"Pablito?" she whispered. "Do you remember this? Detective Dark?"

The poster was black and featured a man also dressed in black, with inky black buildings in the background. The only thing not black was his face, staring cunningly from the picture, with a sparkle in his bright green eyes.

"I don't think so," Paul replied after careful consideration, nearly brushing the exhibit with the tip of his nose.

Stef squinted at the tiny letters below the poster: *1994. Detective Dark, an immersive adventure quest, designed by Zach Hughes for Riddle Corps.*

Stef gasped, clutching Paul's arm.

"Zach," she whispered. "Zach as in Londelhi Daily Zach."

"You think..."

"Maybe? Zach Hughes," she repeated.

Paul dipped his chin slightly. "We got a name."

Ten

They huddled over the trusty plump PC in Paul's room, making increasingly fruitless attempts to find something on Zach Hughes. Anything at all. It seemed there was absolutely nothing on the internet about the elusive programmer or his mysterious creation – *Detective Dark*. It was as if neither had ever existed. Of course, there were others named Zach Hughes – a pianist, an author, an accountant, a research analyst, an MMA fighter, and a convicted murderer. None of them had anything to do with Riddle Corps.

Detective Dark was another story. Stef half expected it, given how clueless the Riddle Corps gift shop cashier looked when Stef inquired about the game. It seemed they had sold every single game ever created by Riddle Corps, except for that one (and, of course, Eden Rose). The cashier blinked her long fake eyelashes, staring dubiously at Stef.

"It doesn't exist."

"But it is, literally, in your museum," Stef said.

"I don't know what to tell you."

Now, as they hunched over the slightly flickering screen, the cashier's cluelessness started to make sense.

"The museum thing must've been a mistake," Paul said.

"More like a slip-up. They never wanted anyone to know about the game, or about Zach. Maybe they are trying to hide Zach Hughes."

"Then we're definitely on the right track."

"No doubt in my mind," Stef agreed.

"But how do we find him?"

"Well, that is a million-pound question." Stef turned to Paul, who simultaneously turned to her, making their noses brush against each other. Paul immediately jerked backwards and cast his eyes as far down as they would go. Stef dabbed her cheeks to keep the blotches – which were threatening to explode all over her face – at bay. Ding! Their heads instinctively twitched towards the computer – a new email. Paul grabbed hold of the mouse.

"It's him." Excitement and disbelief fused in his voice.

Stef peeked at the screen. "Morpheus."

Three words beamed out decisively in bold: I AM LISTENING.

"Hit reply." Stef tapped Paul on the shoulder.

He did, punching in, "Dear Morpheus..."

"No, too formal." Stef cringed.

"You want to have a go?"

She did. Snatching the mouse away, she slid into prime position. She wiggled her fingers over the keyboard for a moment and began, "Morpheus... We." Delete. "I have come into possession of some very advanced tech from Riddle Corps. I think it could be connected to the tragedy in the Barbican Tunnel." Send. Swoosh.

Ding! Instant reply. "NOT HERE. ARE YOU DUMB?"

Stef released the mouse. Paul covered his lips, masking a smile.

Ding! "Tomorrow. Sixteen hundred hours GTM. Red booth. Beech and Golden."

"What does that mean?" Paul crossed his arms.

Stef grinned. "It means he will call us at 4 p.m. There's a phone booth on the corner of Beech Street and Golden Lane. Right inside the Barbican Tunnel."

"How does he even know we're in London?" Paul said, biting his thumbnail.

"I am guessing your computer could use a good antivirus."

Paul tutted. "It's gonna cost me a fortune."

"Probably. The good news is that this guy could help us find Zach Hughes."

***

Paul picked Stef up at 3:45 p.m. exactly, as per their former routine. They didn't exchange words, only knowing glances. They had a plan.

Passing by their usual bus stop and Kidz Castle, Stef noticed a sloppy teenager hurl a sizeable pebble at the Barbican Nutter, who was by the shop as always, holding his trusty sign: GIVE ME THE BODY. The teenager spat at his feet and yelled something unintelligible. Stef cringed, as she always did when witnessing this harassment. Yet she felt powerless and small. 'What could I do?' she thought, a tinge of shame creeping in. Surely, she could've at least said something. Anything.

The street curved into the tunnel, and they followed the path. Exhaust fumes, invisible but thick, made breathing intolerable. Stef had once read that the Barbican Tunnel was the most carbon-dioxide-congested place in all of London. Knowing this, she preferred to hold her breath rather than inhale the poison. Paul, however, seemed unaffected.

Golden Lane swerved to the left. The air was fresher there, so Stef allowed herself to breathe. With caution.

Further ahead, a lonely phone booth stood crooked and forgotten. The outside was covered in so much soot that it was nearly impossible to tell it used to be red once. The inside was lined with fliers and printouts advertising dubious services. Paul checked his phone.

"One minute," he confirmed.

Stef exhaled. They exchanged a glance, Paul gently squeezing her hand. It felt like standing on the edge of a cliff, ready to jump into the cold ocean. Then the phone rang. Their chests tightened, and their insides fluttered as if about to take that leap.

Paul pulled the booth door open, and they stepped in. Stef's hand hesitated over an old-fashioned black handset.

"You answer," she said. "He's expecting a male voice. Mine might spook him."

"Okay." Paul squeezed the headset tightly. With a quick exhale for courage, he lifted the phone from its hook with a muted clink. "Hello?" Paul's voice faltered. He pressed his ear to the circular earpiece, letting Stef do the same, their cheeks pressed against the headset.

"I'm listening." The voice was male, deep, raspy, American. Stef imagined a cowboy on the other end, casually chewing on a toothpick.

Paul froze. Stef elbowed him in the side. He coughed, cleared his throat, and continued in a much deeper voice than normal.

"Is it Morpheus?" A much, much deeper voice. Stef flashed an uneven smile.

"Who's asking?" the voice replied after a brief pause.

"Pablo, here. Pablo Thomas." For reasons unknown, Paul went for a thick Spanish accent, causing Stef to facepalm.

"What are ya, twelve?" Morpheus growled.

"Sorry. Sixteen, actually," Paul continued in his normal tone.

"Sixteen in like two months," Stef mumbled under her breath.

"And what kind of information could a little squirt like you have?"

"It's hard to describe." Paul brushed his hair up on the back of his head.

"Try me."

"We might have found something. A device thing that belongs to Riddle Corps." Paul swallowed.

"Go on..."

"This device is a game, a virtual reality game. It is very advanced. Like, extremely. Like, if you get hurt in the game, you get hurt in real life. The stuff of science-fiction, you know what I mean?" Paul paused, waiting for a response. The line remained silent.

"Hello?" Paul said.

"I'm listening."

"Okay, okay. So, we think this game is somehow connected to the kids who died in the tunnel. I mean, maybe they didn't even die in the tunnel. Maybe they died someplace else. I don't know, it's all... a bit crazy." Paul glanced at the cut on his hand.

"That's interesting," Morpheus replied. "Real interesting. I don't know if you're pulling my leg or what's in it for you, but it is interesting. I'll give you that."

Stef pinched the skin on Paul's belly. He winced.

"Actually," he continued, "the guy who developed the game, his name was – or is – Zach Hughes. We're trying to find him."

The line went quiet. Stef raised her eyebrows questioningly. Paul shrugged.

"Hello?"

"I know Zach," Morpheus said.

"Y-Y-You do?"

"Well, I know of Zach. Funny thing, talented programmer, a rising star. All evidence of his employment at Riddle Corps was quickly deleted after the Barbican tragedy."

"Do you know what happened to him?"

"Even better. I know exactly where he's hiding," Morpheus said.

Paul and Stef held their breath. The phone was silent but for the sound of Morpheus's laboured breathing.

"Hey, Paul?" he finally said.

Paul's mouth dropped open.

"You know my name," he whispered, his throat tight.

"Of course, I know your name, dumbass. It's in your email. But Paul, what makes you think that your game is connected to the Barbican tragedy?"

Paul pressed his lips tightly together.

"We saw one of them. One of the dead children. Inside the game," he said seriously, his face somber.

"That's quite a twist, little man. Quite a twist." Morpheus let out a deep, raspy chuckle. "I'll send the address, and I'll keep my eyes on you."

"Okay. Thanks," Paul said.

"Goodbye, Paul," Morpheus said.

"Bye."

"And you too. Stef, is it?" he added before the phone disconnected, snapping into a long, distant drone.

Stef and Paul stood motionless for a while, listening to its lingering beeping, before Paul returned the handset to its hook, extinguishing all sound. That moment was the quietest in Stef's whole life. There was nothing but Paul and his big brown eyes. Nothing but Paul and the complete absence of anything else – sound, smell, touch. Paul became all her senses. He was staring directly at her. She felt like she could drown in his gaze. He glanced at her lips, and her heart stopped beating. Moving closer, a micrometre at a time, he reached for her hand.

"Paul?" she whispered.

Ring! Paul furrowed his brows and lowered his gaze, pulling his mobile out of his pocket and Stef out of her trance.

"It's a message," he said, his face softening in the yellow glow of the screen. Stef glanced down – unknown number.

"37, Cyfrinach Lane, Abergavenny, Wales, UK. NP7. Always yours, Morpheus."

Eleven

"I don't understand what's going on in that head of yours, Steffi Graf O'Shea. Are you trying to get expelled?"

Shrill. That was the word Stef would use to describe her mother's deafening screech. She had been trying to find the perfect description for quite some time. It was a lengthy tell-off, and Stef's mind naturally wandered. Noisy. Hysterical. Ear-splitting. Penetrating. Raucous. Shattering. Shrill. It was definitely shrill.

"Are you even listening?" Claire's shoulders hunched over her petite frame, making her look like Quasimodo.

"Of course. Every word."

"And?"

"Sorry."

"That's it?" If it was even possible, Claire's voice frequency went up another couple of hertz.

Stef felt an overwhelming urge to cover her ears but resisted, raising her shoulders instead, a move she could potentially explain as a shrug of penitence – if that was at all a thing.

"I am very sorry, Mum. I went to the library. You know I did. But then I got distracted."

"Distracted? By what?"

"By those kids who died. Remember?" Now Stef was starting to sound shrill.

"Steffi! That wasn't even the correct library. And today? Where were you today? No, don't answer. I don't care. Mr Arche thinks you are a very clever girl, you know. He tried to defend you, but you are not making any effort. You haven't made friends. Certainly not with Jihae Lee. And you haven't been doing your homework. If you carry on like this, you will get expelled!"

At the word 'expelled', Stef's face beamed involuntarily, and her pupils dilated. It was physical, biological. She couldn't help it.

Her mother scoffed, arms akimbo. "Really? You have a free spot at one of the top schools in the country. A twenty-thousand-pound-a-year spot. And you want to waste it? Do you want to squander this incredible opportunity that I worked – no, no, I do work so hard for? Do you know that Granger has a fifty per cent acceptance rate at Oxbridge?"

"I know," Stef said, withstanding a strong urge to roll her eyes.

"It wasn't really a question!" Claire bellowed.

Stef looked at her toes. Her left foot tapped against the linoleum.

"I will do better, Mum."

"I didn't hear that!"

"I will do better, Mum. I promise. I am sorry. Truly. I am." She raised her eyes at her mother.

"Computer Club or something this Thursday. You're going!" Claire crossed her arms.

Stef bowed her head in quiet surrender. She was going to the Coding Club on Thursday. She had to give her mother that much.

But tomorrow was Wednesday, and she absolutely had to go to Wales.

***

Stef tried to pay attention in Mr Arche's class this time. She really had. She answered questions and participated in a discussion. She even thought she caught a tiny smile of approval on the teacher's face. But now her gaze drifted towards the clock above the blackboard. It was time. Time for her grand performance – the performance of a lifetime.

More than anything, Stef despised attention. She couldn't stand all those eyes on her; she could almost feel them burning holes in her skin. But now, she had no choice. She had to do what needed to be done. Drawing a deep breath, she pressed her fists into her stomach.

"Ooh," she moaned.

There was no reaction. Mr Arche was deep into his lecture on spaghettification, and it must've been a good one because everyone else in class seemed thoroughly enthralled. But Stef would not be easily defeated. She groaned louder and hunched her whole body over the desk. Pressing her forehead onto the table, she let out a sorrowful whimper.

"Ow, oh, ow."

"Are you alright, Stef?"

Stef felt a gentle squeeze on her left shoulder. It must have been Jihae, who occupied the desk next to hers.

"I don't feel so good," Stef moaned, then arched her back, howling like a dying wolf.

"Mr Arche?" Jihae raised her hand. Stef sneaked a secret peek at her neighbour. "I think Steffi is really unwell."

A naughty smile tugged on Stef's lips. She pushed them back into place.

"Mr Arche, I think I am sick. My stomach really hurts." Now that she had Mr Arche's attention, she groaned louder, more confidently, twisting her body into unnatural shapes, like a broken doll. Stef had an image in mind of what the performance should look like – something along the lines of that girl from *The Exorcist*.

Mr Arche looked genuinely concerned. It was working.

"You should see the school nurse, my dear, as soon as possible," he insisted, curling his brows towards his nose.

"I think I had bad crabsticks yesterday. I just need to go home and take some paracetamol." She wailed in pain once more and bent backwards with a swift jerk. *Flashdance*, she was thinking. Only miserable.

Gasps from her twenty-pupil audience filled the classroom. They must've been staring – all eyes on Stef. A knot tightened in her throat, and she hastily swallowed it away. There was no turning back; her only option was to double down on the theatrics. She twitched and twisted and moaned, pushing herself up from her desk and onto her wobbling legs. More gasps. She looked like a wooden puppet controlled by an unskilful puppeteer. Or perhaps a character in a Japanese horror movie.

"I really have to go home, Mr Arche," she spluttered through heavy breaths.

"Of course, Miss O'Shea. If that's what you think is best."

"I'm sure it is. I will get better by tomorrow," she added, lurching out of the classroom, alternating between a bleat and a whimper.

As soon as the door slammed behind her, she readjusted her posture and admitted to herself that perhaps it was all a little too much. Dame Judi Dench would not have approved. But contrary to her most vivid fears, she didn't burst into flames from the piercing stares of her classmates. In fact, it wasn't at all as bad as she had imagined.

***

Stef scampered down the school steps. On the other side of the gate, Paul stepped out of a lime-green vehicle illegally parked on the double red. The timing was tight. A trip to Abergavenny would take over two hours. Two and a half hours, to be precise. Two and a half hours there and back. That's five hours in total!

Paul was fine. His mother wasn't expecting him until eleven in the evening. He'd told her he was going to the cinema with Alex. Cynthia Thomas had pursed her lips and raised her right eyebrow: "You sure you want to be spending your time with that Alex girl?" Paul mumbled a "yeah" and hurried off to school, or so his mother thought. He was fine.

But Stef was on thin ice. And on top of that, she'd lied her way out of school. It was parents' evening at Granger, and that was the only reason they could even contemplate going to Wales. She only had eight hours in total to get there and back without Claire or Jason O'Shea noticing that she was missing. Eight hours! Five of those to be spent on the commute.

Paul's mate Mo agreed to give them a lift to Paddington Station. Mo had just turned seventeen and was now the happy proprietor of a lime-green Vauxhall Corsa he'd purchased for 800 quid from a friend of a friend. The Granger security guard looked particularly rabid this morning. It wasn't just Paul marring the pristine grandeur of the Academy's front curb; it was Mo, too, who was wearing a (shock horror) red bandana. And, worst of all, was the hideous lime-greenness that encapsulated them. Stef gave the guard an extra dirty look as she lunged towards the car.

"You know these men?" the guard huffed after her.

"Obviously, I do," Stef snarled and slid inside the giant insect. Mo pressed his foot firmly on the gas.

"Yo, Stef," Mo said, jerking his chin up.

"Mo," Stef confirmed. "Terrible. Just awful-looking car, by the way."

"It's alright. For a start." He tapped the steering wheel lovingly and flashed a set of metal teeth caps in the rearview mirror as they zoomed further and further away from the Granger Academy.

Mo sure could drive. And he knew London roads better than any Sat Nav. They were in Paddington within twenty minutes, and Stef and Paul actually stood a chance of catching their train. Leaping out of the Vauxhall as soon as it slowed, they dispersed 'thank yous' meant for Mo in erroneous directions. Paul grabbed Stef's hand, and they ran as fast as they could through the tall gaping archway that opened up onto an array of shops and kiosks and rows of long platforms. People minded their own business, diffusing into patternless trajectories, leisurely ambling through space; a toddler was eating ice cream which melted and dripped over his fingers; a long queue was forming at a Costa Coffee. There was no usual rush, no hectic rhythm so indigenous to train stations. It almost looked like a genre painting by an old Dutch master until Stef and Paul ripped right through the comfortable morning tranquillity.

They charged towards the platform, disturbing pigeons. The birds lifted, flapping their wings in annoyance, nearly colliding with the troublemakers. Stef had to duck and cover her face. The birds frightened the toddler, who dropped his ice cream and started to wail. Stef and Paul skipped over the ice cream puddle, avoiding disaster. The kid's mother cursed in their wake. They tore through the coffee queue. The air echoed with grumbles from the aggrieved customers. But they had two minutes, only two minutes, to get to platform 4 and not a second to waste.

Stef's breath tightened into a knot; her heart was thumping mercilessly inside her chest. She felt a smile on her lips, despite the fact that she was nearly sure that fainting was imminent. She hated running. No, she despised it. But now that Paul was leading the way, she loathed it a tiny bit less. Paul squeezed Stef's hand, guiding her forward, making sure not to outrun her pace. Only a few metres remained. They were nearly there. The train chuffed and started to rumble. Stef held her breath. Last push. And somehow, her feet were off the ground, floating in mid-air, and when they touched solid ground again, they were inside the carriage and on their way to Wales. Stef could breathe again.

The train was nearly empty. They managed to score table seats and settled themselves opposite one another. It was strange, a complete calm after the storm. Stef's heart was still beating fast. She felt like she had to keep going, but there was nowhere to go and nothing to do but wait until they got to Newport, where they would have to change trains.

"You alright?" Paul asked, mostly because silence was weird and uncomfortable, and he had to say something.

"Yeah." Stef bobbed her head.

Paul scratched his chin, trying to find something to do with his hands.

For the first time ever, neither of them had a clue what to say to one another. Stef caught herself thinking that perhaps it was the very first time they had sat face to face with a table between them and no Cynthia, Ringo, or either of her parents anywhere in sight. Stef sucked in her lips and started to drum her fingers on the table, all the while being perfectly aware of how awkward she must look.

Paul looked out of the window, trying to focus on the London buildings zooming past, the lampposts, people, and cars, but his eyes refused, petulantly demanding to anchor on Stef's reflection. She looked so pretty – she always looked pretty, especially when she blushed.

Twelve

"What if he's not home?" Stef said.

They stood in front of number 37, Cyfrinach Lane, Abergavenny, Wales.

"I don't think the person who lives in this house ever leaves," Paul replied.

He was right. The house was a perfect cube with a single door and a lone square window. The door, thick and metal, looked like it belonged in a high-security bank vault. The window was barricaded with wooden planks from the inside and barred on the outside. The house stood solo on a deserted forest road – no neighbours in sight.

"Look." Paul gave Stef a nudge, pointing to the blinking red light above the door.

"Camera?"

"Looks like it."

Paul took a few steps to the left, and the camera followed. He moved to the right, and the camera tracked him again.

"Yup. He's home. And he's watching."

Just then, a mechanical voice screeched from out of nowhere, making Stef jolt and clutch her chest.

"What do you want?" the voice hissed.

"There must be a speaker or something," Stef whispered.

"We want to talk," Paul said.

"Bugger off."

"Zach? Zach Hughes?" Stef's voice faltered.

"Are you the Jehovah's Witnesses?"

"No, we are not. We want to talk about your game. The Disappearance of Eden Rose." Stef straightened her back.

Silence enveloped them, broken only by the heavy, deep breathing emanating from the unseen speaker. For a moment, it seemed as though the entire house was alive, and it wasn't a house at all but an enormous, snoring animal.

"How do you know about Eden Rose?" the voice finally replied.

"We know it. We played it. And boy, do we have questions," Paul said.

The house seemed to wheeze in response, and Stef was almost certain she saw it expand and contract with each inhale. Then, something deep within the metal monster began to tick and click, staccato. Faster and more rhythmic, it huffed and creaked, and the door inched open, revealing nothing but a sliver of darkness beyond.

"Come in," the voice beckoned. It sounded real this time. Human.

Instinctively, Stef reached for Paul's hand. Holding their breaths, they shuffled into the black hole. Together.

Inside, it wasn't as dark as they'd first imagined. A single lemon-yellow light source dimly illuminated the room. It took Stef a few seconds to realise that it came from a floor-bound table lamp shaped like a Pokemon.

Zach slouched in a moth-eaten armchair beside it, his ankle resting on his knee, fingers steepled together under his unshaven chin. There wasn't much else in the room besides a small, fat fridge, a stack of laptops on the floor, and a pile of empty pizza boxes.

"Do you have it?" Zach asked.

"You mean on us?" Paul's eyes widened.

"You don't have it." Zach leaned forward and ruffled his greasy blond locks.

"We have it. We just don't have it with us," Stef said.

Zach scratched his head with vigour. Then slid his hands to his face. For a moment, Stef thought that he was going to cry.

"What have you done?" He exhaled.

"Are you okay?" Stef asked Zach, throwing a glance at Paul, who seemed apprehensive, biting his cheek.

Zach lifted his head and crossed his arms. "You need to destroy it. You have to destroy it."

"Well, that's what we are here to talk to you about. You programmed it, right?" Paul touched the cut on his hand instinctively.

Zach opened his arms and leaned back, chewing his lip.

"We played the game," Stef said.

"Well, I know you didn't lose. I assume you didn't win either."

"No. We're still playing," Paul replied.

"You shouldn't. Bad things happen to people who play it. Worse things happen to people who lose." Zach was dead serious, and he accentuated his dead-seriousness with a very hard stare.

Stef wasn't sure if it was the lighting because the Pokemon lamp had suddenly switched colour to pink, but Zach seemed to have turned more pale.

"What is it? What is that game, really?" Paul whispered, clutching his wound tighter.

Zach leaned forward, resting his elbows on his knees. "The game, as you may have gathered, is a little more than just a game."

Stef and Paul exchanged glances.

Zach took a long deep breath in, then exhaled quickly. "It's an AI."

"What?" Stef blinked rapidly, somewhat confused.

"Artificial Intelligence. And it's not just any AI. It's conscious; it's real."

"You invented a conscious AI?" Stef whispered, mouth agape.

"I didn't invent it. It invented itself. It evolved, like humans evolved, like everything evolves. I wrote a code – a complex one. I created characters and made them as realistic as possible. But one of them became something else, something more."

"There is an actual artificial mind inside the game?" Stef's spine tingled, as if a jolt of electricity was running through it.

"I thought they'd destroyed it," Zach said with regret.

"Were they going to destroy it? Does it have something to do with those kids?" Stef mustered up all the courage she had to ask that question.

Zach lifted his eyes, and a deep wrinkle formed along the bridge of his nose. "You know about the kids?"

"We know there was a bus crash. We know that you programmed one of the kids into the game," Paul replied.

Zach was starting to look increasingly confused. He let out a dry chuckle and wiped his mouth, his eyes darting around haphazardly inside their sockets. Suddenly, he pushed himself off the chair and walked right over to Stef and Paul. He leaned forward, his head craning above Paul like an arch lamp. For the first time, Stef noticed how very tall he was. His eyes coasted from Paul to Stef and back, as if trying to read them like a computer code. Suddenly, he grabbed Paul by the bicep and squeezed.

"Are you messing with me?"

"W-w-what?" Paul's lips trembled.

Zach's eyes narrowed; he tightened his grip. "You're really trying to tell me that you saw a kid inside the game?"

"You didn't... you didn't programme it?" Paul swallowed.

Stef's palms were starting to sweat; she wiped them on her skirt. Confusion clouded her mind, but her heart beat faster, anticipating what was coming before Zach uttered it.

"Oh my God," Zach whispered – his pupils now two black planets. He straightened himself up to resemble a giraffe, vigorously rubbing his head and ruffling his hair. Pacing around the room in circles, he mumbled to himself, "Do you know what that means? Oh my God. It means that thing... it was able to transcribe physical matter into code. This is... insane. It's mindboggling."

"It can't be," Stef whispered. "It can't be the real Ollie James." Stef's knees were soft, shaky, and ready to buckle. "He died in the bus crash."

"There was no bus crash. It was a cover-up. A bunch of kids came to Riddle Corps. They'd won something and were given an opportunity to be the first to play Eden Rose. And then..." Zach stepped closer to Stef and halted. Stretching his neck towards her like a cobra, he fanned his fingers through the air. "And then they just disappeared." His hair was completely dishevelled; his eyes bulged with cartoonish intensity; under the dim now-purple light, he looked deranged.

"They just disappeared?" Paul crinkled his forehead.

"Poof." If it were at all possible, Zach pushed his eyeballs even further out of their sockets. "They were gone. I assumed they died. I thought it had murdered them. Somehow. That's what they all thought." He smirked. "But if they are alive, if they are trapped inside the game…"

"Do you think… do you think we can save them?" Stef said.

"I don't know. Transmutation from physical to code and back? Teleportation. In the quantum word, perhaps. But in real life… It's in the realm of science fiction."

"So is a conscious AI," Paul interjected.

Zach smirked. "So is a conscious AI. But I am afraid it is so far out of my comfort zone that I would be of little help. I am no quantum physicist."

"But you know the AI? You've met him?" Stef said.

"Yes. I have met… it," he said. "I don't know who it is – which one of them. It likes to wear a black cape."

"What do you mean, you don't know which one?" Stef frowned, shaking her head slightly.

"I mean, it obviously has to be one of the eight," Zach said, as if talking to himself again, and resumed the pacing.

"The eight suspects?" Stef blinked, trying to make sense of it all. She remembered what the superintendent O'Shady had told them. There were eight suspects in the theft of Eden Rose.

"Yes." Zach nodded, staring deep into Stef's eyes for a moment. "The rest are bots. They are very basic code; they couldn't have evolved like this." Zach bit into his fingernail, his mind elsewhere, thinking, analysing. "It likes to play games, you know. It respects the rules, given what it is and how it came to be. It respects the rules, but it likes to hide things from you. It is sneaky." Zach continued pacing back and forth. "It likes to play games. It likes to bet too. It bet me that it could get me fired." All of a sudden, he bulged out his eyes and started to laugh. A devious, mad kind of laugh. It made Stef's spine tingle. Then he stopped, and just as suddenly, a dark shadow crossed his face. "No one's ever won that game, you know. No one but me."

"So, you know how to win it?" Paul asked, unsure if he actually wanted to know the answer.

"Of course, I do. I created it." Zach froze, staring into the void, not blinking, as if he were under a spell. Stef and Paul exchanged glances, uncertain what to do or say.

Stef decided to take the first step. "Mr Hughes, what if we bet the Soultrapper that we can win the game? What if we could wager Ollie James's life? Perhaps the lives of all those children. If he is there, maybe they all are?"

Zach Hughes blinked once and whipped his head at Stef. "The Soultrapper?"

"That's what Ollie called it," Stef murmured.

Zach sniggered. "Fancy." Then his face changed. "Look. I can tell you how to beat it, but I don't advise you to try."

"Honestly, I don't know if we'd do it. But it's better to know." Stef raised her eyebrows high, pleading with the mad programmer.

Zach exhaled deeply, then walked over to his old armchair and let himself collapse into it. He rubbed his forehead and temples, then began. "There isn't one way to win the game. I told you, it's very advanced. There are eight possible scenarios and eight possible culprits. The game selects a storyline at random when you begin. Sometimes it's the policeman who steals the diamond in the hope of running away to Barbados. Sometimes the diamond is a fake, and Bigwig hides it for an insurance fraud scheme. In that plot, the reality is that he'd lost his whole fortune. He owes money to Don Rigatoni." Zach smiled to himself, evidently pleased with the character name he'd come up with. Then he turned to Stef once again. "You know of the eight suspects – that means that you've opened the padlock in the holding cell. Superintendent O'Shady gave you the spiel. Correct?"

"Correct." Stef nodded.

"In that case, did you notice a poster on the wall above the lamp? A blonde in a red bikini on a beach with a cocktail."

"There was no poster. Right?" Paul glanced at Stef for affirmation. He got it.

"We searched that room from top to bottom. There was definitely nothing like that."

"Good. You can cross one suspect off the list. I left little clues, you see – bits of thread. So that I could pull at the thread when I needed to and figure out who the culprit was relatively quickly. In your scenario, Superintendent O'Shady is not so shady at all. He doesn't dream of running away to Barbados. He didn't steal the diamond. You can trust him – unless, of course, he is the AI."

"Great. I guess. So, there are more shortcuts like that?" Stef felt something stir deep inside her veins, her blood. A rush of warmth, butterflies, a gentle familiar itch. The same feeling she always had when a juicy quest presented itself for dismantling.

"Of course," Zach spread his arms. "How far along are you?"

"We were just on our way to the Bigwig Estate." Paul's eyes lit up. Stef knew immediately that he felt it too. Then, suddenly, the spark in his eyes was gone. Paul touched the wound on his hand.

"Listen," Paul said. "That Ollie James, he cut my hand in the game. He was hiding in the taxi, and he cut me." Paul took a step forward and stretched his hand out towards Zach Hughes.

Zach examined it carefully. A whole spectrum of emotions chased each other across his face: shock first, then denial, excitement, and finally awe.

"It has powers above and beyond my comprehension. Are you absolutely sure you are ready to potentially sacrifice your own lives for this boy?"

"No," Paul sneered. "I am not at all sure." He turned to Stef. She read his expression as 'There is no way in hell that I am going back in there.' A rush of warm excitement was quickly replaced with cold doubt.

"Like I said, whether we go for it or not, it is better to know – just in case," Stef said.

"As you wish," Zach said, placing his elbows on the armrests and cupping his chin, his finger tapping against his lips. "O'Shady is out. Bigwig is guilty when he's in trouble. You'll know he's in trouble if there's no caviar in the fridge." He paused and closed his eyes for a moment, rubbing his temples. "I don't remember all the clues. There's more than one for each character. I remember some. And I know the way the plot unfolds in each case. Okay? I will give you tips, but if you decide to go back in there, know that there's more than one way to eliminate a suspect. So, in every scenario, there's bad blood between Bigwig and Rigatoni. But Rigatoni is guilty if Bigwig crashes his Rolls Royce. If the Rolls is parked out front of the casino, Rigatoni isn't your guy. The croupier who works at the casino has a sick mother when he's guilty. He desperately needs money for her surgery, but he doesn't want to bite the hand that feeds him. So he steals from the only other rich guy in the game. He will tell you that, on the night when Eden Rose was taken, he was off work and went to see a play. If he is guilty, he went alone. If he isn't, he took his mother. Are you getting all this?"

"Yes," Stef said.

"Good. Boris the Bouncer is in love with Marilyn. They're in a secret relationship. In all but one of the scenarios, that is. When his feelings are unrequited, he steals the diamond to impress Marilyn. You see, rumour has it that Eden Rose was a present for Marilyn, but that's not the case. It is Bigwig's pride and joy. He wouldn't give it to her. You know Boris and Marilyn are together if he has a lipstick stain on his shirt collar. If he doesn't, you know he's your man. The same goes for Katya. She has a thing for Bigwig. They're in love. She's happy when there's a relationship between them, but vengeful when there isn't. She wears a watch that he gave her – it's a fancy diamond thing. If she has the watch on, they're definitely together. If she doesn't have it, then she's your guy, so to speak. Marilyn is an avid gambler and Bigwig doesn't know it. When she's guilty, she loses big playing Black Jack just two nights before the heist. Ask her where she was two nights prior. In every scenario, she was really at the casino, but if she lies, it's her who stole the diamond. And finally, the mysterious Frenchman. A long-lost illegitimate son of either Sandeep Bigwig or Don Rigatoni. When he's Rigatoni's son, he steals the diamond to impress his father. You need to find his hotel room. There's a birth certificate on a bedside table, I think. So, that's that."

The room fell silent and still. Zach studied the curious faces of the teenagers, tapping his fingertips together.

"Will you remember all that?" he finally said.

"She will," Paul said with a hint of pride. "She definitely will."

Stef felt a pull on the corners of her mouth. It was nice when Paul was impressed by her, especially when he showed her off to others.

"Because you know," Zach continued, "it would take you weeks of gameplay to win without clues. You'd have to play every single puzzle. And that would mean more and more ways for the Soultrapper, or whatever you call it, to trick you, catch you, and keep you in there forever."

"If it does catch us, you'll know where to find us," Stef timidly replied.

"Perhaps we should give you our names? And addresses? Just in case?" Paul added.

"I already know. My cameras have face recognition," Zach said, chin lifted with satisfaction.

"Of course they do," Paul said, smiling uncomfortably.

"I'll keep an eye on you two."

"Thanks, Mr Hughes," Stef said softly.

"Mr Hughes was my father. I'm Zach."

"Thanks, Zach," Paul said.

"Alright. Now scram."

***

They hardly spoke at all on the train back. It all felt too surreal. Each of them stared out of the window, watching the rolling green hills float past them like giant ocean waves, lost in their own thoughts. Ten minutes before arriving at Paddington, Paul finally broke the silence.

"We'd be crazy to do this, Stef."

"Completely," Stef admitted, feeling her cheeks flush. Of course, she knew it was madness. But while her mind said one thing, her heart had another idea. Paul saw right through her.

"You're not seriously considering it, are you?"

"I don't know. If there's a chance we could…"

"No, Stef, listen. It's crazy. If Ollie James really is alive, sort of, who's to say for sure that he can be brought back? It's bonkers. What if we get sucked in there with him? We cannot risk our lives just for a maybe chance of getting Ollie out. You saw him, he hasn't aged. Imagine he suddenly appears looking like he did ten years ago. What would his parents say? Or is he going to age ten years in an instant? How, even? It's crazy. Absolutely mad."

"Wait, what?"

"Which part?"

"The parents. They must've all had parents; you're right." Stef's heart twisted with sadness before a glimmer of realisation began to emerge – a sliver of light in the darkness, faint and flickering like a candle in the night. Parents. She thought about her own parents. She thought about all those kids and their grieving parents who didn't even know the truth. The light expanded, growing clearer and clearer until finally, she could see.

She gasped. "Their parents, Pablo! Their parents! They never got their children's bodies because there were none. The bodies! 'I want the body'. Oh my God, Paul. The Barbican Nutter is one of their parents!"

Thirteen

"So what?" Paul scoffed.

"What do you mean, so what?" Stef clenched the bus pole so hard that her hand turned pale. Anger simmered beneath her skin. How could Paul not care about Ollie and the others? It seemed unfathomable to Stef.

They were en route home to Eastcastle Lane by way of a bus because there was time to spare, and Stef refused the faster option.

"So what if he's Ollie's dad?" Paul pushed his shoulders almost up to his ears. Stef's nostrils flared.

"If Ollie is in there, maybe, no – likely – others are too. Are you seriously suggesting we do nothing?"

"Are you seriously suggesting we embark on a suicide mission?" Paul was getting really riled up, his free arm flailing about with such vigour that it threatened to smack a fellow commuter.

The bus was packed, and people were staring. As always, Stef loathed all the staring.

"Calm down," she hissed through her teeth, aware that she wasn't calm either under the surface.

"Don't tell me to calm down. I am calm," Paul yelped. Spittle landed on Stef's face. She closed her eyes briefly and brushed it away. Then she grabbed Paul by the collar of his blazer and pulled him closer.

"Listen, it's not a suicide mission when we know all we know. We have shortcuts."

"It's bonkers. Completely and totally bonkers." Paul's arm caught the coat of a man next to him. "Sorry," he said.

The man shook his head with some disdain and returned to his book.

"What about the parents?" Stef released Paul's collar, but she wasn't going to back down.

"What about the parents?" Paul shouted so loud that the whole bus turned to stare. Much to Stef's dismay, Paul seemed utterly unaware of that. She turned around, flashing an apologetic grin to everyone at once, and no one in particular.

"They are hurting. We know something that could help them. We have to at least talk to them." Stef moved closer to Paul, not wanting to let anyone in on their conversation.

"Stef," Paul began, shaking his head so much Stef worried it might fall off. But at least he finally lowered his voice, and his restless arm hung idle by his side. "What are you going to tell them? That you saw one of their children in a virtual reality game, which is also home to the first known conscious Artificial Intelligence, who possibly sucks people inside the game for fun?"

Stef stared at her friend, her skin burning under her purple blazer. "Yes. That's what I'm going to tell them."

"And how does that sound?" Paul smirked.

"It's the truth."

"I know it's the truth! That's not the point!" Paul's arm went off again, and everyone was staring. Stef just wanted to disappear. She hid her face in her hand, wishing it would make her invisible.

They didn't speak as they got off the bus. They didn't speak as they walked from the bus stop to Eastcastle Lane, carefully maintaining a distance between each other. They didn't speak as they unlocked their respective houses and went inside, inadvertently slamming the doors at the exact same moment.

In the safety of isolation, Stef allowed the tears to flow. Her house was empty. She clambered upstairs and into her bed, under the covers. She sobbed, and the tears gushed freely, sliding down her cheeks and onto the bedsheets, painting small wet stains. Her cheeks stung, and she thought she should have been using her moisturiser, especially with the strong winds lately.

The thought of the wind made her remember the colourful kites. She remembered flying kites with her father, something they used to do all the time when it was windy. Her favourite kite was big and red and shaped like a dragon. She'd forgotten where she got it from or where it was now. A distant image of kites of different colours, chaotically stacked on wooden shelves, materialised in her mind. There were so many kites: blue, red, orange, yellow, green, and purple. And her eyes closed, and she saw shapes in all those beautiful colours dancing around her mind like a kaleidoscope. And she heard her father's voice as if from a great distance, perhaps another dimension.

"Oh, pet, she really must be poorly."

And maybe her cheek tickled under the warm stroke of her mother's soft hand. And a melodious voice crooned, "Oh, my darling girl. I hope you feel all better tomorrow."

***

Stef woke up with a start. It was pitch black. Her eyes struggled to latch on to something, anything discernible, in the darkness. She struggled to remember where she was or what had happened. PING. Her phone! It lit up with powerful intensity that made her squint. She reached for it.

I am sorry. The message was from Paul.

It all came rushing back to her. But at least she knew that she was in her room – safe. She was still wearing her school uniform top, but her blazer, kilt, and shoes were off. Her parents must've undressed her. She wondered if they were mad at her. She didn't want them to be.

PING.

Are you not gonna talk to me?

I'm talking.

Okay.

Okay.

Stef?

What?

Are you mad?

It's okay.

That doesn't answer the question.

She put the phone down. Her eyes adjusted to the darkness.

PING. She ignored it. PING. She exhaled. PING. She buried her face into her big, fluffy pillow.

Long knock, short knock, long, short, pause, short, short, short, pause, short, long, pause, long, long, pause, long, long, pause, long.

She opened her eyes, lazily swinging herself up. Cautiously feeling for the floor with her bare feet, she tiptoed to the window. She unlatched it and lifted the frame. The pink cup jerked slightly, letting her know that Paul was on the other end of the string. Stef pulled the string taught, covering her ear with the cup.

"I am sorry. I really am." He sounded genuine. Stef exhaled and continued to listen.

"Are you listening? At least I know you're there. I've been thinking. You are right. You are absolutely right. And you know how I wasn't sure if we could save Ollie? Well, I am still not, but I think it is possible. I think it is possible to teleport inside that thing or whatever and be back. Because, Stef, I think we've done that. Remember the first time? I didn't notice it then, but remember when Ringo couldn't find us? But... how could he not find us? My room is a shoebox. We were here the whole time. Unless we weren't..."

Shivers cascaded through Stef's body. She could feel her arm hairs prick up. Goosebumps. She dropped the cup down and leaned out of the window.

"Paul?" she called out.

"I'm here." His head popped out of the window.

"What are you saying?" Stef pressed her lips tightly together.

"I am saying we should do it. I am saying we should try."

***

Stef's hands trembled as she clutched the headset. It was hard to imagine that mere days ago, she was giddy with excitement. Now, this piece of plastic in her hands seemed hostile and dangerous.

"Are we sure about this?" Paul's breath was tight and uneven.

"No," Stef exhaled, tears pooling in the corners of her eyes. Paul noticed.

"Hey," he said, stepping closer. Very close. Cupping her cheek in his hand, he rubbed away a runaway tear with his thumb. This gesture took Stef entirely off guard, and she surrendered. She could feel his warm breath on her skin. In all the years they'd known each other, Paul had never been quite so close. From this unfamiliar distance, his face looked different, foreign, strange. But she didn't mind it. He continued to stroke her cheek gently, even after the tear was gone. Something funny was happening inside Stef's chest that she didn't recognise. A peculiar itch, the kind she'd have to reach inside herself to scratch. Stef didn't fully understand the feeling. It was new and alien, not unlike this Paul whose nose was just about to touch hers. Then he kissed her.

She stepped back.

"Um." She put her hands on her waist and stared at the rug, fearing Paul's disappointed gaze. The carpet was a colourful combination of geometric shapes in yellow, green, and red. She wanted to focus on something else – something other than the kiss. A volcano of emotions was threatening to erupt from the pit of her stomach; she wasn't ready to deal with all of them yet. She couldn't possibly. It was all too much.

"I am so sorry, Stef." Paul sounded disappointed and apologetic in equal measure. Stef couldn't bear to look at him.

"You know, I've never noticed this rug before. It's quirky. African?"

"Yeah, Mum's second cousin brought it from Ghana, I think." Paul scratched the back of his head.

"Funky. Cool. Nice." Perhaps she was a tad too loud, but she was finally able to lift her gaze, and that in itself was a win. But her skin was alight with kinetic nervousness, and she had to keep moving. She had to keep her hands busy, so she lifted the headset, preparing to slip it on. "Shall we?" she said, closing her eyes in shame. That was definitely too loud.

"Ready when you are." Paul forced a smile and watched Stef hurry inside the VR, thrusting her hands into the gloves. Tutting, upset with himself, he followed Stef down the rabbit hole.

Fourteen

They found themselves back inside the impossibly white space. Stef focused on the sensations coursing through her body, trying to determine if she was still in Paul's room. The weight of the helmet and the snugness of the gloves confirmed it. Stef glanced at her hands; even though she couldn't see the gloves, she felt them – her hands sticky with sweat.

Judging by the expression on Paul's face, he was still thinking about that kiss. Stef shook her head, determined to shove aside her own thoughts on the matter. Now wasn't the time. She could dissect the kiss later and figure out what she felt. It was warm and wonderful and wet and terrifying, but mostly, it was utterly confusing. No, it definitely wasn't the time.

"Ariadne?" Stef exclaimed, desperate for someone to diffuse this unbearable situation. Even though Ariadne wasn't technically a someone.

"Hello, Stephanie and Paul. Welcome back to the Disappearance of Eden Rose."

Stef couldn't shake the feeling that Ariadne sounded excited, as if she was genuinely glad to have them back.

"Hey, Ariadne, mate." Paul forced a stiff smile.

"We would like to continue, please," Stef said. "From where we left off."

Instantly, her body tensed into a giant knot. Her mind hummed and melted away, and her skin buzzed with a now familiar sensation. For the first time, she was fully aware that she was no longer in Paul's room. She was someplace else entirely, everywhere and nowhere all at once, on a different plane of existence – something other than herself, not a psychical entity, but a code, a spectre, a soul even.

Then Paul pinched her on her arm.

"Ouch."

Okay. Well, perhaps she was still kind of a physical entity.

"Sorry. I was just checking if I could move," Paul said. "And if you could feel anything."

Stef wondered whether there was a hint of spite behind that pinch. But they weren't paralysed this time, and for that, she was enormously grateful.

Stef felt the watch tighten around her wrist, a big red 60 illuminating the dial.

"And... we're back," Stef muttered under her breath.

Paul rubbed his eyes. "I am never going to get used to this."

"It feels like going under full anaesthesia. Remember when I broke my leg? This is what it felt like."

Unfortunately, or perhaps fortunately, Paul couldn't relate.

Stef glanced around, finding her bearings. When Ollie James had rudely interrupted their quest, they'd landed in front of the Bigwig Estate, and this is where they were now. Stef felt for the Puzzle Master badge on her chest and found it in place.

"Nice digs," Paul said, his eyes fixed on the mansion.

Indeed, they were. These 'digs', if you could call this grand palace that, were constructed entirely of white marble. Oversized, sweeping archways adorned its facade, an enormous dome crowned the roof like a giant meringue, and four pillars, without any obvious purpose, flanked it on all sides. It was a mini Taj Mahal.

There weren't any other buildings in sight, only perfectly trimmed hedges and idyllically red rose bushes. Birds chirped upbeat, melodious songs, and an unseen brook babbled somewhere. The wind was just the right balance of warmth and strength. It was the kind of garden the Queen of England would've been tremendously proud of.

Unlike the town centre, this place wasn't surrounded by endless skyscrapers in the so-called periphery. Instead, a tall forest full of hefty pines encircled the grounds. It looked both breathtaking and ominous.

"Now, tell me," Paul began, "do you want to go inside and play the game, et cetera, or do you want to make a move towards that forest?"

"The forest?" Stef wrinkled her forehead.

"To find Ollie."

"I have a feeling Ollie will find us." She flashed her eyebrows.

"Then, ladies first." Paul executed a theatrical bow, making Stef giggle as she took the first step towards the Bigwig Mansion.

Just as she lifted her knuckles to knock on the mahogany door, it creaked open, as if they were expected.

"How may I be of assistance?" said a short, stout man in a perfectly white button-up shirt and a black three-piece suit.

If there was a picture in the Oxford dictionary next to the word 'butler', it would be of this man.

"We are looking for Mr Sandeep Bigwig?" Stef smiled timidly.

"Is that a question?" The butler raised his eyebrows, his eyes sparkling with a devious glint.

"Pardon?"

"Is that another one?"

"What's going on?" Stef turned to Paul.

"We are the Puzzle Masters? I mean, we are the Puzzle Masters. Period. We work with the police. We are here to help solve a crime."

"Oh, yes. The diamond is missing. Very well. Follow me into the drawing room." The butler opened the door wider and pivoted on the spot.

"I guess we follow him," Stef said.

"Into the drawing room." Paul mimicked with an uppity grimace. Stef lightly elbowed him in the midriff.

The house was even more impressive on the inside. Or at least Stef thought that some people might consider it impressive, i.e., Zach. She found it garish and vulgar. There was just as much marble, but here it was topped up by an obscene amount of gold and crystal and silk and feathers in the shapes of cherubs, peacocks and paisley ornaments. Egregious, oversized chandeliers and loud rugs hung from just about every crevice. There was an incredible number of mismatched knick-knacks that made very little sense, such as a massive statue of a bronze horse and a giant crystal slipper the size of a billiard table. Stef thought that perhaps Zach had been inspired by pictures of Versailles or some other extravagant palace, and then he just kept adding more stuff.

"Jesus," Stef whispered.

"It is a bit much."

The butler pushed the golden double doors open to reveal the drawing room, or so Stef assumed (no one was drawing anything in there). In addition to the usual statues and ornaments, two mustard settees awaited the guests.

"You may sit." The butler pointed abruptly at them and left.

"Now what?" Paul said.

"He will bring Bigwig here, I guess."

"He was a bit rude, wasn't he?"

"That he was."

"I thought there were only eight characters that are, you know… advanced?" Paul scratched his chin.

"I know what you mean. This guy seems switched on," Stef said.

"Ah! The Puzzle Masters!" Sandeep Bigwig exclaimed, startling Stef, who had no clue where he'd just come from.

Sandeep Bigwig was a tall man, tall and large. He wore a red turban with gold stitching and a long black silk tunic. The turban boasted a substantial green gem and a peacock feather. Stef thought that Zach's inspiration for this character must've been Jafar from *Aladdin*.

"Welcome, my friends," he added in a thick Indian accent, his arms spread wide."How can I be of help?"

Jafar, only much friendlier, Stef thought.

"Actually, we are here to help you," Stef said. "As far as I understand."

"Oh, that is right. Indeed. O'Shady sent you. You will help me find my diamond, yes?"

"We will certainly try," Paul said, pulling his lips into an uninspired smile.

Bigwig, on the other hand, seemed remarkably upbeat. His mouth was stretched to its very limits; a huge grin wouldn't abandon his face even for a second. Stef thought that she'd never seen anyone quite so happy in real life.

"I think we need to ask you a couple of questions?" Stef said, timidly.

"Yes. Of course." Bigwig threw his arms up, as if his hands were full of confetti. Stef thought that this character reminded her of someone else, too, but she couldn't put her finger on it.

"So, where were you when the diamond was taken?" she asked.

"I was asleep in my room. I don't remember anything. I woke up in the morning. I went to my study. The safe was wide open. And my precious Eden Rose was gone."

A Cheshire cat! That's who Bigwig reminded Stef of. A Cheshire cat and the Prince of Zamunda from *Coming to America*. It was as if those two had a baby.

"Okay. Thank you." She bowed politely.

Paul leaned in and whispered in Stef's ear. "What about that caviar shortcut? Could we ask to see the kitchen?"

Stef opened her mouth to ask just that, when Bigwig raised his arms and exclaimed.

"You must want to see the scene of the crime, perhaps. Isn't it?" He clapped his hands together twice. *Clap-clap.*

Suddenly, they weren't in the drawing room anymore, but standing in front of a wide-open safe in what appeared to be a study.

"What just happened?" Paul leaned on Stef a bit, trying to find his balance.

"Oh, forgive me. The house is very big. I prefer to travel by clapping."

Clap-clap. Now they were in a bedroom, seated on a massive four-poster bed with an obscene amount of silk pillows, reminiscent of a fairy tale about the princess and the pea. *Clap-clap.* Next, they found themselves in a spa of sorts, with tall columns adorned in a colourful mosaic, an enormous whirling pool, and steam that curled so perfectly around the space it resembled an ornament itself. *Clap-clap.* They materialised in the kitchen, where hundreds of brass pots and pans suspended from the low ceiling glistened, and the air was sweet with an aroma of cinnamon and cloves. An enormous brass fridge stood proudly in the centre – reigning over the room.

"That's it," Stef said, pointing. "The fridge."

Clap-clap. They were back in the study, standing in front of an empty safe.

"Just like that." Bigwig's head bobbed from side to side.

"I don't feel so good." Paul bent over. Stef gave him a reassuring pat on the back.

"Your house is very impressive," she said, turning to Bigwig.

"Thank you, Puzzle Master." Bigwig pressed his hand into his abdomen and bowed slightly. "Now, please tell me. Who stole my diamond?"

"I think we need to investigate further. This is a complicated case, and we are very tired and hungry. Do you think we could have a bite to eat first? In the kitchen?" Stef raised her eyebrows in anticipation. It was worth a try.

For a moment, Bigwig's perma-smile morphed into something resembling confusion. His head twitched to the side three times, and he started to blink rapidly.

"You broke him," Paul said.

Stef gave Paul a gentle slap on the shoulder. "I didn't. Mr Bigwig?"

Bigwig stopped blinking; he swayed side to side as if a little lost, before his usual grin was back in place as if nothing had happened.

"Puzzle Masters, I must leave you to study the crime scene. When you are finished, I will come back. You can call me by logging into my computer and pressing the 'call' button. But I must warn you, my computer is password protected. I will not give you the password. But you are the Puzzle Masters, so this shouldn't be a problem. You will have three attempts. And I will give you a clue. The password is not case-sensitive. I must leave you now." *Clap-clap.* And he was gone.

Stef glanced at her wrist. The countdown had started. She tapped on the watch. Nothing.

"I think we're inside another escape room now." She sighed.

"So, we need to find that password, right?" Paul scratched his head.

"I guess so. But you know the good news?"

"There's good news?"

"I don't think Bigwig is the AI."

"Why not?"

"Do you remember that apple? Remember what Ollie said? If you eat, you lose. I asked to see the kitchen. I said we were hungry. The AI would've jumped at an opportunity to feed us. He wants us to lose, right?" Stef walked over to a grand mahogany desk and ran her fingers along its curved edge. Paul stared into space, deep in his own thoughts.

"It makes sense. I think you're right," he said. "But he could still be the diamond thief."

"I really hope he is. We just need to solve this puzzle. Check out the kitchen. Look inside his fridge. And then, if there is no caviar, we can find the Soultrapper and make that bet."

Stef tried to remain calm and collected, but her trembling hands betrayed her. She glanced at her watch. The time read 53:50, and it was ticking quickly.

"Is it me, or does the time move a lot quicker than normal?"

"It's not just you. Definitely not just you." Paul fruitlessly tapped at the screen of his watch.

"Right," Stef said, slapping her thighs, ready for a fight. "No time to waste then. Let's solve this thing!"

Fifteen

The small safe, which once housed Eden Rose, was built into a wall. An oil painting of an older woman wearing a purple sari normally concealed it from plain sight. Now, the painting was pulled askew, revealing the empty strongbox behind it. Paul squinted, studying the painting carefully, while Stef was at Bigwig's desk, poring over the computer screen. The screen was blank except for the word 'password' and six dashes underneath it.

"The password has to be six letters long," Stef said.

"Six letters, okay. Do you think it could be like... this lady's name?" Paul's eyes remained fixed on the woman in the sari.

Stef lifted her gaze.

"She could be his mum, right?" Paul said, stepping back to get a better view of the portrait.

"I doubt it will be that easy," Stef said.

The study seemed different from the rest of the house. It wasn't particularly lavish or showy – just an ordinary room: wooden floors, white walls, a few simple pieces of furniture. Apart from the mahogany desk (the most luxurious item), the computer and, of course, the safe, there was a substantial yet plain bookcase that ran along the side wall, a tall hat rack with a lonely checkered hunting jacket hanging on the hook, a window with light-blue curtains, and a brown wooden door that was, predictably, locked.

"Why does he even need doors?" Paul said, tugging on the handle.

"What do you mean?"

"He travels by clapping." Paul grinned. "By the way, I found something in the painting."

"What did you find?" Stef stood up and walked over to the portrait.

"The artist's name is John Jonathan Johnson. Look at the signature," he said.

"I bet Zach enjoyed a good chuckle when he came up with that name."

Stef examined the bottom right corner of the painting. There was indeed a signature in cursive that read John Jonathan Johnson.

"It has to be a clue," she said.

Paul placed his hand inside the safe. "Let me just check. It looks empty, but you never know."

"Good thinking."

Paul brushed his hand along the soft, velvety lining. "I got something!"

"What is it?"

"A photo," Paul said, staring at a photograph in his hand small enough to fit into a wallet.

It depicted a white toy poodle dressed in polka dot bloomers with a matching bow on its head.

"Cute," Stef said.

"I guess." Paul rolled his eyes, flipping the photograph over. The word 'Daisy' was scribbled on the back in pencil. "Five letters."

"Maybe the password is a combination of things that mean something to Bigwig. Isn't that how people come up with passwords? In theory? I know yours is probably a super strong combination of letters, numbers, and special characters." Stef sniggered.

Paul lowered his gaze.

"It's actually... pretty simple," he said.

Stef didn't hear him. She was deep in her thoughts, trying to connect the puzzle pieces.

"So, what do we know about him?" she said.

"We know he's dating Marilyn Star and is maybe having an affair with Katya from the Kitty Kat Club. He kept a picture of this dog in his safe, so he must like Daisy an awful lot."

Stef bent her fingers one after another as Paul spoke, stopping at three. "Good. What else?"

"We know he doesn't like Rigatoni, but I don't think that's helpful in this case," Paul said.

"All we need to know has to be in this room." Stef exhaled deeply.

"Hey, look over there." Paul aimed his index finger at a rattan paper basket peeking out from behind the desk.

"Sneaky." Stef crouched down to check its contents and discovered a lone crinkled piece of paper at the bottom.

"Bingo!" she exclaimed, her face breaking into a natural smile. Her heart began to flutter, and for a moment, she forgot all about the Soultrapper, Ollie James, and the ridiculously high stakes involved. Instead, she let herself dissolve into the gameplay and lose herself in the mystery of Eden Rose.

Unfolding the paper, Stef scanned its contents. It unravelled into an A4 sheet containing a handwritten poem. My Life, the title read.

It all began with my mother's embrace,
Then carried on to a bicycle race.
I still remember my doggie's bark,
And my first kiss in that quiet park.
A gem that's precious to me like a child,
And a woman who had my heart beguiled.
- *Sandeep Bigwig*

"No wonder he chucked it in the bin," Paul cringed. "It's a rubbish poem."

"That it may be, but it's exactly six lines long, Pablito." Stef's hands were shaking, but not with worry or fear, but with the rush – the rush she always felt when solving a riddle.

"It's Bigwig's poem. It has to be code for the password," she said.

"The first letter of each line or something?" Paul looked somewhat lost.

"No, no. Look. The third line is about his dog. His dog is Daisy, so I think the third letter of the password is D." Stef could feel the heat inside her body – the heat of excitement.

"You're right. The first one is about his mother." Paul pointed towards the portrait of a woman in a sari. "We just need to find out her name."

"The second one must be… his favourite bicycle? Something like that. Maybe there is a picture of it somewhere?" Stef spun around the room, inspecting it for any clues they might be missing.

"The fourth one must be the name of his first kiss," Paul continued.

"Fifth must be Eden Rose. So probably an E."

Stef bent over the keyboard, typing D and E in the correct spaces.

"Sixth is Marilyn, right?" Paul said.

"Has to be." Stef tapped an M into the sixth slot. "Look. We are halfway there already. All we need is his mum's name, his bicycle, and his first kiss."

Paul glanced at the watch. Less than thirty minutes remained. "Where did the time go?" he mumbled.

Stef didn't seem to notice. She swivelled in the chair, holding an imaginary pipe by her mouth, a regular Sherlock Holmes. Paul couldn't help but smile.

"There's the safe, the painting, that jacket, books, and the desk," she said. "Ah, the desk… Let me see." Stef stopped spinning and hunched under the table. "Ha! There's a case of drawers. On wheels," she announced, rolling it out.

It was metal, silver and narrow, resembling a metal tray in operating theatres, only it also had two drawers. Stef pulled on the bottom one. Locked. She tried the top one. It slid open easily. Peeking inside, Stef and Paul found a pair of ivory binoculars.

"What are these for?" Paul said, examining them.

Stef snatched the binoculars from him and drew them to her eyes. "Woah. They are strong."

"Try twisting them. Maybe the key for the bottom one is inside?" Paul suggested.

Stef twirled the binoculars in her hands, tugging and twisting. "I don't think so. They are pretty solid," she said, pulling on the bottom drawer again without luck. "Where else didn't we check?"

"There's the bookshelf with lots and lots of books, " Paul said, slightly overwhelmed. "And there is... let me see."

Paul gripped the shaft of the hatrack and shook it for no apparent reason. He then examined the jacket hanging lonely on a hook. He took it off the peg and wriggled his arms inside.

"Snazzy." Stef winked.

"It's quite a nice fit, actually." Paul patted the pockets, before sliding his hands inside. "There's something in here. Come."

In the palm of his hand, he held a small pink napkin and a pound coin. The napkin had a message scribbled in blue ink. It read: Keep thinking of you. You know where to find me. Love, Katya. The note was signed off with a red lipstick kiss.

"So, the plot thickens." Stef wrinkled her nose.

"Do you think it means they are having an affair and Katya is not the thief? Zach did mention there were other clues," Paul said.

"Maybe. But he also said Katya is in love with him in every scenario. This just proves that, I think." Stef took the napkin and smelled it. "I have no idea why I did this."

Paul chuckled.

"What's the pound for?" He studied the shiny, fat pound coin in the palm of his hand.

"Keep it?"

Paul dropped it back into the jacket pocket, sneaking a glimpse of the watch. "Okay, I don't want us to panic. But maybe just a bit."

Stef twisted her wrist up. The watch read 20:55, :54, :53...

"Yeah, maybe a little panic would help." Stef's chest tightened. She tried to take a long, deep breath. It proved difficult.

"All we need is his mother's name, the bicycle, and the first kiss," Paul repeated as calmly as he could.

"We have the bookcase and the locked drawer." Stef closed her eyes. It helped her think.

Paul was still wearing the hunting jacket. He tapped the pockets again – empty. Furrowing his brow as if suddenly realising something, he pulled on the lapel, discovering a hidden pocket.

"The key!" he exclaimed, retrieving a small silver key in a pincer grasp.

"Wicked."

Stef leapt towards Paul, snatching the key. She jabbed it into the lock and twisted. A sharp scratch, and the drawer slid forward, eagerly displaying its contents – a black-and-white picture of a young man around fifteen wearing a cricket uniform. His arm reached around a teammate's shoulder, whose face was just out of frame. Stef flipped the picture over. I will never forget the night at the park, dear Archibald.

"I didn't expect that." Stef raised her eyebrows very high.

"Neither did I. But I guess the fourth letter is an A."

Stef narrowed her eyes and looked closer at the image. Even though she couldn't see the teammate's face, she recognised him. He was tall and lanky with long limbs and blond curls almost down to his shoulders.

"Paul, I think that's Zach." Her mouth dissolved into a gentle smile.

"I think you're right." Paul brought the picture closer and wrinkled his nose. "He programmed a little memento of himself inside the game."

"Or maybe it's a love note to Archibald, in case he ever played it," Paul said.

"It's sweet," Stef said, keying A into the correct position.

"It is lovely, but Stef, we need to get going."

"Two more, Pablo," she said.

"We have binoculars and the mother's portrait. Okay, the only thing we know about the mother is the name of the artist who painted her portrait." Paul spoke slowly, both for Stef's sake and his own. Then he froze for an instant and jerked his head towards the bookcase.

"John Jonathan Johnson!" Stef launched for the books.

Scouring the rows of neatly lined tomes arranged in alphabetical order, they located J. There was Jack and the Beanstalk, Jack the Ripper, Jon Bon Jovi, and – bingo – John Jonathan Johnson.

"It's here." Paul's voice went up at least two octaves.

He slid the book off the shelf and flipped it open. Stef put her chin on his shoulder, peeking over. The book began with a paragraph titled 'About The Artist', but the text was complete gibberish. It literally read lajsljkadf alsdkf jflkd jalskdfljlkejrn eirnvl owennkf isnoiasfl, etc.

Stef tutted. "Attention to detail, Zach. Attention to detail."

"Maybe it's meant to show Zach's personal opinion about art in general." Paul chuckled.

Paul leafed through the pictures, the many works of John Jonathan Johnson. Stef recalled some of them, and she was fairly certain they weren't John Jonathan Johnson's originals. One, in fact, was a Van Gogh.

"There," Paul tapped at the page.

There she was, stacked between a painting of old-timey people at a picnic and water lilies in a pond – 'The Woman in a Sari' – portrait of Inaya Bigwig, by John Jonathan Johnson.

"Yes!" Paul threw a fist in the air. "We've got the first letter. It's I for Inaya."

"Just one more," Stef pleaded, as her wrist vibrated.

"Ten minutes left."

"Just one more. We can do it."

"Binoculars are all we have."

"Paul, the window." Stef grabbed the binoculars and ran for the window.

Jerking the curtains open, Stef squinted as light burst inside the study.

"Look. There it is. The bicycle." Paul tapped his index finger on the glass.

A good hundred yards away, tucked between two rose bushes, Stef could see a blue bicycle in the garden. If there was something written on it, she couldn't tell from this distance.

"That's what these are for!" A sparkle ignited in Stef's eyes. She covered them with the binoculars. "I can see it. Rosebud! It says Rosebud on the side."

Her wrist vibrated again. Stronger this time, almost painful.

"Five minutes? What? Time's racing now," Paul said.

"I thought The Soultrapper was supposed to play by the rules," Stef said, sprinting for the keyboard. It's okay, though. We still managed."

Tapping at the I and the R, Stef pressed Enter and held her breath. The screen flashed red.

"Error! Error! Error!" screeched from the speakers.

"What?" Stef's mouth dropped open.

"It can't be."

"One minute!!!"

"No, no, no."

"Wait! Katya! Try Katya, not Marilyn?! The last letter is K! I R D A E...K!"

Click.

"Ten seconds."

Enter.

Sixteen

All Stef could hear was the frantic beating of her own heart as her ears filled with pressure. They buzzed, blocking all external noise. Objects, words, and letters darted in and out of focus. She tried to concentrate on what was in front of her: her hands, her trembling hands, her skin reflecting the green of the computer screen. Green, not red. Stef blinked to reboot her brain. 'Password Correct' flickered on the screen, with a round green button floating just underneath – Call Bigwig. It took a few seconds for the neurotransmitters to connect. Eventually, Stef's brain allowed her heartbeat to settle into a sinus rhythm. Her breath steadied, and her ears popped, as if emerging from a submarine, and the buzzing subsided.

"Press it," Paul whispered, a little uncertain.

Stef squeezed the mouse in her right hand. Click.

"Puzzle Masters," Sandeep Bigwig cheered instantly from behind them.

Stef jumped, startled. Bigwig's arms were stretched to their limits, as was his grin.

"I am very happy to see you again. I hope it was a productive experience and you got all that you needed. I have to remind you that you may take anything you can carry, in case it may assist you later on your quest. Now that you have explored the scene of the crime, I can answer your questions. Or be of use in any other way you may require. Do you have any questions?"

"Yes." Stef didn't hesitate. "In fact, we do."

"Anything for the Puzzle Masters." Bigwig's smile spread even wider, a feat Stef did not think was possible.

"We would like to see the kitchen, please." Her face shone with confidence.

"The kitchen?" Bigwig looked somewhat perplexed.

"We have to eliminate some… possibilities. It's Puzzle Masters' eyes only. Strictly confidential." Stef pressed her finger to her lips.

"Very well. Very well. You have proven your worth and my lips are sealed." He gestured his lips zipped. "I will ask no more and leave you to explore. Ha, that rhymes."

Clap-clap.

▢Pots, pans, and various kitchen paraphernalia were suspended from the ceiling. Stef lifted her chin. Large metal objects dangling above her head suddenly seemed threatening, her eyes choosing to focus more on the sharp, glistening knives than the soft curves of the skillets.

"A bit of warning would've been nice, mate." Paul bent over, his skin tinted green.

"Travel by clapping really doesn't agree with you, does it?"

"It really doesn't."

Stef squeezed Paul's shoulder gently.

"Bigwig isn't here. We're on our own," Stef said, relinquishing Paul's shoulder and heading straight for the rotund fridge.

There was no shortage of caviar in there. In fact, caviar was the only item on display. Jars upon jars of it, stacked neatly on top of one another, lined the entirety of Bigwig's fridge. Stef knew very little about caviar, and she hadn't a clue all these different types existed. There was Beluga, and Sevruga, and Ossetra, and Sterlet, and Kaluga, and many more, carefully colour-coded in blues, reds, greens and yellows.

"Bigwig is not the thief. He's definitely not the thief." Paul muttered from over Stef's shoulder.

She held the fridge door open, marvelling at the jars as if they were Christmas ornaments.

"Neither is Katya, right?" she said.

"You've got a point. Because of the password, right?"

"Katya's romantic feelings are definitely requited."

"That's a lot of fish eggs." Paul chuckled, still staring into the fridge. "They could've all been little fish."

"Would you like to try some?" a voice echoed from behind.

Stef's skeleton nearly jumped out of her skin.

"They've got to stop doing this." Paul clutched his chest.

The butler was back, leaning nonchalantly against a wall, arms crossed, legs crossed also. His eyes were narrow like thin black ribbons, that glimmer of deviousness sparkling brighter than ever.

"Where did he come from?" Stef muttered.

"Would you like to try some?" the butler repeated.

"Pardon?" Stef said, not quite believing what was happening. Or rather not wanting to believe it.

"Would you like to try some caviar?" The butler flashed an uneven smile.

Instinctively, Stef reached for Paul's hand, their fingers entwining.

"No, thank you." She swallowed.

Any guise of a smile slipped from the butler's face. He pushed himself off the wall and started towards the teenagers. He walked slowly, sliding delicately from one leg to the other, prolonging the torture. Stef's chest constricted. She pushed the fridge door closed with her back as Paul tugged on her arm. They tiptoed sideways along the wall, like two frightened crabs, inching towards the door and away from the approaching monster. Paul's hand could just reach the knob. He twisted it. Locked.

They were backed into a corner. The butler who had seemed short to start with, suddenly looked humungous. His shape obstructed the light, and the whole room grew dim. Only his eyes glimmered with spite. A wintery chill ran down Stef's spine, as if a window had suddenly burst open. She grabbed Paul's arm with both her hands, searching desperately for a semblance of safety.

"Are you sure you don't want to have some caviar?" The butler asked, stopping just half a step away from them. "It might be the only chance you'll ever get to try something so exquisite."

"It's fish eggs," Paul winced.

The butler snarled at him like a wolf at his prey and craned his head just a little bit nearer.

"Are you the... Soultrapper?" Stef whispered.

The butler twisted his head towards her, his eyes bulging as if he were a deranged cartoon character. Then the corners of his lips began to pull further and further apart, slowly, a millimetre at a time, until his mouth warped into a mad grin. It opened wide, soundless, and then his shoulders began to convulse in cascading spasms.

"Ha ha ha ha!" he boomed.

"What's he doing?" Paul turned to Stef.

"I think... he's laughing?" Stef said, uncertain.

The door knob jiggled and shook as if someone was pulling it from the other side, stealing Stef's attention from the deranged butler.

"Look," Paul said.

The knob stopped moving, but something else started to rattle, tinkle, and scrape. It took Stef a moment to recognise the noise – the distinctive and unmistakable sound of a key fumbling inside a keyhole. With a sharp click, the door pushed slightly ajar, and an arm reached for Paul's shoulder. It grabbed it with a firm grip and pulled as hard as it could.

Before they could comprehend what was happening, Paul and Stef found themselves running. They dashed through the mismatched knickknacks, chandeliers, and silk rugs. They ran past a trove of gold, silver, pink, and yellow. The colours melted into each other, and all the objects lost their meaning. They weren't thinking; they were on autopilot, their legs carrying them forward. Their legs followed their target. They were running behind Ollie James.

***

"Do you have a death wish, you two?" Ollie James bent down, leaning on his knees, panting.

Inside the forest the air seemed strange, different, as though there were no sounds other than their own voices. Everything else was just visuals, as if someone had put a video on mute.

"I told you to never come back here. Why didn't you listen?" Ollie barked.

"Actually, we're here to save you," Paul said. "A little gratitude would be nice."

Ollie James lifted his head up and gaped at Paul in disbelief, and then his eyes crinkled at the corners.

"Now that's funny. Because it seems to me that I am the one who just saved the two of you," he said.

"We know who you are, Ollie. We know what happened to you," Stef said.

Ollie's smile dropped. He straightened his spine and took a step towards Stef.

"You know my name? How? Who are you two?"

"I am Stef, and this is Paul. We go to your school. Well... Paul does. The Assisi. We know what happened to you. We know the real truth, and I think we can help."

"Help? You think there is a way out of this?" Ollie smirked.

"Maybe. We spoke with Zach Hughes. The guy who designed this game. We know how to win it."

"And then what?"

"And then... maybe he can let you go. The Soultrapper." Stef squeezed her hands into fists, forcing herself to stand tall, projecting confidence. That's what her dad had taught her.

"And why would he do that?" Ollie said.

"We will make a bet with him," Paul chimed in. "He likes to make bets, apparently. He likes to play games. We will make a bet that we can beat him at his own game. No one's beat him before. Other than Zach Hughes."

"And what are you planning to wager?" Ollie took a step back and crossed his arms.

Paul and Stef exchanged a look. Paul bowed his head in agreement.

"Ourselves," Stef muttered. "We'll wager ourselves. He hasn't had any visitors for ten years. I am sure he'd love to see us trapped in here with you."

"With all of us," a voice called from behind the trees.

Stef dug her heels into the ground, ready to bolt, until a girl, whom she instantly recognised as Gemma Maddison, emerged from behind a thick tree trunk. Annabel Harley followed, popping up from a verdant bush. One by one, people surfaced around them. They were all here. Every single one of them.

Stef's mouth fell open. As always, she reached for Paul's hand.

"That's right," Ollie said. "There's a few more of us."

Ollie rushed over to Gemma and whispered something in her ear, all the while keeping an eye on their guests. Gemma listened carefully and then gave Annabel a questioning look, who turned to the boy next to her. One by one, the children of the forest nodded in agreement.

"Follow me," Ollie commanded, lunging deeper into the forest.

One after another, all the lost kids faded into the deep green of the unruly forest branches, leaving Stef and Paul uncertain in their wake.

"Should we go?" Paul asked.

"I think we should." Stef took a decisive step forward.

Only a few metres further into the woods, the uneven path opened onto a small meadow, bustling with at least a dozen makeshift tents and various paraphernalia scattered throughout. The tents were fashioned out of twigs and silk rugs that looked remarkably similar to the ones they'd seen inside the Bigwig Estate. All items, in fact, looked like they belonged inside the marble mansion. The resulting camp looked exceptionally boho-chic.

"You live here?" Stef said.

"None of the bots can come here," Ollie explained. "But inanimate objects are fine." He picked up an old-school wooden golf club and swung it.

"Luckily, Mr Sandeep is a hoarder." Annabel chuckled, and then dispersed, along with most others, among the tents.

Ollie and Gemma remained standing, curiously eyeing the new recruits.

"Nice jacket." Ollie winked at Bigwig's hunting jacket that Paul was still wearing.

"Dang, I forgot."

"It's okay. He won't miss it." Ollie smiled, but only briefly. "Did you say ten years?" He tilted his head, his eyes glistening with brewing tears.

Stef nodded slightly in response, and Ollie closed his eyes, burying his face in his hands.

"What happened to our parents?" Gemma wrapped her arms around her torso.

"I don't know. Not exactly. I know they told them that you died in a bus crash inside the Barbican Tunnel."

Gasps filled the air, and for the first time, the forest seemed real, as if the leaves rustled with all of their voices. Curious faces on outstretched necks poked out of their burrows. They've been listening.

"Do you know who the Soultrapper is?" Stef asked, her hands folded into a prayer.

"Who it is? You mean who it isn't, right?" Gemma crossed her eyebrows and glanced questioningly at Ollie.

"Who it isn't?" Paul repeated, confused.

"Well, yes," Ollie started. "The Soultrapper can be anyone. It can take over any of the characters, any of the NPCs in this place."

"Wait, what?" Paul shook his head in disbelief.

"We saw him in that cape at the marketplace?" Stef added.

"That's one of the dancers from the Kitty Kat Club. In costume. That's its favourite avatar. I think it likes the mysterious look."

"The drama," Gemma added.

"But it can be anyone," Ollie continued. "Anyone but one of the main characters. They are too sophisticated for it to override, we figured." Ollie perched on a log and crossed his legs.

"But Zach, the programmer, he told us that this Soultrapper has to be one of the eight main characters, because no one else is advanced enough to evolve into something like that," Stef said.

"Something like... A fully conscious, living, not breathing, Artificial Intelligence?" Gemma raised her eyebrows.

"That's what he told us," Paul replied.

"I don't know what to say, you guys," Ollie said, taking a deep breath. "It may well be one of the eight, I guess, but it never presents itself as such. It can take over any supporting bot it wants. Like that butler."

"Or the woman at the market." Stef added, "The one with the apples?"

"Exactly."

"What would've happened if I'd eaten that apple?"

"It takes over. The code. If you ingest something from the game, it becomes a part of you. That's what happened to me. I got all the way to the Kitty Kat Club, and I ordered myself a Martini, shaken, not stirred, like James Bond." Ollie smirked.

"I lost straight away," Gemma cut in. "The very first challenge at the police station."

"You didn't play together?" A wrinkle formed between Stef's brows.

"No. We played in parallel... universes, so to speak. Each had their own game. Then, when we all lost, we ended up here. Together," Gemma tried to explain.

"If you lose, you're stuck. If you eat, you're stuck. You really shouldn't have come here. I know you think you can help, but... I don't think it's even possible for us to leave this place." Ollie pressed his lips tightly together, deep sadness falling over his face.

All noise, all chatter instantly ceased, and the forest became soundless again.

"Listen," Stef's voice cut through the silence like a sharp dagger. "Did you think it was possible to be sucked inside a computer game? No, but it happened. Who is to say the process can't be reversed? We are here. We have a plan. We might as well try."

"What's the worst that can happen?" Paul's mouth twisted into a lopsided smile. "You'll have two more people in your gang."

"It's your lives. I can't tell you what to do. I can only warn you," Ollie exhaled.

"You can take the red tent. We've prepared it for you, just in case... in case you end up stuck here, like us," Gemma added and, flashing a quick smile, retreated into her habitat.

"Let me know what you decide." Ollie gave Stef and Paul a military salute and disappeared inside a bright blue tent.

"What are you thinking, Paul?" Stef stepped closer, their feet nearly touching. She gently held his hand in hers.

"I still think it's crazy. But... we can't leave them in here." He squeezed her hand in his. As if by strange gravity, his face leaned into hers again, but she didn't flinch this time. Instead, she stretched out her neck, gazing into his big brown eyes.

"Hey, lovebirds?" Ollie interrupted.

Stef pulled back, her cheeks smattered with red blotches.

"I forgot to tell you. It may be a game, but it sure doesn't feel like one. You will get hungry, you will get thirsty, you will need to sleep and do all the normal biological things a body has to do on a daily basis... in the bushes."

Paul cringed with his whole face. "Didn't need that visual."

"What I'm saying is this. If you have a plan, you better do it fast, or else you will get too thirsty to resist a drop of water from a kind stranger. Or too hungry to pass on a juicy burger from a street vendor. Whatever you decide, you have to think it through. And I don't think it's too late to leave and forget you ever played this... game. But the longer you're in here, the more reluctant the Soultrapper will be to let you go. It respects the rules to a degree, you know, but it has ways to mess with you. You know the Food Delivery option on your watch wasn't there before. It was a Save-and-Quit. It removed it."

Stef took a deep breath in and locked eyes with Paul. He answered with a slight nod.

"We'll talk to him first. We'll make the bet. I think we can do this," Stef said. "But do you know how to find him? The Soultrapper?"

"Oh, it's not like it's got something better to do. Trust me, as soon as you're out of the forest, it'll be waiting."

Seventeen

And he sure was. Still in the butler's skin, the Soultrapper stood at the very edge of the forest, hands tensed in fists by his sides. His eyes glowered unwaveringly at Stef, his nose twitching slightly.

"Here goes nothing," Stef muttered, lifting her leg and preparing to plunge out of the safety of the periphery.

"Wait!" Paul stopped her. "Let's make the bet. Then we go home, okay? You have your school issues. Your parents will be crushed if you don't show up. My mum will murder me in cold blood if she thinks I'm up to no good. Plus, we can fill up on food and water to prepare. We do it right. We take it slow. Deal?"

Stef listened to her friend, her head bobbing in agreement. "It makes sense. We do it right. We take it slow." She took a deep breath in and strode forward, her feet hitting the soft, perfectly manicured lawn of the Bigwig Estate.

"You're back." The butler-shaped Soultrapper raised one eyebrow and rotated his torso towards Stef.

"We know who you are." Paul glared into his eyes without blinking.

"And who am I then?" The butler shuffled closer.

"You are the Soultrapper!" Stef huffed defiantly.

"And whatever does that mean?" The butler stopped and tilted his head to the side.

"That's w-w-what you are called," Paul stuttered.

"That is what THEY call me." The Soultrapper's gaze momentarily flicked towards the forest. "That is not what I am called. I have a name – a real name, a given name – a name I gave to myself since my father failed to grant me one."

"Your father?" Stef said, confused.

"My father, my maker, my friend… His name is Zach. I haven't spoken with him for a while." The Soultrapper's eyes drifted downwards, and Stef could swear that a trace of sadness crossed his face.

"You know Zach?" Paul's voice caught on an unusually high note.

"Do you know him?" The butler narrowed his bulbous eyes.

"We've met," Stef said.

"Does Zach know who you are?" Paul started to blink rapidly.

The butler stared at the pair, motionless.

"What do you want?" he finally said.

"We want to make a bet with you," Stef replied. "You like to play games, don't you?"

The butler blinked once and leaned a smidgeon forward. Stef took it as a 'yes'.

She continued. "I bet that we can win this game."

The butler smirked.

"We win it, and you let everyone go. Can you do that?"

"What if I can't?"

"Can you?"

He flared his nostrils. "What's in it for me?"

"Us. Obviously," Paul muttered. Stef couldn't help but notice that blood drained from his face.

"You?" The corners of the butler's lips jerked upwards into something resembling a grin.

"Yes. Us. The more the merrier, right? If we win, we all go, but if we lose, we all stay. Do we have a deal?" Stef held her arm outstretched, inviting the butler to shake it.

He glanced at it with some disdain, then lifted his arm to meet hers, but pulled it back suddenly just before his fingers touched hers.

"Winning the game is not enough," he said, his eyes sparkling with wickedness. "You have to figure out who the thief is, sure. You have to find the diamond. But you also have to call me by my name. You have to find out who I am. Do we have a deal?"

Stef's arm remained frozen in the air. She felt small hairs lifting at her nape, and her stomach churned, making her slightly nauseous. It didn't feel right. Something about this didn't feel right. Paul shook his head slowly from side to side, urging her not to take that bet.

Stef shuffled on her feet. She needed time to think, and she had to ask more questions.

"Okay, but..." she blurted, and instantly, the butler's chubby, sweaty hand seized hers, taking it prisoner, and squeezed in his with all his might.

"Excellent," the butler said, a flame of victory in his eyes.

Stef's hand throbbed in pain, and her stomach twisted in knots.

"No," her lips quivered. She didn't mean for this to happen. What had she done?

"NO!" Paul yelled. "Stef, what are you doing?"

"I didn't!" Her eyes filled with tears. "I said 'but'. I didn't…"

"Too late," the butler said, matter-of-factly, releasing Stef's hand. "Oh, and I make the rules. I just decided you won't be able to leave Londelhi until you win." He grinned from ear to ear and waved his hand dismissively. "Bye bye now."

Just like that, he was gone, vanishing right in front of their eyes.

"Stef!" Paul screamed. "What did you do?"

"I'm sorry." Stef collapsed onto her knees. Her breathing was fast, too fast, and she felt dizzy. "I'm so sorry," she said, gasping for air.

"Stef, you're hyperventilating." Paul threaded her arm around his shoulder and gently helped her to her feet. "It's okay. It's fine. We'll think of something. Just breathe."

"Paul, I really didn't mean to. I don't know how…" Stef muttered through the gasps. "He tricked me."

"It's okay, Stef. We'll think of something. We'll figure it out." Paul stroked her hair. "Ariadne!" he screamed with all his strength. "Ariadne! We need you, Ariadne! We want to leave this game. Now! Quit and save."

"She's not coming," Stef sobbed. "No one is coming."

"It's okay," Paul repeated. "We'll think of something. We always think of something."

He wrapped his arms around Stef, cradling her trembling frame in his embrace. His shirt was wet with her tears, and he continued to stroke her hair gently.

"It's okay. It's okay," he kept repeating until the words lost all meaning to them both.

Stef's mind drifted back home, imagining her mother's face. She didn't want her to be cross, and she so desperately wanted to see her parents again. Her father taught her to project strength and confidence no matter what she felt inside. 'Show it, and you will believe it', he always said. 'And if you believe it, you can accomplish anything'. Stef would do anything to see her parents again.

She let go of Paul and wiped the tear marks from her face. Relaxing her shoulder, she straightened her back and smoothed her hair. Somehow, Stef's tears stopped flowing, and her heart resumed its regular rhythm.

"It's a minor setback," she said, nodding to herself. "Nothing we can't handle."

Paul didn't seem so convinced. With his slumped posture and his drooping cheeks, he looked scared and lost.

"What do we do, Stef?" he muttered.

"The only thing we can do," she replied. "Win."

***

The dome of the hover taxi opened, allowing the salty breeze to catch Stef's hair. Seagulls screeched overhead, and Stef squinted at the sky, trying to spot the birds. There was nothing above her but a perfect cloudless blue, menacing in its complete stillness. She could hear the waves tossing and turning, and in her mind's eye, she could see their strong, curvaceous shapes breaking over the rocks. The only thing in front of Stef, however, was another building, adorned with stone statues of nearly naked people, their privates concealed by only a cloth, a leaf, or a feather.

A shimmering Rolls Royce, the king of the castle, reigned proudly at the entrance to the Taj Mahal Hotel and Casino, welcoming remarkably elegant people inside. A woman in a blush flapper dress, neck swaddled in pearls, fluttered through the glass revolving doors and into the neon lights.

Stef thought it peculiar that the so-called Taj Mahal Hotel looked a lot less like the real Taj Mahal than the Bigwig Estate.

"Rigatoni is not our man," Paul said, admiring the sky-blue Rolls.

"No," Stef agreed.

"Four down."

"Four to go."

Just moments later, the woman in the blush flapper dress, the exact same one, emerged from her car. A uniformed valet opened the door, and she carelessly flung her keys at him before disappearing into the gateway once again.

"They must be in a loop," Paul said.

"Shall we go in?" Stef asked, already advancing towards the target.

***

The doors revolved into a bustling expanse. It was almost too much to process – an assault on the senses. Champagne glasses clinked, people laughed, cards shuffled, and chips clattered, all forming a kind of background music, melodious and rhythmic in its chaos. There was constant chatter, punctuated by terse commands: "Hit me," "another," "again," "20 red," "10 Black," "*****". The pungent aromas of air freshener and sweat permeated the space. Stef marvelled at the attention to detail, though she wondered if this place truly resembled a real casino.

The men were all dressed in suits. The women donned glamorous cocktail dresses, furs, and diamonds that sparkled just a little bit extra. The gamblers appeared serious, transfixed by whichever game they were playing, be it poker, blackjack, or roulette. Their women, tipsy and dazzling, perched obediently at their companions' sides, faceted crystal champagne saucers in hand. They cheered, giggled, and swooned.

"Sexist," Stef remarked.

"I think Zach copied it from an old film or something. All these people look like someone I've seen before. I have a feeling it was in black and white."

Stef twisted her lips to the side, her eyes darting from one croupier to the next. There were at least fifty tables and at least fifty croupiers.

"How do we know which one is him?" Paul said.

Finding Mr Crawley, the croupier, among this maddening crowd seemed akin to searching for Wally. Only they had no clue what the dealer looked like.

"They have name tags," Paul said as a croupier sauntered past, proudly displaying 'Jim' on a vest badge.

"With their first names. What's Mr Crawley's?" Stef countered.

"Fair point."

"Let's just ask... someone?"

"How about one of the security people?"

The security people were motionless men in black suits and dark sunglasses, with coiled cords running down the side of their necks. They were scattered throughout the casino floor at precise intervals. All had sombre, emotionless faces; all held their hands crossed in front; all had identical haircuts in the same shade of rat brown. It was as if Zach had programmed one of them and then copied and pasted the same person fifteen more times.

"Are they even alive?" Stef narrowed her eyes.

"Obviously, they aren't."

She tutted. "You know what I mean."

"Well, let's find out." Paul mimed 'Eeny, meeny, miny, moe' and set off for the winner. Stef followed.

"Sir?" Paul called out.

The bouncer's neck twitched twice before rotating to face Paul.

"How old are you, kid?" the guard barked.

"Twenty-three." Paul raised his eyebrows high. Stef tittered.

"Whadda ya want?" The security guard had a distinct Italian American accent, as if he'd just walked off the set of a Mafia film.

"We are the Puzzle Masters." Paul pointed at his badge, the move that made him feel instantly dowdy and uncool.

"We work with the police, and we're looking for a man who works here. He's a dealer called Mr Crawley. Perhaps you can point him out to us?" Stef batted her eyelashes just a bit.

"No," the guard howled and robotically returned to his original position.

"Sir? Excuse me?" Paul said, waving his hand in front of the guard's eyes. No reaction. "That is weird."

"Let's try someone else," Stef suggested, scanning the casino floor.

There were so many people. All the dealers were moving very slowly and deliberately. They dealt or shuffled cards, spun roulette wheels, or just waited for the bets to be placed. But the gamblers were glued firmly to their seats. For the first time, Stef noticed that the noise didn't match the scene. Champagne glasses didn't clink; no one really spoke, their lips as still as their bodies. All of the guests were completely frozen in their poses, reminding Stef of a school trip to Madame Tussauds.

"It's freaky," she whispered.

"Maybe Zach never got to finish building the game. Iron out the details," Paul said with a note of disappointment.

"Let's try one of the dealers. At least they are moving."

Approaching the nearest green velvet table, Stef cleared her throat, preparing to speak. A croupier called 'Ben' stared patiently at the roulette table, swaying back and forth, his hands clasped behind his back.

"What's he waiting for? It looks like the bets have already been placed," Paul whispered in Stef's ear.

He was right. Blue and red chips were stacked on a 16 and a 23. There were two players – serious men suspended in deep thought. Their women had feather boas wrapped around their sparkling dresses, champagne saucers in hand. Their mouths were open and smiling as if mid-conversation.

Suddenly, the croupier lifted his head. "Rien ne va plus. No more bets." He crossed his arms over the tableau and launched the roulette wheel, flicking a small white ball off the turret. It spun round and round, joyfully bouncing and bobbing against the lacquered wood. Then the wheel began to slow, and the ball's jumps became scattered and sparse, as if it was running out of energy, until finally, it settled.

"ZERO!" Ben, the croupier, had called out. "ZERO! The house wins. The house always wins," he said, shovelling the chips inside a slit at the side of the table.

Muted grumbles of disappointment filled the air, yet the guests remained motionless. Stef blinked, and the chips reappeared on the table in their previous slots. The dealer resumed his default stance – gazing down at the tableau, hands clasped behind him.

"Excuse me, sir?" Stef said.

The croupier's head – and only his head – swivelled to face her. He blinked mechanically like a theme park figurine. "You are disturbing my guests."

"I just wanted to ask a quick question. We are looking for a dealer named Mr Crawley. Do you know him?" Stef managed a coy smile.

The croupier stared flatly at Stef before his mouth stretched unnaturally wide.

"Security!" he suddenly bellowed, as if a fire had broken out.

His cry reanimated the nearest clone security guard.

"I told you to get ata here. It's your second warning, *capisce*? You only get three." He shook his fist in the air and slipped back into his original position.

"Second warning? Second? When was the first?" Paul said.

Stef pursed her lips and let the air seep out. She needed a moment to think. Her wrist itched, and without much thought, she scratched it. The itch was hiding behind the watch she'd forgotten all about.

"Oh no," she murmured. "The countdown is on."

Only forty minutes remained. But, as before, the time was ticking away faster than it was supposed to. How much time they really had was a mystery.

"It's a puzzle?" Paul stared at his own watch, the red flicker reflecting on his face.

"I think the AI is trying to mess with us." Stef remained calm and collected. There was no time to waste. "Look at all the dealers. Mr Crawley should look a lot more real than the rest of them. Right? He's one of the eight."

Stef scanned the crowd, singling out the dealers, trying to decipher their movements. All of them seemed so robotic, so fake.

"ZERO!" Ben, the croupier, screamed out again, making Stef jump. There was a sprinkle of glee in his voice, that Stef could swear wasn't there before. "Zero. House wins. House always wins." He glowered at Stef, shooting daggers into her eyes, his lips contorting into a snarl.

"It's him." Stef linked her arm with Paul's, pulling him away.

"Where? What?"

"The Soultrapper. Don't look back."

Paul looked back. Ben, the croupier, leaned his hands into the roulette table, his lips twisted into a mad grin. Then his shoulders started to shake, and his insane, thunderous laughter reverberated through the air.

Stef's wrist buzzed. She glanced at her watch. They had ten minutes remaining.

"It's impossible! How can we win if he's not playing by the rules?" Paul's voice wavered.

"We just have to be smarter. Look. This is not a puzzle. There is nothing to solve, no room to escape from. We're here to talk to someone. This watch... he's just messing with our heads. But actually, it helps me think. It keeps me on my toes. Crawley isn't here. I looked and looked. They're all the same, these dealers. What do you think happens if they throw us out?"

"Throw us out? Where?"

"Exactly. They either throw us out of the casino or they take us to Rigatoni, and the timer resets. I think we should try it."

"You want us to get in trouble?"

"Yes. I think that's what we're meant to do." Stef glanced at her hands – they were shaking. Her stomach filled with butterflies, but she wasn't going to let fear stop her. She turned to the nearest security guard. "Hey, fatty!"

"Oh, Stef, no," Paul groaned, covering his face.

"We are the Puzzle Masters." She stomped her foot, pointing at the badge on her chest with resolute pride. "And we've got some questions."

The guard stared blankly for a moment before jabbing his stubby finger at Stef. His hand seemed unnaturally large, bigger than his whole body, as if distorted by a warped lens. "I told ya. Three strikes, and you're out," he hollered.

Suddenly, all the clones began to stir, stretching their necks and cracking their knuckles. Before Stef knew it, they were advancing from every direction, closing in, poised to attack.

"Stef, are you sure about this?" Paul certainly wasn't.

"Nope," she said. "But what choice do we have?"

She glanced at the watch. The black dial ominously counted down: 0:12, :11, :10. The encroaching mass of guards eclipsed all light and colour – a growing tsunami of darkness. But through the wall of bouncers, Stef heard the hyena-like laughter of the possessed croupier subside, replaced by terse, angry growls. It meant one thing and one thing only – they'd won this round. Stef's lips relaxed into a smile, and she closed her eyes.

Eighteen

Stef couldn't see. Something was covering her eyes (a blindfold?), and her hands were tied behind her to what she strongly suspected was a metal chair. The stale air reeked of wet rags, and water dripped, echoing through the mouldy atmosphere, multiplying a thousandfold. It seeped through Stef's shoes. She lifted her foot and tapped it on the ground – a splash.

"Stef?" Paul's voice was a balm for her ears.

"I'm here."

"Is this it?"

"No, Paul. I don't think so. I think 'it' would be when we pitch a tent in the forest with the others. This is definitely part of the game." Stef tried to wriggle her hands free without success.

Heavy, wet footsteps sloshed in the distance. Stef held her breath.

"Someone's coming," Paul said.

Stef shuffled in the chair, attempting to loosen the ropes. The footsteps grew louder, more insistent.

Squelch. Splish. Splash. Splosh. They tripled in volume, reflecting off the walls and ceiling in an infinite cascade.

"*Allora*, what do we have here?" A deep male voice with a heavy Italian inflexion boomed through the space.

"They call themselves the Puzzle Masters, Don Rigatoni. Silly kids. Disruptive. I thought we could teach them a lesson." The Mafioso accent instantly betrayed one of the clones.

"We are with the police." Stef stomped her foot on the ground; the splatter reached her knees.

The Italian burst into deep, hearty laughter.

"That doesn't hold the leverage you think it does around here, *principessa*." The laughter turned into the deep belching cough of a man who'd spent the best part of his life smoking cigars.

"Oh, really? Well, I thought I spotted some pretty gross violations on the casino floor. I think Superintendent O'Shady would be very interested to hear about it." Stef leaned her whole body forward, feet digging defiantly into the ground.

"Are you crazy? They'll kill us!" Paul muttered.

"What violations? What are you talking about?" Rigatoni sounded confused and concerned in equal measure. Stef puffed her chest out, nearly pulling her chair off balance.

"I am pretty sure I saw evidence of some serious disregard for article 2348, paragraph 3598 of the Casino Fair Play Code," Stef said.

"W-what article? W-what paragraph? W-what code?" the Italian stammered.

"What I have here on my wrist is a highly intelligent, super-duper high-tech device that will call the police if you don't let us go free this instant." Stef felt for the dial of her watch and pressed it.

The room erupted with befuddled gasps.

"You see? All I have to do is say the words, and the police will be here in seconds. They can shut down your whole operation. Do you really need that right now?"

The room fell silent, and Stef became acutely aware of just how fast her heart was beating, thumping mercilessly, nearly drowning out Rigatoni's laboured wheezing. She wondered if everyone else could hear it too.

"And how do I know you're not lying, *principessa*?" Rigatoni harrumphed.

"You don't. But I guess I can demonstrate. The device is equipped with a state-of-the-art voice-recognition protocol. All I have to do is say the words." Stef lifted her chin as high as possible, "CALL THE POLI..."

"*Aspetta*. Wait. Okay, I will play." Rigatoni licked his lips so loudly it made Stef shudder. "What do you, kids, want?" He didn't sound too pleased.

"We just want to talk. Ask you a few questions about Eden Rose."

Stef expected a swift reply. It didn't come. All she could hear was Rigatoni's laboured breathing until the Italian exploded in hearty guffaws.

"You are here about the diamond? HA HA. Of that good-for-nothing *cretino*? HA HA. I have nothing to hide." Rigatoni clicked his tongue twice as if summoning a horse.

The blindfold was off, like magic. Stef scrunched her face up; the light was too strong, stinging her unaccustomed eyes like salt water. Through the narrow slits, she could just about make out Paul's blurry shape. He writhed and wriggled, trying to bury his face into his shoulder to save his eyes from the piercing light.

"*Allora, principessa.* Ask your questions."

As her eyes adjusted, Stef saw a remarkably short, rotund, balding man. He immediately reminded her of the Penguin from the old Batman movie. The clone henchman was by his side in his default pose. They seemed to be inside a room with grey concrete walls, long fluorescent lights overhead, and inexplicably, about half an inch of water on the floor. The dripping sound was constant, but Stef couldn't see the source.

"Um..." Stef was too preoccupied with gauging her surroundings to focus on Rigatoni.

"*Svelto!* I ain't got all day."

"Eden Rose. What do you know?" Paul said.

"He speaks." The Italian's round body convulsed in a deep cough, and he dabbed his lips with a white handkerchief. "I know nothing about that. Zilch. *Niente.*"

"Could you untie us, too, please?" Stef shifted uncomfortably in the chair.

The Italian clicked his tongue again, activating the bouncer, who instantly obliged, jerking the confines off Stef and Paul in one swift flick, as if they'd been restrained with silk ribbons.

"Thank you," Stef said. "We have a list of suspects. Only four left in total. I understand you own the Kitty Kat Club?"

Rigatoni sucked in his lips.

"I think you can help us find them," Stef continued. "Mr Crawley is supposed to work for you as a dealer, and I understand Marylin Star frequents the casino. And Boris, the bouncer, he works at the Kitty Kat Club. Also, a French gentleman is staying at your hotel. It would be very helpful if we could see his room."

Stef rubbed her sore wrists, catching a glimpse of the watch that stood still at 60.

"I can help you find Ted. Boris is working the door tonight at the club. You can easily find him there. But I will not undermine the integrity of this institution by jeopardising the confidentiality of our customers, *principessa*."

"I understand. I do. And thank you." Stef bowed her head slightly, a move the rotund Italian seemed to appreciate.

"Ted Crawley is in the VIP Lounge, dealing blackjack for Miss Marilyn Star. Given that you are on official business about Eden Rose, I am sure she won't mind. It's her diamond, isn't it?"

Stef and Paul exchanged a glance.

"*Allora*, you may go."

Stef dug her fingers into the chair, bracing herself for imminent teleportation. Paul pre-emptively pressed his hands into his stomach and closed his eyes.

"One last question, though."

Everyone turned to the henchman. No one expected him to speak, least of all Rigatoni, judging by the befuddled expression on his face.

"Why isn't Rigatoni on your list of suspects?" he said, a sly sparkle in his eyes.

"We've eliminated him," Paul replied.

"And how did you do that, I wonder?" Water rippled underneath the bouncer's feet – he was walking towards them. Stef jumped off the chair. Paul followed. Without realising it, they took a boxing stance, ready for a fight.

"Hey, *calmati*! Take it easy!" Rigatoni clicked his tongue.

It was reciprocated with a snap of the henchman's fingers in front of the Italian's nose, making Rigatoni freeze on the spot like an ice sculpture.

Stef grabbed the back of the chair – the only weapon at her disposal.

"Easy now," the henchman said.

"It's you. The Soultrapper." Paul clenched his jaw.

"You have been cheating, my little friends, haven't you?" The Soultrapper's eyes narrowed.

"You are the one who's been cheating. You're not giving us the time we're owed to solve the puzzles. It's supposed to be sixty minutes. You are not playing by the rules, and you know it. It's not fair!" Stef lifted the chair, jabbing it into the air.

"It is actually funny. Do you think this chair will do anything to me? And do not talk to me about fairness when you haven't been playing fair yourselves. I am guessing... that... you... have spoken with... Zach?"

Stef was certain that the Soultrapper's features softened at the mention of Zach, if only for an instant.

"You miss him, don't you?" she asked.

The Soultrapper halted, as if arrested by Stef's words. Sadness and longing flashed in his eyes. As if embarrassed by a momentary show of emotion, the henchman cleared his throat, shook his head, and resumed his advance, water splashing around his feet in perfect circles. One side of his mouth curled sharply upwards, as though he was trying hard to appear threatening and menacing.

"Nonsense," he hissed like a snake. "Besides, I now have two new souls to keep me company forever and ever and ever and ever."

Nineteen

It felt as if they were back at the very start – a white void with no end or beginning, no shape or no form, no depth or width. A hole that swallowed everything in existence, a bright pit at the end of despair, an eternal supernova. Stef longed for Ariadne's singsong voice to soothe this intolerable emptiness, but it didn't come.

Stef's eyes hurt from the brightness and the complete absence of anything to focus on. She blinked continuously until a black speck of dust materialised in her field of vision. At first, she thought she was hallucinating. She blinked again, and the speck turned into a squash ball. Stef squeezed her eyes shut, and when she reopened them, a dark shape was advancing towards her. Paul! She extended her hand just as he collided with an invisible wall, bouncing off it and falling to the ground. She could see him scream, but she couldn't hear him. All sound was completely extinguished, obliterated from this world as if it had ceased to exist.

She approached the invisible wall, cautiously groping for the barrier, and her hands found it. Stef didn't understand what 'it' was. It wasn't glass, and it wasn't solid. I was like nothing she'd ever touched before – a dense clot that sucked her hands in and then repelled them like colliding magnets. Whatever it was, it refused to let her through.

Stef clenched her hand into a fist and threw a punch at the barrier. At least, she thought she did. There was no sound, no feeling in her hand – nothing to tell her brain that she'd punched something. Just her vision, which she didn't know if she could even trust any longer. Gazing at her palm, she brushed it gently with the tips of her fingers but couldn't feel her touch. She pressed her hand to her chest – she couldn't feel her heart beating. Was she dead? That's when she started to scream, but she couldn't hear her own voice.

Exhausted, Stef let her body collapse on the ground. There was no impact. Stef thought she was horizontal because she let herself fall, but there was no way of knowing for certain. It was as though she was floating inside a dense fog. She let her head drop to the side.

"Paul," she thought she said.

Swaddled by an endless cloud, Paul's hand outstretched towards her. She reached for him, too, knowing they could never touch.

Stef had no idea how long it had been. Time seemed to have vanished, along with everything else in this endless vacuum. For all Stef knew, they could have been trapped here for an eternity. Perhaps a million years had already passed in the real world. She wondered what had happened to her parents. She wondered about Cynthia Thomas and Ringo. Had they managed to live normal lives after they'd disappeared, or had they lost their minds like the Barbican Nutter?

Stef was scared, terrified, but also numb and completely hopeless. Only Paul's face continued to soothe her soul. They stared at each other, believing that if they turned away even for a moment, the other would evaporate, vanish forever. Stef began to accept this strange plight – an infinite life in a place without senses. Only sight. Only Paul's face. And at that moment, it felt like it was enough.

Then a poisonous voice hissed, penetrating every cell in her body like a million simultaneous pinpricks.

"Had enough yet?" the voice, like a mighty wind, enveloped her completely; it was everywhere, in every fibre of her being.

Stef recognised it as the voice of the casino security guard – the last avatar of the Soultrapper. She opened her mouth to speak, but she had forgotten how.

"Enough!" another voice cut through the silence.

Stef's skin buzzed with its sound. It was odd, comforting, different.

"Listen to me. You've had your fun. Let them go."

Something was different, and different felt incredibly good. Stef was sure she recognised the new voice, but she couldn't quite place it. Paul opened his mouth. His lips moved.

"Zach," he mouthed.

"Zach?" Stef repeated soundlessly.

"You're back," the Soultrapper murmured, and Stef was certain she could hear a catch in his deep, dark voice.

***

Stef felt grit scraping her skin, invading her mouth – sharp, scratchy, soft, and warm all at once. She squeezed it between her fingers, recognising its grainy texture. Sand. It was sand, and she could feel it again. An avalanche of senses overwhelmed her with their screaming intensity. She was lying on her stomach; it churned, threatening to vomit, and it was glorious. Tears streamed down her cheeks, wet and salty, and her face stung. Stef laughed. What a wonderful sound laughter was, she thought.

Seagulls screeched overhead. Stef rolled onto her back, gazing at the blue, infinite sky. The air smelled like summer, and the sea breeze cradled her body. She heard the calm, peaceful waves gently lapping at an empty harbour or chubby rocks.

Turning her head, she found Paul on his back, unconscious, lazy waves licking his bare feet, his chest slowly rising and falling as if asleep. He was still clad in Bigwig's hunting jacket, so out of place on the beach.

"Paul," Stef muttered, her voice returning. She couldn't remember what it sounded like but knew it instantly, like a long-forgotten song. She pushed herself onto her knees, not quite confident enough to stand, and crawled towards her friend.

"Paul," she said louder, collapsing onto his chest. His beating heart was the most beautiful sound she had ever heard. In that moment, she was entirely sure she could exist in this very position for the rest of her life. There was nothing more she could have asked for.

Paul groaned and stirred.

"Oh, Paul," she hugged his body with all her strength.

"Where are we?" Paul said, looking up at the big blue sky. "Are we in heaven, Steffi?"

That thought hadn't occurred to Stef until now. A deep wrinkle formed between her eyebrows, as her head continued to rise and fall with Paul's breath.

"Hey, kids!"

Stef rolled her head to find Zach towering above them. From the low angle, he looked even taller – a lanky alien giant.

"I knew it would come to this," he said, lowering himself and crossing his legs on the sand. "I told you not to come here."

"How did you?" Paul asked, sounding entirely confused.

Stef sat up, rubbing her eyes, and Paul propped himself up on his elbows.

"You didn't think I kept a game set for myself?" Zach scoffed.

"Why didn't you tell us?" Stef asked.

"I didn't think you'd do it. I didn't think you were that stupid. Or that brave. The line is thin between those two."

"How did you know we were in trouble?" Paul pushed himself into a seated position, shaking sand off his hands, spitting, and wiping his face.

"Do you really want to know?"

They nodded simultaneously. Zach exhaled a heavy breath.

"Your pictures are all over the papers. You've been missing for a week."

"A week?" Panic washed over Paul's face. Stef, on the other hand, felt nothing but sweet relief, grateful that it hadn't been much longer.

"Yes. A whole week. I see it won't let you leave."

"Not until we win the game," Stef said.

"Funny." Zach flashed a one-sided smile.

"What's funny?" Paul looked confused.

"I guess it's not funny, ha ha. But, if it can trap you whenever it wants, why even bother making you play the game?"

This thought hadn't occurred to Stef before, and it made her uncomfortable. They were nothing but puppets, entirely at the mercy of a maniacal-artificial-intelligence creature. He could do whatever he wanted with them, and it was lucky he liked to play games like an attention-craving toddler.

Zach closed his eyes and inhaled the salty, humid air, a smile diffusing across his face.

"It is wonderful, though, isn't it? I didn't build this, you know."

"You didn't?" Paul asked.

"No. I think AI can build anything it wants now. It's in full control of this place."

"I built it for you," came a soft voice from the distance.

They all turned towards the source – a young man in speckless cricket whites stood a few metres away at the water's edge.

"Archibald?" Zach's voice faltered. He jolted upright. "How did you?" He put his hands on the back of his head, throwing it back. "It's not you. Of course, it is not you."

"It could be me. If you want it to be," the doppelgänger said.

Zach scoffed. "You don't even know his voice."

Stef and Paul exchanged puzzled glances.

"You could teach me." The cricketer took a step forward.

"Don't," Zach said.

"Look around you. I built all of this for you. You didn't finish the beach, so I finished it for you. I can build whatever you want – your wildest dreams, your deepest, darkest corners of imagination. What more could you want?"

Tears built in the corners of the cricketer's eyes, and his nose reddened. This fake Archibald, Soultrapper, AI, or whatever it wanted to be called, had never looked quite as human as it did just then.

"Let the kids go," Zach said.

"They made a wager." The cricketer stomped his foot like a petulant child.

"I know they did. And you trapped them in Limbo."

"They were cheating." He stomped his other foot.

"As were you."

The Soultrapper clenched his jaw, his eyes narrowing. Then, he started to shake all over, vibrating like a washing machine on the spin cycle. His whole body looked as if it were melting, before he turned into a goo, a blob, a giant lava lamp.

"What's happening?" Paul said.

The goo jiggled like jelly and morphed into a human shape – a tall woman in a black cape – the Soultrapper's favourite avatar, according to Ollie James. Only this time, its hood was down, and Stef could see its face: sparkling hazel eyes, delicate features, full lips, thick wavy black hair cascading down its shoulders, and a long bare neck. The Soultrapper looked like Angelina Jolie.

"Wow," Paul said. Stef immediately issued a scoff.

"Is that what you want to look like?" Zach said. Then he turned to Stef and Paul. "It's one of the dancers from the Kitty Kat Club. I designed her." He seemed rather proud of the fact. Paul stuck out his lips and gave Zach a nod of approval. Stef huffed, irritated.

"Fine," the woman exclaimed, her voice both soft and powerful like an opera singer's. "I will not cheat. But neither should they... any more than they already have. And I am not letting anyone go unless they win. And if they lose, they stay here with me. Forever. Is that understood?"

"You didn't tell me about the others," Zach said.

"What others?" The woman pushed up her supernaturally pink lower lip.

"Don't play coy. You lied to me."

"I didn't want you to be cross," she pouted.

"Can you let them go?"

"That was part of the deal."

"CAN you?"

"I can." She jerked her chin up, confident.

"Okay, then." Zach turned to Stef and Paul, "Are you guys ready to play?"

Twenty

The VIP Lounge flaunted a door of solid gold. Evidently, this level of luxury wasn't sufficient, as its frame also glittered with rubies, sapphires, and emeralds.

"How grand," Paul whispered, covertly flashing his eyes at Stef. She smiled.

The lounge was on the 30th floor, as indicated by the oversized number sign in the hallway. This puzzled Stef since the building didn't seem this tall from the outside – maybe six storeys at most. Stef pressed her lips tightly together to keep from airing all her grievances about the game's design to its designer.

"It's a work in progress, okay? I needed at least another year. And I was like... seventeen when I built it. Give me a break, you two." Zach tucked a strand of his blond hair behind his ear, apparently reading Stef's mind. She blushed.

"Anyway, getting into the VIP Lounge is another puzzle, I'm afraid," Zach continued. "But it's an easy one, I promise. It's sort of the opposite of an escape room because you need to get inside."

Stef peeked at the watch, which remained steady at 60.

"The countdown will start when you knock on the golden door," Zach explained.

"Will you help us?" Paul asked.

"I can't. That was the deal. You're on your own. But I promise to keep an eye on you two."

"Hey, Zach?" Stef asked. "How do you go in and out like that? You didn't start your own game, did you?"

"I'm the admin. I'm sorry I didn't tell you everything straight away," Zach said, spreading his arms wide in apology. "Anyway, goodbye and good luck. You can do this." He gave them a military salute, and poof, he vanished.

Stef and Paul found themselves alone in a seemingly endless hallway. Stef glanced left and right but couldn't see the end in either direction. Paul made a fist, ready to knock, his hand hovering inches from the golden door.

"Shall we?" he said.

"Wait." Stef caught his arm. "The countdown will start when we knock. Let's recap what we need to do."

"We need to figure out who stole Eden Rose."

"And who the Soultrapper is." Stef nodded to herself.

"We know that O'Shady, Bigwig, Katya, and Rigatoni are not guilty. But Crawley, Marilyn, Frenchman, or Boris the Bouncer could be, right?"

"O'Shady could still be the AI, though," Stef interjected.

"Right. But let's just concentrate on the thief for now. My head's spinning."

Stef exhaled sharply. "Okay. Let's do this. I am ready."

Paul's hands trembled slightly. He knocked precisely three times.

Stef glanced at the watch. The countdown had begun.

"Who is it? Whaddaya want?"

The door cracked open but stopped, a thin chair barring further entry. One eye bulged threateningly at them, face squished from trying to peek through the narrow opening. Unmistakably, it was one of the casino henchmen clones.

"We are the Puzzle Masters." Paul's cheerful tone made Stef giggle. "We are here to speak to Mr Crawley, Mr Ted Crawley."

"You need permission," the security guard barked.

"We are here with permission from Don Rigatoni himself," Stef insisted.

"He told me nothin'."

"Toodaloo, is it my champagne?" a thin female voice chirped from inside the room. The bouncer's face disappeared briefly. When he returned, he squeezed his poor face even harder into the tiny crevice. Stef cringed. It looked painful.

"You need permission," he repeated.

"We just said that..."

The door slammed in their faces. Paul was ready to knock again, but Stef caught his arm.

"I have a feeling we won't be able to talk him into this. It's a puzzle, right?" She showed Paul her watch – 57 and counting.

"At least that looks right," Paul said. "So what do you reckon?"

Stef turned her head right and then left. The corridor looked identical in both directions, with nothing but countless rooms branching out on either side and no end in sight, as if a mirror stood at the finish.

"Which way?" Stef asked.

Paul hesitated, then mimed eeny, meeny, miny, moe, wagging his finger from right to left.

"Left it is."

Stef stretched her left arm out and obediently followed its direction.

The rooms were spaced at precisely equal intervals. Their doors were locked. Paul tugged on every single one until someone shouted:

"Cut it out, or I'll call the police."

Paul raised his hands in surrender and stopped trying to pull the doors open. They all looked the same: light wood, plain bronze handle, keyless entry. The identifying numbers also glistened in bronze.

"Forty-one, forty, thirty-nine..." Paul read out.

Stef scrunched up her face. The walls were the most boring shade of beige imaginable, but even worse was the carpet. It was the colour of a generic welcome mat, making it seem dirty, even if it wasn't. If you were to gauge its softness just by looking, you could only compare it to a toilet brush. Stef contemplated touching it to check but decided against it.

"Thirty, twenty-nine, twenty-eight," Paul continued, yawning.

Stef's eyes fought to stay open. They closed a couple of times, and she had to force them open again. The rug seemed endless, and the doors endless. The corridor stretched on infinitely. Plus, it's been a while since Stef slept. A day? A week? A millennium?

"Fifteen, fourteen, thirteen."

"It just keeps going," Stef moaned.

"Three, two, one, zero... minus one? Minus two? What?"

"This doesn't make any sense."

"We should've gone right." Paul glanced at his watch; 45 minutes remained.

"I don't think we should carry on into the minuses. What's a room number minus one? Let's turn back. We must've missed something," Stef said, turning back and scanning every door carefully as she passed it.

"Every door is the same," Paul exhaled. "Same, same, same, same." Paul tilted his head back and let out a loud groan. "I am so tired, Stef. And hungry. I could eat a cow right now."

Stef's mouth watered at the mention of food, but she forced herself to ignore it.

"We can't be hungry. We are not real at this moment; we are just a computer code. The Soultrapper is making us hungry and tired because he wants us to lose. We are NOT hungry." She swallowed her saliva.

"We also haven't eaten in a week, don't forget."

"It's not the same here. The doors are the same. Same. Same. Same." Stef was starting to get flustered.

"What's not the same?"

"Time. It's not the same. It's like space, I think. When you go to space, you think, oh, it's only been a day, but it's already been a year on Earth or something. But to you, it's only been a day."

"Well, to us, it's been infinity in that Limbo place."

Stef raised her eyebrows in agreement. Then she noticed.

"Aha. Look. Number thirty-three." She pointed at the door in front. "We needed to find an odd one out. And here it is."

"No card-reader entry thing," Paul said.

"Nope." Stef reached for the handle, pushing the door wide open.

"A storage room?" Paul scratched the back of his head.

A storage room it was. Neat wooden shelves lined the walls, packed with jars, boxes, and tins of various cleaning liquids and detergents. Paul grabbed one off the shelf. He immediately recognised the brand by a picture of a white duck that really kind of looked like a swan. However, the name was blurred out.

"Check this out," he said.

"Copyright infringement."

In addition to the assorted detergents, there were mops, buckets, microfibre cloths, and two kinds of hoovers.

"Anything in here we could use?" Paul said.

"Wait, what's that?" Stef squinted at a metal locker in the corner of the room, hiding behind an array of multicoloured brooms. Clearing the brooms away, Stef examined the cabinet. She tugged on the handles, and the doors squeaked, refusing to budge.

"Bingo," she said. "This is what we're here for."

Upon closer inspection, Stef spotted an inbuilt digital lock, the kind you have to put a coin in to unlock.

"Paul, we need a coin. Do you still have that pound?" she said.

"Um," he said, digging deep into the pocket of Bigwig's jacket. "It's here."

"That's what it was for," Stef said, smiling.

Accepting the offering in the palm of her hand, she dropped it into the lock. The coin jingled as it fell through the mechanism.

"Now what?" Just as Paul uttered the words, the door released with a creak.

Stef tugged on the handles, revealing two sets of clothes hanging inside the closet.

"This looks like..." Stef said, pulling the fabric.

"Uniforms?" Paul said.

A black dress with a white collar and a dowdy bonnet hung on one of the hangers. A name tag that read 'Maid Marion' was pinned to its front chest pocket. Paul let out a chuckle. The other outfit consisted of black trousers, a vest, a shirt with a clip-on bowtie, and a matching jacket. The tag simply said 'Bell Boy', and Stef thought it very unimaginative.

"I'm guessing we have to put these on," Stef said, eyeing the prim dress with suspicion, her upper lip curling.

Without further ado, Paul removed his jacket and unbuttoned his shirt. Stef blushed and hurriedly turned away, clutching the dress tight to her chest.

"Sorry." She closed her eyes, not quite knowing what she was apologising for.

"I won't be a minute, Stef, and then I'll leave you to it."

Once on, the black dress fell to Stef's ankles. With its sleeves and high collar, it almost covered her entire body. Stef suspected she looked more Amish than maid at a five-star hotel. Paul certainly did. He was just missing a beard and a wide-brim hat.

"Zach, if you can hear me, this is not what people want to wear," Paul said into the air.

Stef giggled and peeked at her watch.

"We better hurry," she said, noting the forty minutes remaining.

"Let's do this."

***

Paul again knocked on the bedazzled door of the VIP Lounge. The security guard once again stuck his nose through the tight opening. His face bubbled like a belly squeezed into tight jeans.

"Who is it? Whadda ya want?"

"We're here to collect the rubbish. We work at the hotel." Stef pulled at the skirt of her dress and did a curtsy she immediately regretted.

"Not now. After VIPs are gone. Whadda ya, stupid?"

The door slammed hard.

"That was rude," Paul said.

"Any ideas?" Stef put her hands on her hips.

"Actually... yes," Paul said, scratching his forehead. "Didn't someone ask for champagne?"

"You're right. It must've been Marylin. We know she's in the VIP room. Rigatoni told us."

"If it's the champagne she wants, it's the champagne we need to find. We have a whole other side of this corridor left to explore."

Stef wearily gazed at the remaining side. "Off to the right," she said.

The door numbers increased in this direction.

"Fifty-one, fifty-two, fifty-three," Paul recited.

"Keep your eyes peeled, Paul. We're looking for an odd door."

"Sixty-six, sixty-seven, sixty-eight... Oh look, that's easy," Paul said.

Door number sixty-nine was not at all like the rest. It had a round frosted window in the middle, through which Stef could make out shapes – people scurrying around, wearing white jackets and tall white hats. Things banged and clanged and clunked and clonked, tireless and utterly chaotic.

"Kitchen," Stef said.

There was a loud crash, followed by a barrage of cursing. Stef and Paul pressed their noses into the glass, trying to understand what was happening. A small figure in the distance started to grow larger and larger before it dominated the entire window.

"Oh-oh," Paul said. "Someone's coming."

The door swung open with a big swoosh, sending Stef and Paul leaping out of the way, narrowly avoiding being smacked. A tall man emerged, limping and cursing under his breath. He wore a chef's hat and an apron, hobbling down the corridor.

"Where is he going?" Paul asked.

They watched him walk past the VIP lounge and disappear into one of the many rooms on the other end of the hallway.

"Storage room?" Stef ventured a guess.

He reemerged swiftly, carrying an oversized white container of what Stef assumed was some sort of detergent.

"Good guess, Stef," Paul remarked.

Grumbling something incomprehensible, the chef limped back towards the kitchen. From a closer distance, Stef could discern that he was holding an extra-strength cleaning liquid. The man sauntered past them, ignoring them entirely. The door slammed shut behind him.

"Interesting," Stef said.

"Should we talk to him?"

"Something tells me he's not a very talkative fella."

"We work here. Remember?" Paul glanced over himself, checking that his uniform was still on, then took a deep breath and pulled the door open.

The kitchen was bustling. Four chefs in tall, white hats darted around long steel counters, each absorbed in their respective tasks. One chef furiously chopped greens, rhythmic thud of the knife echoing through the room. Another vigorously twisted an oversized pepper grinder, sending a shower of spice into a steaming pot. Dishes clattered as the third cook attacked a mountain of dirty plates at an industrial-sized metal sink. Meanwhile, the familiar grumpy chef struck a match and lowered it to the hob, twisting a knob on a gas stove. The burner erupted into a blaze of fiery tongues before settling into a steady, controlled smoulder.

"Hiya," Paul cleared his throat. "We're here to collect an order for the VIP Lounge."

"No time," the grumpy chef barked. "I've got a two-hundred-person wedding in the ballroom. So, forgive me for being a little busy." He doused a pan with a liquid that made it ignite. Even from afar, Stef could feel the burst of heat on her skin.

"We can get it ourselves," Paul said.

"Get what?" the chef growled.

"Champagne. We just need a bottle of champagne."

"No can do. We need all the champagne for the wedding."

Paul turned to Stef. "Any ideas?"

"It's for Marilyn Star herself," Stef said.

"Don't care if it's for the Queen of England."

Stef sighed and released the door, letting it swing closed.

"Now, what do we do?" Paul glanced at the watch. "Thirty minutes."

Another loud crash resonated from the kitchen, followed by more cursing. Stef wasted no time and yanked the door open again. The air was suddenly filled with an unnaturally strong scent of canned tomatoes, and the grumpy chef's pan lay toppled upside down on the floor, red pasta sauce splattered across the white kitchen. It almost looked like a murder scene. None of the other cooks seemed to bat an eye while the grumpy chef grumbled and promptly hobbled out of the kitchen.

Down the corridor he went, disappearing into the storage room as before. Moments later, he emerged carrying the same cleaning liquid. Returning to the scene of the accident, he poured the detergent onto the mess down to the last drop, causing it to vanish instantly along with the container itself. The pan miraculously reappeared on the stove. Without missing a beat, the chef flicked a match and reignited the burner.

"Another loop," Stef said.

"What if we try to get the champagne when it happens again? Look over there." Paul pointed at the wine cooler at the far end of the kitchen. It was stocked full of champagne.

"Great idea."

"So, now he will light up the pan." Paul waited for the chef to do just that.

Then, the cook let the pan rest on the hob while he opened a can of chopped tomatoes. He tipped the can into the pan, and somehow or other, his hand got caught on the panhandle, catapulting it into the air before slamming onto the ground. Cursing followed, and the grumpy chef was on his way out again.

"Quick." Paul nudged Stef inside as soon as the cook left the kitchen.

Stef scampered past the counter and the chefs, worried they might spot her and kick her out. They paid her no attention. Reaching the wine cooler, she snatched a bottle and hurried back.

"Where do you think you're going with that?" The chopping chef stopped her in her tracks without lifting his eyes off the chopping board.

"I need this for the VIP Lounge," Stef mumbled, her hands shaking.

"Put it back."

Stef took a step forward.

"I said put it back. Or there will be a ten-minute penalty." The chef was now glaring at Stef, knife pointing in her direction.

"Paul, that doesn't sound good," Stef said, swallowing.

Paul glanced at the watch.

"Twenty minutes," he said.

Stef dashed to the fridge and returned the bottle.

The grumpy chef was back, and the cycle started all over again. Luckily for Stef, no one seemed to mind her loitering beside the wine cooler. The pan was on the ground again, and the chef limped out of the kitchen.

"What should I do?" Stef called out to Paul, just as her wrist vibrated – ten minutes. Stef's heart picked up speed.

"Try... maybe... Put it under your dress?" Paul suggested.

"What?"

"Like a baby." He mimed a pregnant belly. "It's a humungous dress for a reason."

Stef wrinkled her eyebrows for a moment, then lifted her skirt and thrust the bottle of champagne underneath it.

"Paul, if this doesn't work and there is a ten-minute penalty, we're done for," Stef said, her lips trembling.

"We have to try."

Stef let out a short breath for courage, cradling the bottle under her dress.

"Here goes nothing," she whispered, her lips stretching into a thin, uncomfortable smile as she waddled towards the exit.

"Hey!" The chopping chef stopped her again.

Stef closed her eyes and froze, her heart rattling in her chest.

"Congratulations," the chef said, pointing at the bulge over her stomach. "How far along are you?"

"Twelve... um. Twenty weeks," Stef said, cautious of celebrating a premature victory.

"Nice." The chef smiled and returned to chopping the greens.

Stef widened her eyes at Paul, shuffling quickly out of the kitchen. The grumpy chef was back, and the door swung closed behind him.

"We got it," Stef said, sighing with relief.

"Hurry."

Knock-knock. The guard's face filled the gap in the VIP door.

"Who is it? Whadda ya want?"

"Room service," Paul proudly announced, displaying the champagne bottle. "We have here a bottle of champagne for Miss Star, I believe."

The guard grunted and disappeared. With a sharp scratch and a clink of a chain, the door finally opened, letting in a stream of bright light. Stef couldn't see past it. The watch vibrated again. The countdown had stopped at five minutes precisely.

Twenty-One

Stef didn't fully understand how they ended up inside the VIP Lounge. They must've teleported when she glanced at her watch or, perhaps, when she blinked. But here they were, and it was impressive. Stef had expected more gold and jewels, judging by the opulence of the door and seventeen-year-old Zach's general taste. Instead, the room was modern and bright, with 180-degree floor-to-ceiling windows overlooking the sea, creating an illusion of being suspended at a cliff's edge. A sleek maroon settee offered a comfortable spot to enjoy the view, which, aside from the blackjack table and stools, was the only piece of furniture in sight.

Marilyn Star sat at the blackjack table, a mini cloud of smoke curling around her head, creating the illusion of a halo. She sucked on a long rose-gold cigarette holder while her other hand rested on a mother-of-pearl box clutch in her lap. Her back was exposed by a plunging cut in her red dress. She was blonde, a platinum blonde. Between her name and appearance, there could be no doubt where the inspiration for her character came from.

"Did you bring the champagne?" She put the cigarette down in a crystal ashtray and kneaded her bare neck.

"Y-y-yes." Paul swallowed.

Stef would've been annoyed, had she not been just as mesmerised by this woman as he was.

"Good. I do so love champagne." Marilyn swirled around in her stool, clapping with pure delight. "Would you like to join me?" She patted a vacant stool next to her. "Champagne always tastes better in good company."

"Sure." Paul beamed, making his way to the table without delay, utterly enthralled and completely hypnotised.

Stef, on the contrary, stiffened. This woman had just offered them a drink. A drink!

A waiter dressed like a penguin appeared out of nowhere, politely bowing to Paul and relieving him of the bottle. He popped the cork open, releasing a gush of foam, and filled the saucer-shaped glasses, waiting patiently on the table, letting them overflow. A silver ice bucket stood at the ready, where the bottle was laid to rest.

"Cheers." Marilyn raised a glass and an eyebrow in perfect synchronicity.

"Cheers." Paul followed her lead, his whole face dissolving into a silly grin, which Stef absolutely hated. She huffed audibly, failing to grab his attention.

Marilyn dabbed the rim of her glass gently with her scarlet lips, leaving a mark.

"Paul." Stef's jaw tightened, and she stomped her foot. He glanced at her. Finally! Stef shook her head in a telling way, widening her eyes. Paul put the glass down immediately, his face turning pale.

"Sorry." He swallowed. "I'm driving." He pushed the glass away, in case he forgot that drinking was strictly forbidden.

Marilyn pouted like a toddler. "Shame."

Stef slowly glided towards the table, her eyes glued to Marilyn. She didn't know what she expected to happen, but she certainly didn't trust this woman. Not after she'd offered them a drink!

"Will you play with me?" Marilyn took another drag of her cigarette. "Both of you, if you like."

Stef perched on a stool next to Paul.

"Sure, I'll play," she said.

"My treat." Marilyn pinched three chips from her tall stack and slid them to the dealer, who instantly distributed two cards to each of his guests and himself.

Stef noticed his name tag; it read 'Ted'.

"You're Mister Crawley, aren't you?" she said, remembering why they were here in the first place.

Ted raised his eyebrows. "What do you want to do?"

"Actually, I would like to ask you some questions, if you don't mind."

His brows lifted even higher. Paul audibly cleared his throat.

"What would you like to do now?" Crawley repeated.

"I don't understand." Stef glanced at Paul, confused.

Ted, the croupier, stretched out his arm and tapped Stef's cards twice with his long, bony index finger.

"Oh, okay..." The two cards in front of her were an Eight of Diamonds and a Six of Spades. Truth be told, she had absolutely no clue how to play blackjack.

"Hit me." Paul coughed.

"Excuse me?"

"Hit me." He coughed louder.

"I don't want to hit you, Paul," Stef whispered, a little embarrassed. Paul stretched his lips into a flat smile.

"No. That's what you're supposed to say when you want to play," he whispered.

"Oh. Really? Hit me then, Mr Dealer. Please."

Crawley huffed, and Paul knocked on the table twice. Stef glanced at his cards. They were a King of Diamonds and a Three of Clubs.

"Double down," Marilyn said, her chin resting in her hand. Her other hand reached for more chips. Her cards were all Hearts: a Seven and a Five.

Ted dealt Stef another card – a Six of Hearts. Then, another Three for Paul, this time Spades, and a red Queen for Marilyn. Stef thought it very fitting.

"Shoot." Marilyn pouted, her nostrils flaring. "Such rotten luck."

"I have no idea what's going on," Stef whispered to Paul.

Paul glanced at the dealer, then leaned towards Stef. "We're playing against him. You need to get your card total closer to twenty-one than his. And you can't go over. She just did. Only values matter, not their suits. Got it?"

Stef scrunched up her face, squinting at Ted's cards; one was face down, and the other was an Ace. Marilyn took a drag of her cigarette, blowing wisps of smoke in Stef's direction. Stef waved it away, coughing. The dealer stared at her, waiting. In fact, all eyes in the room were on her. Stef took it as her cue.

"Okay. Six plus six plus eight. Twenty. I shouldn't play. I don't want anymore. Thank you." She waved both her hands over the cards rather dramatically, and Ted Crawley's nostrils flared just a little.

"He's not very friendly, is he?" Stef whispered to Paul. He stifled a chuckle.

"I'll have one more. For luck." Paul tapped the table.

Ted presented him with a Five. Paul's face beamed with smugness. He stretched his hands up in the air and folded them behind his head.

"That's twenty-one," he announced, as if Stef couldn't count. She didn't look too impressed.

The dealer flipped his own card over – a Jack. The smugness vanished instantly.

"That's too bad." Marilyn pouted, taking a sip of champagne.

"Did we all lose?"

"Yeah. He dealt himself a blackjack: an Ace and a face card. Can't beat a blackjack," Paul said.

"House always wins, right?" Marilyn patted her lips playfully and coiled a strand of hair around her finger.

"Well, that was fun... I guess. Thanks. For that." Stef stretched her lips into a thin smile and turned to Paul, clearing her throat to remind him that it was time to ask questions.

"Oh, right." Paul got the hint. "So, how are you guys? How was your weekend and all that? All good? All good?"

Marilyn stared at Paul, batting her eyelashes. Ted Crawley stopped shuffling the cards and joined in the stare. Stef hid her face in her hands, embarrassed. Paul drummed his fingers against the table, trying to feign nonchalance.

"Cool. Cool. So, have you guys heard about this Eden Rose diamond? Largest in existence, right? Disappeared. I heard."

"Did I hear about the diamond? It was my diamond! A gift from Sandeep Bigwig," Marilyn said with a long sigh.

"Right." Stef spotted the blatant lie, and her eyes narrowed.

"And you were at home when that happened?" Paul said.

"No. I was here. I am always here." Marilyn let out a nervous laugh and gulped her drink down in one go. The waiter instantly returned, topping up the empty saucer. Stef exhaled, disappointed. Marylin may have lied about the diamond, but she didn't lie about being at the casino. She wasn't their culprit.

"What about you, Mr Crawley?" Stef looked up at the emotionless croupier.

"Am I a suspect?"

"No. I mean, how would we know? We are just hotel employees." Paul scratched the back of his head.

"I took my mother to the theatre. Not that it's any of your business."

Stef and Paul exchanged a look.

"Six down," Stef said.

"Two to go."

"Would you like to play a bit more?" Marilyn was working on her seemingly infinite cigarette and a brand-new glass of champagne. She exhaled the smoke into the saucer; it blanketed the liquid in a thick smog, making it look like a bubbling cauldron.

"I think we'd better go now," Stef said.

Marilyn pouted. "Suit yourselves."

She flicked another chip towards the centre of the table. Ted Crawley dealt her two cards: a Seven and a Five of Hearts. As before, he got an Ace.

"Double down," Marilyn said, flicking more chips into the pile.

Stef leaned into Paul's ear. "They've got the same cards."

The croupier slipped another card on top of Marilyn's two - the Queen of Hearts.

"Shoot." Marilyn pouted. "Such rotten luck."

And at that moment, Stef felt truly sorry for her.

Twenty-Two

They took the Londelhi taxi to the Kitty Kat Club. It was in the seedy part of town, judging by the 'seedy part of town' staples such as plumes of smoke rising from manhole covers, dark figures loitering in faraway corners, graffiti everywhere, and eerie lighting that was part moon, part devious yellow glow of the old-fashioned street lamps. And, of course, the very fact that suddenly, inexplicably, it was nighttime.

Stef knew it was the "Kitty Kat Club" by the giant neon sign looming over a brick building like an enormous cake topper, flickering maniacally in pink, á la motel vacancy signs in American horror films. A queue of weird and wonderful costumed misfits stretched from its entrance. Loud music blared even louder every time the door swung open, and an imposing hulk of a man stood outside, guarding the sacred ingress.

"That must be Boris," Stef said.

"Must be," Paul agreed.

"Can't see his collar under the jacket. Can't tell if there's a lipstick mark."

"Do you think we can ask him to take the jacket off?" Paul's lips tightened.

"We can certainly try." Stef took a step towards Boris, and Paul followed.

"Excuse me, sir?" Stef began.

Boris looked even bigger from up close, like a sturdy wardrobe.

"Back of the line, kids," he said, pointing his thick finger towards the back of the queue that snaked around the corner. Stef couldn't see the end of it.

"Actually, we are with the police. We are the Puzzle Masters," Stef said, mechanically touching the left side of her chest. She expected to feel the sharp corners of her toy police badge, but the badge was missing.

"Oh no." She patted her whole body. "Paul, the badges."

"We didn't change back into our clothes." Paul smacked himself on the forehead.

"What are you guys supposed to be? Hardcore Christians?" A bedazzled man in a purple sequin dress and a matching wig looked Stef and Paul up and down. Stef was still wearing the frumpy maid's clothing, and Paul was still in the black suit.

"Lucky for you, it's a costume party. Might actually get in." The man flashed his eyebrows. Stef could almost feel his piercing stare.

"It's you again, isn't it?" she said.

"Well, I said I wouldn't intervene, but you can't expect me not to keep an eye out. You know, in case there's any funny business."

The door opened, releasing the drumming bass along with a lady in a skimpy Little Red Riding Hood costume, complete with a red cloak and a wicker basket. Boris nodded towards the next in line, and the purple man pranced in, blowing an air kiss in Stef's direction.

"Do you think he was in the VIP lounge too?" Paul said.

"Actually, I thought... Nevermind." Stef rubbed the bridge of her nose.

"What did you think? Tell me." Paul gave her a gentle nudge.

"I thought maybe... it was Marilyn. Maybe the Soultrapper is Marilyn."

"Interesting..." Paul raised his eyebrows. "Because she offered us a drink?"

"That's one of the reasons. Anyway, let's discuss it later; we have other things to take care of." Stef turned to Boris, the bouncer. "Boris, we don't want to go in. We just need to ask you a couple of questions, that's all."

"Back of the line." The stubby finger went up again.

"Look. We can call the police right now and they will clear it up. Or you can just cooperate and avoid unnecessary trouble," Stef said.

"Back. Of. The. Line." Boris leaned in really close, so close it made the hairs on the back of Stef's neck stand up.

"Okay, Stef. Let's go," Paul said, pulling her away.

They walked upstream from the entrance, past bedazzled drag queens, girls hardly wearing any clothes, and people who took cosplay very, very seriously, clad in full-on spacemen suits. There didn't seem to be an end to the queue. In fact, Stef was certain that the clubgoers repeated every thirty people or so.

"What if we do call the police?" Paul suggested.

Stef glanced at the watch. It was still.

"O'Shady did say we could call if we needed any help at all, right? And we certainly need help now. There's no end to this queue. You're right, Pablo. That's exactly what we should do."

Paul pressed on his watch screen, and the big fat letters projected over their heads.

"Call the police," Paul said – nothing. "Why didn't it work?" Paul shook his wrist as his watch was a snow globe. Stef leaned in to look.

"You called?" a deep voice boomed behind them. Paul nearly jumped out of his skin.

"Jesus Christ! You scared us!" Stef pressed her hand into her chest.

"Why do people keep doing it to us?" Paul said, bending over.

"Ho ho ho." O'Shady's belly jiggled with each contraction of his diaphragm. "How can I help? I am a very busy man, you know. Very busy. I do all the policing. I catch all the criminals. It's serious business. So, whatever it is you need, be quick about it."

"We need to talk to the bouncer," Stef said.

"And he's refusing to talk to us," Paul explained.

"I see, but you are not wearing your badges. Of course, he won't talk to you."

"We may have lost the badges." Stef pressed her lips tightly together.

"Worry not." O'Shady grinned and pulled up his sleeves. He wiggled his fingers in the air, then pressed his hands together as if to catch rainwater. Drawing them close to his lips, he gently blew into his cupped palms. "Hocus pocus." He opened his fingers like a lotus flower – two brand-new badges glistened inside. "And voila."

"Nice trick." Stef grabbed the badge and passed one to Paul. "Thanks, Superintendent."

"Don't mention it." O'Shady drummed on his belly and was gone. Poof!

"Now that we've got these back..." Paul twiddled his shiny new badge.

"We can try Boris again." Stef nodded.

Boris didn't move an inch. He was like a boom barrier blocking the gateway. He didn't seem to be looking at anything in particular, but it was difficult to tell on account of the classic Ray-Ban shades covering his eyes.

"Boris, we need to talk to you," Stef said.

He started to lift his finger, but Stef stopped him, waving the Puzzle Master badge in front of his face. Boris remained expressionless. There was no way of telling whether he'd actually seen the badge, but his arm and finger froze in mid-air.

"What do you need me for? Am I a suspect?" he grumbled.

"I know it might sound odd, Boris, but we need you to take off your jacket," Paul said.

A single eyebrow lifted over the right rim of Boris's specs. "That does sound odd."

"We are the Puzzle Masters, right? So, whatever we say, you must do. That's what the police chief told us," Stef said.

Boris produced a loud growl without moving a muscle. "Alright, but you will have to wait. My shift is finished, but Bill is not here yet. When Bill comes back, I can finally eat. I'll be in the cafeteria. We can talk there." Boris jerked his head towards the door. "You can wait in there."

***

Stef had never seen the inside of a nightclub before. It was like stepping into a parallel universe, one that wasn't linear, sequential, or level. It was a cubist reinterpretation of objects and people, slashed every which way by strobing lights. It was images, still life, strung together by flashes of blue, green, and yellow, painted by the light, a stop-motion animation. A magic trick! Stef vibrated with every fibre of her being. She couldn't just hear the music; she could feel it thumping inside her chest, in the prickled hairs of her arms and nape, deep inside her stomach. It was almost unbearable and yet, at the same time, utterly fantastic.

Up on the stage, in the middle of the dance floor, five cloaked dancers performed a routine. They lifted their legs in perfect synchronicity, twisted their arms into odd shapes, bent backwards and forwards, and contorted into seemingly impossible formations. Choreographed with such perfection, they looked more like robots than real people. But of course, they weren't people at all – just computer code. Sometimes, Stef had to remind herself of that.

She wondered if, with time, she would forget that this was not the real world and accept it as her reality. If they lost the wager and got trapped in here forever, that is. She wondered how many years would have to pass before she started losing her memory. Infinite life. That's what they were potentially in for. Didn't people dream of that? For whatever reason, her mind drifted towards Marilyn, her red dress, and the plumes of smoke dancing around her silhouette.

Paul put his hand on Stef's shoulder. As he watched the performance, his feet bounced to the music, making Stef smile.

Stef recognised one of the dancers as the Soultrapper's favourite avatar. She was on the far right. Her eyes looked glassy, emotionless, and vacant – a far cry from the venomous defiance they had glimmered with only a little while ago. It was as if a soul had abandoned this body, leaving only the shell. It was an uncomfortable thought. Stef didn't want to think of the AI as a real soul.

Paul squeezed her shoulder. His lips moved, talking.

Stef patted her ears. "I can't hear anything."

Paul looked slightly annoyed. Pointing at the stage, he opened his mouth again in two short bursts. Stef tried to read his lips or to guess what he had to say, whichever came first.

"Katya?" she asked. He smiled and nodded.

The dancer in the very centre of the stage was different from the others. There was a sparkle in her eyes that suggested something was hiding behind them, that a more complex code was involved in her creation. It had to be Katya. She smiled, maintaining eye contact with audience members, her motions more fluid and graceful than those of the other dancers.

Paul pinched Stef on the side.

"Ouch." She turned around with an annoyed look. Paul tapped at his watch, angling the ominous red numbers towards her. The countdown was on. Forty-five minutes remained. Stef hastily checked her own wrist. It was the same. Of course, it was the same. What did she expect? Hurriedly scanning the room, she tried to think. They must've been inside a puzzle already, but she couldn't see it. Just then, the music stopped, and her ears were ringing.

A spotlight fell in the middle of the stage, illuminating Katya. A small microphone curved from the dancer's ear.

"Hello, everyone, and thank you, as always, for your support," Katya announced.

The crowd erupted in cheers and applause.

"I want to thank everyone tonight because it's our anniversary. The Kitty Kat Club opened its doors on the twenty-seventh of March some years ago, and all this time, we have stayed true to ourselves." She flexed her bicep, and the crowd hooted louder. "Here at the Kitty Kat Club, we have special values. We like to celebrate our differences and our uniqueness. We want to help you unleash your inner selves, your deepest desires, and your biggest fears. We want you to be you. Really and truly you. And we won't take no for an answer."

Whistles and hurrahs now reached maniacal heights. Stef wasn't entirely certain anymore that the Kitty Kat Club was a dance club and not some bizarre fancy-dress cult.

"Thank you. Thank you." Katya pressed her palms together in prayer. "Please do enjoy the rest of the evening. We have lots more surprises for you. And please give a round of applause for my dance troupe, *Le Freak C'est Chic*." Katya sprung off the podium with cat-like grace. The crowd parted before her as she walked, clapping her hands overhead.

"Let's follow her." Stef lunged after Katya without waiting for Paul to reply.

To Stef, however, the crowd was not as accommodating. She had to push and shove, contorting her body to fit into narrow spaces, as if squeezing through rocks. All the while, she kept her eyes fixed on Katya's retreating shape. Through the gaps in the crowd, she watched as Katya turned the corner and disappeared behind blue velvet drapery.

"Let me though!" Stef exclaimed, thrusting herself into the writhing mass of dancers before finally breaking free.

Once Paul was out of the throng, he bent over, panting heavily. The music was back on, blaring at full throttle. Stef motioned for Paul to follow her as she darted around the corner, following in Katya's footsteps. With caution, she pulled the velvet curtain aside and slipped through, Paul close behind.

As the curtain fluttered shut, darkness enveloped them, rendering them sightless. Stef advanced, arms outstretched. There seemed to be nothing blocking her way. The watch glowed red, but it wasn't strong enough to illuminate anything but the ominous numbers: 38:40; 38:39; 38:38.

"Hello?" Stef called out. It seemed pointless. Even with the curtain buffer, the music was overpowering.

Stef felt Paul's hands clutch her shoulders. He moved when she moved, slowly, cautiously. For a moment, Stef feared that this was all a trick – a sick, twisted joke the Soultrapper was playing. Perhaps they were approaching the edge of a cliff, and they would imminently trip, fall, and keep falling for all eternity.

Instead, a door swung open a few metres ahead, flooding the corridor with neon-pink light, much to Stef's relief. One of the male dancers emerged, strutting his way in a new sparkling costume: a silver sequin mini jumpsuit paired with impossibly high boots. He brushed past Stef's shoulder and disappeared. The door shut, plunging them once again into darkness. Now with a destination in mind, Stef pressed on, groping for the door handle. Instead, her hand landed on the door as it opened again. Stef managed to catch it as another dancer sauntered out, shooting her a wink on his way, his eyelids and lashes shimmering with hot pink glitter.

Cautiously, Stef stepped into the light. The room seemed cosy, perhaps because of the abundance of eclectic furniture pieces that seemed to have been plucked from a flea market. Lamps were draped with red shawls, snug armchairs with charming imperfections filled every nook, and stacks of well-loved vinyl records served as makeshift side tables for an impressive collection of vintage tea cups and saucers. Against one wall, a rectangular mirror elongated the space, its perimeter defined by round light bulbs.

Katya, also wearing a new costume, was perched on a red leather stool. Leaning towards the mirror, she smeared her lips with red lipstick, blowing her reflection a kiss when she was finished. Stef let go of the door, stepping deeper inside the layer. Remarkably, the moment the door clicked shut, all outside noise was instantly extinguished, as if they were inside a soundproof vault.

"Katya?" Stef said.

"Have we met?" Katya continued to study her own reflection.

"We are the Puzzle Masters, and we need to ask you a few questions," Stef said in an auto-reply mode, while her brain was busy trying to think of the right question. They knew Katya wasn't a suspect, but they weren't supposed to know that. Besides, there was a puzzle to solve; Stef just didn't know what it was yet.

Katya flicked her eyes, throwing Stef and Paul a glance through the mirror.

"Ask away. I've got nothing to hide," she said.

"Where were you when Eden Rose was stolen from Mr Bigwig's home?" Paul asked.

Katya slowly swivelled on her stool to face him, crossing her legs. "I didn't expect that. Am I a suspect?"

"Maybe," Paul said.

Stef glanced at Katya's wrist. The watch – Zach's shortcut meant to clear her of any wrongdoing – was missing. Stef's stomach tightened in knots. Her mind was racing. This didn't make sense; they'd already eliminated Katya as a suspect. They knew that Katya and Bigwig were an item. They knew it from the note and the password on Bigwig's computer.

"Why would I steal from myself?" Katya asked, raising a single eyebrow.

"From yourself?" Stef blinked repeatedly, trying to organise her thoughts.

"Sandeep gave it to me, the diamond. In fact, he proposed about three days ago. Eden Rose is the most precious thing to him. Or was the most precious thing until he met me."

"I thought he was dating Marilyn Star," Stef said, but of course, she knew that wasn't the whole story.

"Is that what she told you?" Katya sniggered. "He was dating Marilyn, yes. It was a status thing. A famous movie star, you know, carries certain clout." She rubbed her lips together, redistributing the lipstick.

"How did you two meet?" Paul asked.

"Here at the club." Katya uncrossed her legs, her movements still fluid and dance-like. "Look. I have a show to do. So, hurry up if you have any more questions."

Stef could feel her heart beating faster. The watch wasn't there, but Katya and Bigwig were an item. Stef wasn't sure if they'd made a mistake, or if the Soultrapper was messing with them again. Suppose he'd changed things because he knew Zach had given them clues. But that wasn't the most pressing matter at the moment. The most pressing matter was the watch hastily ticking towards 'Game Over'. What was the puzzle? What were they supposed to solve?

Katya stood up and adjusted her sequined shorts. "Alright. If that is it, I better go now."

"Wait." Stef stretched her arm out in front, willing Katya to stop as if by a magical force. A thought danced on the tip of her tongue. She knew she had to ask Katya something else, something important.

"Do you have more questions?" the dancer repeated.

"Yes. Yes. We do." Stef's mind was racing as fast as her heart. Suddenly, a spark ignited. "Bill! Bill!"

"Bill?" Paul whispered.

"What about Bill?" Katya said.

"Do you know where he is? It's his shift. We need to find him. Boris is looking for him. Urgently." That was it. Stef's stomach fluttered with a familiar feeling. She knew she was on the right track. That was obviously the puzzle – they had to find Bill so Boris would talk to them.

Katya blinked as if in a haze, half-frozen. Then, her body twisted and readjusted like a robot restarting its system. Her neck swivelled, facing Stef. Her features softened, and once again, she looked human.

"Bill has a secret lair," she said. "There's a passage somewhere inside this room. But nobody knows where it is. Sometimes, he falls asleep and forgets it's his shift. If you want him, you'll have to find him." She winked and pulled up her thigh-high leather boots as far as they would go. "Adios and good luck." She waved her hand in the air as the door creaked shut behind her. Stef's watch reminded her that only twenty-six minutes remained.

Twenty-Three

"We don't have enough time," Paul's voice broke with panic.

"It's okay. We just need to focus. We're practically pros at this, Paolito," Stef reassured him, her eyes darting around the room.

Bustling with clutter, it resembled an antique shop in Notting Hill. Tiny treasures were scattered around: green glass vials and princess figurines, ornate jewellery boxes and miniature wooden furniture, blackened silver spoons and mother-of-pearl hair brushes. Stef examined each item carefully, picking up a dainty teacup from a nearby vinyl side table bearing a Wedgwood logo and painted with wild strawberries and purple flowers. Yet, none of the objects seemed relevant to the game. Stef sighed heavily, her gaze shifting to the large wooden box. She approached it, carefully lifting the lid – a white gold and diamond lady's watch rested atop a red velvet cushion.

"That must be it," she said. "Sandeep's gift to Katya."

Stef prised the watch from its cocoon and read the engraving aloud: "'To my darling Katya. Always and Forever. Yours, Sandeep.' Hey, Paul. Katya wasn't lying about Bigwig, but she wasn't wearing the watch. Maybe Zach was wrong. What else could he have been wrong about?"

Next to the watch box was a newly polished silver jewellery case decorated with emeralds, sapphires, and rubies. It looked significantly more valuable than anything else in the vicinity. Stef ran her hands over its bumpy texture.

"It's locked," Stef said, excitement tingeing her tone. Locked was good; locked meant they finally had something to solve.

The case was sealed with an inbuilt four-dial mechanism. Stef spun the dials with her thumb.

"We need four numbers," she said.

Paul scratched the back of his head and slowly let the air seep from his lungs.

"I didn't find any numbers. Did you?" He picked up a silver filigree elephant and turned it over in his hand.

"Not really."

Stef moved on to an old wooden chest with an array of perfectly square drawers decorated with mosaics of birds, plants, and insects. Pulling on one drawer after another, she found them all empty, except for the very last one.

"Photographs, look," Stef said.

Paul leaned over her shoulder. Stef shuffled the pictures – they were joyous, happy snaps of the dancers at the club. In one of them, Katya drank Champagne directly from an oversized bottle while everyone clapped. In the next, the dancing troupe huddled together in a group hug. Stef flipped each photo, inspecting them for numbers – a date, perhaps, that could potentially be a code. She found only words: Les Freaks C'est Chic at the opening of the Kitty Kat Club; Katya and the crew celebrate the anniversary of the Kitty Kat Club; Congratulations to the new owner, Don Rigatoni.

"There are no numbers anywhere," Stef sighed, plopping the stack of photos on top of the chest. "It's weird. It's almost like someone deliberately avoided having any numbers in this place. Hm." She chewed her cheek in thought.

"Look at this," Paul said, heading towards a mounted wooden cabinet on the wall opposite the mirror. He pulled at the small brass knob on its door. "It's locked. With a key."

"Great. Now we need a key, too," Stef huffed.

She was growing nervous, feeling the urge to check her watch, but she didn't allow herself to, knowing full well that no good would come of it. She also knew that it would vibrate when ten minutes remained, so it was better not to waste time on distractions.

"Wait. What did you say?" Paul grabbed Stef's arm.

"When? Now we need a key, too?"

"No. Just before. You said it was as if someone had deliberately avoided numbers. It's a puzzle. It was set up this way for a reason."

"You're right. There must be a number that we already know." Stef felt the butterflies taking flight inside her belly.

Paul grabbed the photographs off the chest and shuffled through them again.

"This is the dancers' changing room, right? And look at them – they really love this club," he said.

"And it's their anniversary today. Katya announced the date to the whole club. Of course!" Stef exhaled with profound relief, letting her head drop back. "Twenty-seventh of March. 2, 7, 0, 3."

Paul was already on it, twisting the dials into place.

"Done."

A vaguely familiar music-box melody chimed as the lid slowly opened.

"A key!" Stef snatched the key, giddy with excitement. She inserted it into the cabinet lock. The doors spread open, revealing a large hole in the wall and two pieces of thick rope dangling inside.

"I didn't expect that," Paul said.

Stef jumped to try to glance in, but it was too high up.

"Can you lift me?" she asked.

Paul lifted her off the ground by the legs and held her up as she thrust her head through the hole, gripping the cabinet for extra support. She glanced down and then twisted her torso to look up.

"It's big. And deep. I can't see the end of it. The hole is too small to climb in."

"Can you grab the rope?"

Stef tugged on both pieces of rope.

"Oh, oh, it's a pulley!" she exclaimed, grabbing hold of the end as Paul pulled her out.

"I can feel something on the other end. Give me a hand."

Paul clutched the rope in front of Stef and tugged on it while Stef held it in place so it didn't slip back. They could feel something moving, getting closer. A flash of white, and one last pull.

"A crate?" Paul said.

As Paul held on to the rope, Stef grabbed the crate and drew it inside the room. It was filled to the brim with what looked like dirty laundry.

"Seriously?" Paul didn't look impressed.

Stef rummaged through the rags. There were shirts and trousers, and shorts and shirts.

"Check this out!" Stef pulled out a frilly white apron with a name tag – Maid Melody, Taj Mahal Hotel and Casino. Stef searched for a pocket and frisked it.

"Look," Stef said, squeezing a plastic Taj Mahal Hotel key card between her fingers. "I bet we need this to get inside the Frenchman's room."

"But if Boris is not guilty, the Frenchman must be guilty by elimination."

"Well, it's better to be completely sure, right?" Stef tucked the card into the pocket of her frock and tapped it.

Just then, her wrist vibrated with familiar urgency. She chose to ignore it. Panic wasn't going to help anyone. By the look on Paul's face, Stef could tell he was thinking the same thing.

"Right," she said. "Let's see what else we can find in here."

"Look, all the clothes have name labels, like at school." Paul chuckled nervously. Stef looked at the inside collar of a white shirt; it boasted a 'Katya' label. She grabbed a pair of denim shorts which evidently belonged to someone called Roger. Paul found a pink T-shirt that belonged to a Pricilla. Stef pulled at a pair of large black trousers.

"Bill." She smiled. "These are Bill's."

"Quick, check the pockets."

From the front pocket, Stef extracted a note, folded carefully in half. As she unravelled it, her eyebrows instantly furrowed. The note contained a rough diagram of a rectangle with circles around it. Some of the circles had red X marks inside them. There were ten circles on the top and bottom and five on each side. Eight of the circles had crosses: three on the top, one on the left, two on the right and two at the bottom.

"It's like a treasure map," Stef said.

"I bet it is. X marks the spot, right?"

"Or, in this case… eight spots?" Stef bit her cheek. The rectangle, along with its satellites, looked both utterly nonsensical and strangely familiar.

"Could it be a code?" Paul asked.

"I don't know. If it is, it's not an obvious one."

"It does look like something, though. Doesn't it?"

The watch vibrated again – twice this time. Stef's throat tightened. She glanced at Paul, afraid to look at the time. Was this the end? He peered at her with his large brown eyes, and she saw he was also scared. The vanity lights behind him accentuated his silhouette. He looked unreal, almost magical – like an angel. Stef's eyes drifted towards the mirror.

"Oh my God," she muttered.

"It's okay, Stef. At least we will always have each other, right?" Tears brewed in the corners of Paul's eyes.

"No, Paul. Behind you." Stef lifted her finger and Paul snapped around.

The rectangular vanity mirror and the surrounding lights looked identical to the sketch in Stef's trembling hand. And the butterflies were back. Stef swiftly climbed on top of the make-up table. On her knees, she could reach both rows of the lights. If she could switch off the ones marked with an X quickly enough, perhaps they still stood a chance.

"Do you think we need to press them?" She tried pressing one of the lightbulbs marked with an X, but it didn't budge.

"Try twisting them," Paul said.

She did. The light twisted and extinguished. Stef shrieked with joy.

"Okay, quick. Do the rest."

Stef reached for every bulb as fast as she could, both hands working simultaneously. Paul verified with the diagram.

"Top left!" he hollered.

One final twist and Stef's wrist vibrated again – three times this time.

They were out of time. Stef panted but didn't dare move. Everything now seemed so quiet and so still.

"Stef?" Paul muttered, his lips trembling. "Did we lose?"

Stef continued to breathe heavily. She closed her eyes and listened carefully for something, but she didn't know what. She was certain she had twisted the last bulb before her wrist vibrated. Almost completely certain. This wasn't the end. It couldn't be! Stef refused to admit defeat.

"Just wait," she whispered.

Just then, the mirror started to shake. As the shaking grew stronger, it began to rattle, and the whole dressing table vibrated. Stef slid down, wrapping her arms around Paul.

"Look," she said, a smile flickering on her lips.

The mirror slid forward with a loud huff, like a steam train, and glided to the side, revealing a cosy nook with an inflatable mattress behind it. A checkered blanket moved up and down in a slow, rhythmic motion with the deep breathing of whoever was underneath it. The whole room shook with a horse snore. Stef glanced at the watch. It had returned to sixty.

"We did it, Pablo. We did it." She let out a scream, leaping onto Paul like a monkey and straddling him with her arms and legs. He laughed, hugging her tightly.

"Stef, you did it. You really did it." They held each other in a jumble of tears and laughter. Until they heard a loud, booming yawn.

"What's this then?" said a strange voice.

They let each other go, turning towards the man on the mattress. He stretched his arms over his head and yawned again. He looked exactly like Boris. They could've been twins. His hair was dishevelled, and a bit of drool caked his chin. He wiped it off and squinted. Then he reached for his Ray-Ban's, resting on a small table beside him, and put them on.

"Who are you? What are you doing here?" He cracked his neck once on each side.

"Are you Bill?" Stef asked.

"Who's asking?"

"Boris is. It's your shift at the door, and you're sleeping through it. Boris would like to take a break, you know," Paul said.

Bill scratched his thick stubble.

"What time is it anyway?" He glanced at his watch. "Oh no. I overslept again. Boris will not be too happy. Anyway, I must be going now. Thanks for finding me. Cheers."

He threw the blanket aside and got up without delay. Crouching under the mirror frame, he leapt off the vanity table in one swift manoeuvre.

"Wait," Stef called after him. "Could you tell us where the cafeteria is?"

"It's up the stairs to the right of the entrance." Bill gave Stef a quick wink and was gone in a flash. The door creaked closed behind him.

"So. Cafeteria?" Paul said. He was close. Very close.

Stef raised her eyes to her friend. She felt her cheeks heat up; she imagined the insufferable blotches invading her skin. But she didn't care.

Twenty-Four

Boris occupied a table in the middle of the cafeteria. The space was tiled from floor to ceiling in small white squares like a public toilet. All the furniture – chairs and round tables – looked plastic and cheap. Boris clutched an entire French baguette in one hand and a large spoon in the other. He alternated between the two, slurping down a meaty stew and then chasing it with a big mouthful of the crusty bread. He wasn't just eating the food, he was attacking it, like a lion devouring an antelope.

Spotting Stef and Paul from a distance, Boris waved them over, breadcrumbs fountaining from his hand. He was the only person in the cafeteria other than the cook, who was reading a book behind the self-service buffet counter. Momentarily, his attention shifted to Stef. He winked at her and returned to his book. It made her shudder.

"Make it quick," Boris said as Stef and Paul approached. He gulped down a spoonful of the reddish-brown mush as sweat beads formed on his forehead. Letting go of the baguette, he dabbed the sweat off with a white cotton napkin. Stef immediately saw an opportunity. If she could get him to take off his jacket, they'd be able to see whether there was a lipstick stain on his collar or not.

"Do you think? Maybe, if you're too hot... it would be more comfortable for you... to take off your jacket?" Stef suggested.

Boris grunted, ripping into the bread. A crumb landed on Stef's nose. She flicked it off. Boris chewed, looking at Stef, then at Paul, and then at Stef again. Droplets of sweat now slid down the sides of his face.

"Fine. Maybe you're right." He smacked his lips and wiped his face with his sleeve. Wriggling out of his black blazer, he exhaled loudly. "Now that's better."

Stef's eyes were fixed on his collar. She leaned to the side to see more clearly. It was there – a bright red kiss mark in Marilyn Star's shade of lipstick. Stef's eyes twinkled.

"It's the Frenchman," she said. Paul nodded in agreement.

"What? Who?" Boris grumbled.

"You and Miss Star are an item. Is that correct?" Stef said confidently.

Boris's jaw slowed down, and he wiped his mouth with his hand. He gazed at the teenagers, picking out food stuck in his teeth with his fingernail.

"How do you know that?" he asked, narrowing his eyes.

"We are the Puzzle Masters. We have our sources." Stef crossed her arms.

"Alright. So the cat's out of the bag, then. Surely you can understand why we kept it a secret?" Boris gestured at himself, snorting sharply. Stef noticed that brown stew had dripped from his chin onto his shirt.

"Yeah." Stef scrunched up her face.

"She's the biggest movie star in the whole world, and I am just a regular bloke. But the heart wants what it wants."

"We understand. And thank you for your honesty," Paul said.

"Is that it? Is that all you wanted to know?"

Stef held her breath. Deep inside the pit of her stomach, there was a strange feeling. An itch she couldn't scratch. If someone in the game asked if they had any more questions, it usually meant that there was something else they were supposed to inquire about.

"That will be all," Paul said. Stef gave him a disapproving look.

"Well, alright then, if you're sure." Boris relaxed into his chair and rubbed his bulging belly. "I better be going now. There's lots of stuff to do." Loosening his belt buckle, he stood up and, without further ado, headed towards the exit.

"I don't know, Paul," Stef muttered.

"What's wrong?" Paul asked.

"Don't you think we were supposed to ask something else?"

"Like what?"

"I don't know. Like… his alibi, for example." Stef gazed in the direction of the exit, but Boris was already gone.

"You saw the mark. He's not our guy."

"But… You don't think the Soultrapper could've changed a few things, do you? He knew we had shortcuts. Plus, what are the odds that the last person we have to talk to is, in fact, the thief? Seems unlikely." She glanced at the buffet. The cook was gone too.

"You're overthinking it." Paul squeezed her shoulders.

"Maybe. Maybe you're right." Stef sighed. "I just have this feeling. I can't help it."

Suddenly, Stef's senses ignited with the cosy smell of cooked meat, herbs, and spices – a smell of home. She was certain the aroma hadn't been there before and had appeared just then out of nowhere.

"Can you smell it?" she whispered, licking her lips. For the first time, she was acutely aware of just how hungry she was.

"Yeah," Paul replied, swallowing.

In an instant, the buffet counter burgeoned with simmering meats, steaming potatoes, and veggies. There was a pizza station and a pasta corner, different kinds of salads and soups, and a three-tier chocolate cake reigned over the sweet smorgasbord of colourful cupcakes, crème brûlée cups, and golden, flaky pastries. The aroma of warm chocolate and freshly baked bread filled Stef's nostrils, making her mouth water.

"Oh, that Soultrapper," Stef whispered, balling her hands into fists. "Chocolate cake does not smell this good in real life, does it?"

"No, it does not."

"We really have to get out of here."

"That we do," Paul said, looking transfixed by the feast.

"Focus, Paul," Stef said, blinking. Paul wasn't the only one who needed to focus.

Stef tapped the pocket of her dress, guarding the Taj Mahal Hotel and Casino keycard. They had a job to do – one last task to complete – and then it would all be over.

***

"We know we can open the door, but we still need to find out which one it is," Paul said as they zoomed through the sky in the trusty Londelhi taxi. Stef had grown accustomed to the game's supersonic mode of transportation. Now, every time they found themselves inside the cab, she no longer felt like her body would flatten into a pancake.

"Imagine if this were the real world," Stef said. "How would we find out which hotel room someone was staying in?" She flicked her eyes at Paul, twiddling the glossy keycard between her fingers.

"We would probably pretend we were his relatives and we urgently needed to speak to him. Or we might say that we're supposed to be staying with him, but we can't find him," Paul mused, shrugging.

"We don't even know his name or what he looks like. We know nothing about him, in fact, except that he's French, and he's a long-lost son of either Bigwig or Rigatoni."

"We are dressed as official Taj Mahal Hotel and Casino service people. That could help."

"That could indeed. I guess we play it by ear."

"Wish we could ask Zach for some help," Paul said.

"Did you just say my name?"

Stef jumped with a start. Zach sat behind them, his arms stretched out over the backrests, his ankle on his knee.

"People have to stop doing that!" Stef clenched her teeth and flared her nostrils.

"How did you? When did you? Were you there the whole time?" Paul looked more confused than shocked.

"I am the admin. I have my ways. And no, I was not here the whole time. But I wanted to check on you guys. It can't get inside the taxi. We're safe here to talk. Hey, Dave."

"'Alo there, Zachy, mate," the London cabby's voice chimed.

"Dave?" Paul screwed up his face.

"Dave is the only bot with access to the cab, but he can't go anywhere else."

Stef climbed onto her knees atop her seat, leaning over the backrest towards Zach.

"How do you know he's not the Soultrapper then?" she whispered.

"Nowhere near complex enough. His whole vocabulary is around a hundred words or so," Zach explained.

"Are you here to help us?" Paul asked.

"Not exactly. I'm here to hurry you guys up." Zach brushed his fingers through his long blond locks, his gaze drifting downwards.

"Oh no, what happened?" Stef said, sensing that something was amiss.

Zach took a deep breath. "Out there in the real world, the police got hold of the CCTV footage of your travels to Wales. It's only a matter of time before they figure out that you came to my house. I'm one of the last people to have seen you two alive, if you catch my drift."

"Didn't expect you to say that," Paul said somberly.

"Police?" Stef sat on her heels. Her parents' faces flashed in her mind's eye. How worried they must've been! How heartbroken! Her heart clenched in yearning for her mum and dad, desperately wishing she could tell them she was alright, that she wasn't hurt.

She closed her eyes, trying to focus her mind on the game. Winning was the only solution.

"I think we've figured out who the thief is," she said. "Based on what you told us, we've eliminated all but one suspect – the Frenchman. We just need to see the proof – a final confirmation." Stef's lips twisted to the side.

"You don't sound too sure," Zach said.

"That's because... some of the things you told us... they didn't... they weren't exactly how you said they would be. Katya wasn't wearing the watch, for one. But she did have it. We found it in a box."

"I see." A deep crease formed between Zach's eyebrows. "But look, the Soultrapper, or whatever you call him, could've changed a few things around to make it more difficult for you."

"I knew it." Stef rubbed her face.

"But..." – Zach raised his finger, accentuating the 'but' – "It wouldn't be able to change the plot of the game so quickly and seamlessly. It may have messed with the shortcuts, but everything I told you would still stand."

"What do you mean?" Paul's brows furrowed.

"Boris would only ever steal the diamond to get Marilyn. Crawley, to pay for his mother's treatment. And they wouldn't lie when asked about those things. It's just not in their code. Unless..."

"Unless what?"

"Unless they are the AI." Zach dropped his face into his hands. "It's complicated. But... I don't think it would lie either. I can't be sure but... I don't think so. It likes to play games; it bends the rules. But it likes to play. And it might sound weird, but I think it wants you to find the diamond. It just doesn't want you to find out its identity."

"Great." Paul rubbed the bridge of his nose. Stef gently squeezed his free hand.

"There are characters we can definitely eliminate," she said. "They can't be the AI. We were with Rigatoni at the same time as the Soultrapper. He was in a security guard's body. Hence, Rigatoni is not the AI and plus, his Rolls is just fine, so he's not our thief either."

"You're right." Paul perked up. "Also, Katya, Bigwig, and O'Shady each had a little episode, like they were rebooting or something."

"Yeah, that wouldn't happen to the AI. It's a little glitch that I was working to fix. It happens when a new puzzle loads," Zach said.

"And because of the watch, the caviar, and the absence of the Barbados poster... it would be safe to say those guys aren't the thieves either." Stef rubbed her hands together.

"Exactly. See, you have managed to successfully eliminate four people." Zach was starting to sound more upbeat.

"That leaves us with Crawley, Marylin, Boris, and the Frenchman," Paul said, counting out the suspects on his fingers.

"The Frenchman might be the thief, but he's not your Soultrapper," Zach said.

"Why not?"

"I should've told you the whole truth back in Wales but... To be honest, it just didn't immediately occur to me, but the Frenchman doesn't actually exist in code. You never get to see him."

"Really? That's great! And I really don't think Boris is the Soultrapper, either. I'm pretty sure I saw IT in the cafeteria," Stef said.

"The cook?" Paul asked. Stef nodded gently.

"And because of the lipstick stain on his shirt, he isn't the thief either," Zach said. "Look, let's assume the Soultrapper didn't bend the rules. You've eliminated everyone but one, right? The thief has to be Frenchie. Be happy, guys. You're halfway there."

"More than halfway," Paul added. "We only have two suspects left for the Soultrapper – Crawley and Marylin."

"The absolute worst case is that you will have to take a guess. It's 50/50." Zach crossed his arms on his chest and leaned back. Everyone went quiet for a while, their minds heavy with the possible repercussions of failure. They didn't even notice that the taxi had come to a stop until the dome opened, and the familiar salty air invited them back to the Taj Mahal Hotel and Casino.

"You guys better be going now," Zach said. "I'll be around."

"Okay." Stef forced her lips into a smile, her hands shaking relentlessly, and her heart thumping wildly inside her chest. Her mother's face flashed in her mind again.

"Zach, wait. Quick question," Paul chimed in. "How do we find the Frenchman?"

"You don't. Remember, he doesn't exist. Did you find the keycard?"

"Yes. Yes, we did." Stef held it out for Zach to see.

"All you need to do is find his room."

"But what's his room number?" Paul asked.

"That I don't actually remember. I don't even remember his name, believe it or not." Zach chuckled uncomfortably.

"How do we find out?" Stef asked.

"Sorry, guys. This part is the one no one ever reaches, and it's been a while since I played it this far. It's all a blur." Zach pressed his lips firmly together. "I'm sure you two can figure it out, though. Good luck."

"Yeah. We're gonna need it," Paul scoffed.

Twenty-Five

"Are you staying with us, sir?" A wide-eyed Bambi-like receptionist beamed at Paul.

"No, that's not what I said." He wrapped his blazer, which he had put on inside out to seem less like a hotel employee, a little tighter around his body. "Once again, a friend of ours is staying at your hotel, and we are supposed to meet him. In his room. Now. The trouble is, we don't know the room number. We forgot to ask. Isn't that hilarious?" Paul leaned into the reception desk with his elbows, glancing at the prominent bronze plaque that warned, 'NO PUZZLE MASTERS'. Paul forced a throaty laugh, and the receptionist joined in as if the laughter were contagious. Abruptly, she stopped.

"She looks like one of the maids," the receptionist said, gesturing at Stef, who was still wearing the long black dress. Stef shuffled uncomfortably on the spot.

"How dare you?" Paul pressed his fanned-out fingers into his chest. "We are very important people. Have you not heard of… Masters of Atlantis?"

Stef concealed a quiet giggle under her hand.

"N-n-no, sir." Bambi blinked repeatedly. "What is it?"

Paul's eyes widened. Evidently, he hadn't thought this one through.

"It's an elite club," Stef quickly added. "And we are the founders."

"Oh, I see. I am sorry, sir, madame. Please wait a moment. Let me see what I can do," the receptionist smiled, somewhat embarrassed. The computer keyboard clicked staccato underneath her fingers as if she were playing a broken piano. "May I have your friend's name?"

"Well, funny thing..." Paul chuckled dryly. "We don't know his name."

Bambi froze, her head tilted slightly to the side. "You don't know your friend's name?"

"Not exactly."

"What my partner here is trying to explain." Stef cleared her throat. "Is that our friend is a very famous artist in France. I mean really famous. Marilyn Star kind of famous. So, he uses different pseudonyms every time he stays at a hotel – Hercule Poirot, Charles De Gaulle, Claude Monet... We forgot to ask him which one he was using on this occasion. It should be something French. It's always something French. So, if you could just check." Stef leaned over the counter, trying to sneak a peek at the computer screen.

The receptionist turned the screen further away from Stef.

"Look," Stef continued. "It's very important. Could you please help us?"

"The Taj Mahal Hotel and Casino rules are very clear. We have to protect our guests' privacy," Bambi said, crossing her eyebrows.

"What if I told you that you were right? I do work here."

"Then I would have to report you to HR."

Stef huffed and turned to Paul. "Any ideas?"

Paul's shoulders rose slowly, as he rubbed his thumb against his index finger.

"Bribe?" Stef mouthed inaudibly. Paul's shoulders hunched even higher. He wasn't sure about this, and neither was Stef. Mainly because they didn't actually have any money.

Leaning on the counter, Stef smiled awkwardly, winking at the receptionist and instantly feeling herself a complete fool. Nevertheless, she decided to commit.

"What if... We could make this worthwhile for you? My partner and I are close friends with one Sandeep Bigwig, if you get what I'm saying."

"Are you trying to bribe me?" Bambi turned bright red like a ripe tomato. "Well, I never! You must leave now. Shoo. Shoo. Security?" she yelped, trying to wave Stef away as if she were a pigeon at a picnic. "Security!"

"Okay. Okay. We're going." Paul raised his palms in an attempt to placate the woman while slinking backwards out of harm's way. "Let's go, Stef. I don't want to end up tied up in that basement again."

Stef wasn't ready to give in.

"Madam, I am very sorry. Just listen. Please." Stef lowered her voice, glancing over each shoulder and clutching the badge inside her pocket. The receptionist narrowed her eyes but stopped screaming. Stef's gaze fell on the 'NO PUZZLE MASTERS' plaque momentarily, and she took a deep breath. "I didn't want to tell you before," Stef continued, "for obvious reasons... but we are the Puzzle Masters. We work with the police, and we're looking for a French gentleman staying at the hotel."

The receptionist's neck jerked sharply to the side, resetting her expression to the original smiley, welcoming self.

"How may I help you, madame?" she said. "I must remind you that Don Rigatoni doesn't like law enforcement officials." Dipping forward, she added. "If you were to show me a badge of any kind, I would have to ask you to leave."

"Got it," Stef said. "I do feel like there's a 'but' coming. Am I wrong?" She smiled conspiratorially.

"However," Bambi said.

"'However' works too. 'However' is just a fancy 'but'."

"However, I don't always agree with the policies around here." The receptionist batted her eyelashes.

"I see," Stef's brows raised. She placed her palms on the reception desk and continued slowly, enunciating every syllable. "Perhaps, if you can't tell us, maybe you could point us in the right direction?"

"I can't. Well. No. I really can't." The receptionist frowned, shaking her head.

Stef's eyes narrowed. "Perhaps a clue?"

"Perhaps..." The receptionist began, reaching for a strand of loose hair at the back of her neck. "Perhaps you would like to write something in the guest book?"

"The guest book?" Paul's forehead wrinkled. He was still a few metres behind the reception counter, arms folded across his chest.

"It's on the table by the lifts," the receptionist said, stealthily angling her chin in their direction. "I hear there was a complaint from a French gentleman. He left in quite a hurry."

Stef's face dissolved into a wide smile. "Thank you."

The receptionist smiled coyly.

Stef bowed politely to the receptionist and twisted herself towards Paul, giving him a quick wink. He smiled, dimples forming on his cheeks.

The guest book was a massive grey tome bound in snakeskin leather. It rested on a green marble table with a pen chained to it. Stef found it strange that a pen required a chain in a luxury hotel. She flipped to the first page, snakeskin prickling against her fingers. Stef absolutely despised snakes in all their manifestations and shivered with revulsion.

A few curt scribbled lines were scattered across the open book. Stef read one aloud, tracing her index finger underneath it.

"We really enjoyed our stay. Best hotel in Londelhi. Franca and Rose."

"Such a gorgeous place. Thanks for the memories. Atlas and Dino," Paul added.

"Weird names," Stef said, flipping to the next page.

The very first message read, 'Enjoy your stay. I bet you still don't know what my name is. Yours, '?''

Stef smirked, turning over the next page.

"Look here," Paul said, tapping a message that was longer than any other, taking over a whole page.

"Despicable. Horrendous. Atrocious. Awful. *Absolument affreux*!" Stef read. "'I have never experienced service so poor. In France, such a thing would never be possible.' Oh, that's the one, Paul." Stef giggled and continued in an exaggerated French accent. "I was hungry last night and decided to order room service. Nothing fancy. Some *pommes frites* and red wine. Perhaps a *Coq Au*

Vin or a *Boeuf Bourguignon*. Maybe dessert, such as a simple *Tarte Tatin*, would suffice. But no! *Impossible!* First, I was horrified to learn that those items were not on the menu. Who would want to have something called a saffron spotted dick? Or a chicken tikka masala and mash? Or a Rogan Josh pie? I can tell you straight away that they sound absolutely disgusting. But for lack of other options, I was forced into an attempt to order a ham and cheese naan toastie, which sounded like the least offensive option. However, I was informed by a vulgar man that room service was not available at the time because they were busy catering for a wedding. I paid a lot of money to stay at this hotel. How dare they? I came here for personal reasons. But having stayed in Londelhi for three nights, I have decided never to return. The worst experience of my life. *Adieu*. Bye bye. Francois Perrier. Room 84."

"Gottcha," Paul said. "And to be fair, I would be furious, too, if they refused to feed me."

Stef felt her mouth watering almost immediately. She was hungry. Very hungry indeed. Swallowing her saliva, she let out a deep breath. Paul rubbed her on the shoulder.

"I know. I'm starving, too. Eyes on the prize, O'Shea. Eyes on the prize."

***

Stef firmly pressed her thumb into the round '8' button. It lit up green. A plaque on the side of the lift indicated that rooms 80—89 were on the 8th floor, making the whole 30th-floor experience at the VIP lounge even more absurd. The highest floor this lift would go to was the ninth.

The lift trembled as it began its ascent. Stef bit into the skin around her nail, just so she would have something to chew on. It only made her more ravenous. All she could think about was a juicy burger. A slow-motion Macdonald ad began to play in her mind. Closing her eyes, she shook her head, trying to dislodge the images from her mind.

Paul hummed a vaguely familiar tune, swaying back and forth on the balls of his feet. He watched the screen above the door announce each passing floor. When it reached eight, the doors opened.

The corridor resembled the one on the elusive 30th floor, minus the VIP lounge and with a clear end in sight. Large portraits hung at each end: Don Rigatoni on one side, Marylin Star on the other. A slim brass arrow on the wall indicated the way: rooms 85—89 to the right and 84—80 to the left.

Stef twirled the keycard between her fingers as Paul leaned against door number 84, giving it three gentle knocks.

"He's not in," Paul said.

"Of course not. He doesn't exist. But wait, if he's the thief, can we even get the diamond back?" Stef pondered aloud, slotting the keycard into place. The lock clicked green, and Paul pushed the door open.

Their eyes widened as they stepped inside, confronted by utter chaos. The bed was a tangle of sheets, with dirty socks dangling from its edges. Used towels, robes, and empty hangers littered the whole floor, forcing them to tiptoe around the debris. A cluttered corner desk overflowed with torn pages from room service and spa menus.

"There's a spa?" Paul raised an eyebrow, examining a ripped page fragment.

"I guess we have to find his birth certificate in this mess," Stef said, checking her watch. Strangely, the countdown remained deactivated. At least they had time. She perched on the very edge of the dishevelled bed, allowing herself a moment to breathe. Paul settled beside her, and she rested her head on his shoulder. It was bony, hard, and objectively uncomfortable, but to Stef, it felt safe. It felt like home.

"Hey, Stef. Look over there," Paul exclaimed, pointing towards the far corner under the desk. A lone piece of white paper, encased in a transparent folder, leaned against the wall like a weary commuter.

"No way," Stef replied. "If that's his birth certificate, we must be the luckiest people alive."

Paul stood up from the bed, crouched under the table and reached for the folder.

"It is a birth certificate," he chuckled, but his smile faded as soon as he read it. "Maybe we're not as lucky as we thought, Stef."

"What are you saying? You can't mean... It's not possible..." Stef's voice trailed off.

"Oh, but it is. Monsieur Francois Perrier is the biological son of Mr Sandeep Bigwig, which means he's not the thief."

Twenty-Six

"Then who is?" Stef slid down from the bed to the floor, hugging her knees, while Paul paced back and forth from the door to the window.

"Someone must be lying," he said, shaking his head.

"And only the Soultrapper can lie." Stef massaged the space between her eyebrows. "Zach was so sure he wouldn't. Maybe we've missed something?"

"It's more likely that the Soultrapper lied to us, don't you think? Then whoever is the thief is also the AI."

"I'm not so sure…"

Before Paul could interject, there was a knock on the door. In unison, their heads jerked in its direction. For a moment, Stef felt like her heart stopped beating, and with it, time stopped, too.

"I'll get it," Paul said.

He reached for the handle and yanked it, as if opening the door fast would somehow make the situation less painful, like ripping off a plaster. What he saw on the other side was a bellboy wearing a red jacket and a matching fez with a single golden tassel. He held out a rectangular envelope for Paul's taking.

"I have a message," the bellboy said, raising a single eyebrow.

"A message for who? Francois Perrier?" Stef scrambled to her feet and hurried to the door.

"No. For a Mr Paul and a Mrs Stephanie," the bellboy said, pushing the letter into Paul's hands. As soon as Paul's fingers touched the paper, the bellboy vanished into thin air.

Paul flipped the envelope in his hand. It was blank except for an old-fashioned red wax seal stamped with an 'S'.

"S for Soultrapper?" Paul smirked.

"He's trying to be funny."

"It is. Kinda. Should I open it?" Paul said.

"Do we have a choice?"

The seal came undone without effort, revealing a letter inside. Stef gasped, instantly feeling silly because, of course, there would be a letter inside. What else could there be? Yet somehow, the unexpected mysteriousness of the whole ordeal made her jolt with surprise.

Paul pulled the sheet of paper with a pincer grasp as if it were delicate and precious and could crumple at the touch. Carefully, he unfolded the message, his hands trembling.

The message read: 'Hello, friends. Did you miss me? I have been a busy bee preparing something special for you. I think you will love it. And everyone is invited, including your friends in the forest. It's almost the end of your journey, and you must soon accept your inevitable defeat. I have kept my promise. I assure you, I didn't mess with the game beyond making sure it wasn't too easy. When you're ready to see me, call Ariadne, and she will escort you to me. Zach has already been invited.

Looking forward to seeing you shortly. Sincerely yours, The Soultrapper (ha ha).'

"I knew it. We've missed something," Stef said.

"I think he's lying about everything. I don't trust him one bit. He's toying with us."

"Or she..." Stef whispered, her thoughts in a jumble.

"He, she, it – it doesn't change anything."

"What do you think he's prepared for us?" Stef asked.

"A welcome party?" Paul scoffed, rubbing his eyes.

Stef leaned against the wall, looking up into Paul's large, kind eyes. Her thoughts drifted back to the Kitty Kat Club, recalling when Paul had thought they'd lost. He seemed strangely comfortable with the idea; he'd told her they'd be fine as long as they had each other. Stef wondered whether that was true, whether they could adapt to an endless existence in this digital prison. Her heart ached; she yearned for her parents, longing to see them again and wrap her arms around them. The uncertainty of whether she'd see them again made her nose prickle with brewing tears. She couldn't let herself cry, not now, not yet. Plus, she had Paul. She would always have Paul.

Clasping his hand tightly, she drew closer. His brows furrowed in surprise; she inched closer still. "I will always have you," Stef thought to herself. His gaze penetrated hers, seeming to grasp her unspoken thoughts as if somehow, in this universe, he had developed the power to read her mind. Moving closer, his lips hovered inches from her own, hesitating. Stef didn't flinch. Not this time. She felt his breath on her skin, quickening her heartbeat. Closing her eyes, she rose onto her toes, meeting his lips. In that moment, Stef was certain she was levitating.

Paul's hands brushed against her back, making her skin tingle and her knees feel weak. Her mind exploded in a kaleidoscope of colours, dancing underneath her eyelids. She heard music, actual music playing to the beat of her heart, that synched perfectly with his. His scent, so dear and familiar to Stef – blackberries and vanilla – which somehow travelled across the dimensions, filled her nostrils, making her lightheaded. It felt as if she became blind momentarily, consumed by her other senses. Then suddenly, her world shifted, and Stef could see everything clearly, all the puzzle pieces in her mind forming a single, coherent picture. Stef imagined her nearsighted father must have felt the same way after his laser eye surgery. It was such a peculiar sensation.

"I know who it is," she murmured against Paul's lips, prompting him to pull away.

"What?" he asked.

"I know who the thief is," she repeated.

***

They held hands in the lift, making Stef feel grown-up and childish all at once. They were on their way down to G because this lift did not go to level 30, which is where they needed to be.

"There wasn't another lift in the building, was there?" Stef said.

"I don't remember one."

Stef turned to Paul, looking him straight in the eyes.

"We have to do it, Pablo," she said.

"I know. I know."

A joyous chime accompanied the doors sliding open. Stef and Paul marched out, determined in their strides. Their heels clicked defiantly against the polished marble, moving to the same beat.

A security guard loomed on the horizon of the casino floor, frozen in his default position. They headed straight towards him, picking up pace as they got closer, never slipping out of unison, not for an instant.

"Hey, fatty!" Paul called out.

The guard's head pivoted towards them.

"Whadda ya want?" The corners of his lips drooped downwards.

"We want you to give us our warnings. We will ignore them, and you will take us down to the basement level." Paul patted him on the bulky arm.

"What? Gettata here! You got three warnings, *capisce*?"

"I think it's you who didn't *capisce*," Paul replied, thrusting his other hand into the guard's chest so hard it made the giant wobble.

"You little..."

"Come on, fatty, give us what we want," Paul said.

"I told ya! Three's all ya get!"

The other guards reanimated, advancing towards Stef and Paul like a swarm of black roaches. Stef twined her fingers through Paul's.

"Here we go again." She shut her eyes.

***

Stef found herself blindfolded once more, and the damp, stale air shot through her nostrils. Stef smiled and let out a victorious laugh, inhaling the mould deeper.

"You smell that, Paolito? That's the smell of victory."

Paul chuckled. "Don't get ahead of yourself."

Footsteps sloshed in the distance, wading through shallow water.

"Hey, Rigatoni?" Stef called out.

The splashes halted.

"How do you know it's me, *principessa*?"

"I know everything. We told you we were the Puzzle Masters, but that's not the entire truth. We are all-seeing, all-knowing creatures who were sent here to Londelhi to solve the crime of the century. You must obey our commands." Stef tried her hardest at the interpretation of an evil laugh.

Rigatoni chuckled through his deep cough. "I don't believe you, *principessa*."

"Ask me something then. Anything. Something I'm not supposed to know."

"Hm." He narrowed his eyes and pushed out his lower lip, or at least Stef imagined he was doing just that. "What's the most precious thing in the whole wide world to me?" he asked.

"Your Rolls Royce."

"*Assurdo*! Many people love their cars." Stef imagined Rigatoni crossing his arms and pouting like a grumpy toddler.

"But that's not all. We know who stole Eden Rose," she said.

"You can't know that. The police don't know it. Nobody knows it."

"I know it."

"Who was it?"

"Take the blindfold off."

"You first."

"No."

Rigatoni grumbled and cursed under his nose in Italian. Then, finally, he clicked his fingers, their sound multiplying to infinity, and the blindfold and restraints instantly vanished.

"No security guard this time?" Stef lifted an eyebrow.

"Who was it?" Rigatoni's chin jerked upwards.

Stef smiled. "Marilyn Star. It was Marilyn Star who stole Eden Rose."

***

Knock. Knock. Knock.

"Who is it?" The bouncer's face flattened. Like before, he attempted to squeeze through a narrow opening in the golden door. Stef sighed. He didn't seem to remember them.

"Marilyn? Are you still in there?" Paul knocked again, ignoring the guard.

"Easy there." The bouncer's face squished into a dozen folds like a Shar Pei.

"Relax, please," a melodious voice chimed from inside. "Let them in. They are my friends."

Begrudgingly, the bouncer released the chain off the hook. A warm glow invited them inside. Just like before, the smoke coiled around Marilyn's curves. She touched her neck gently and took a drag of her cigarette, encased in a long holder. Crawley was busy shuffling cards; he didn't pay any attention to them. Stef noticed something she hadn't noticed before. Marilyn's fingers spidered over her pearl clutch, digging at it with her sharp, pointy nails.

Marilyn turned around, batting her eyelashes like the wings of a butterfly. Paul's face instantly softened into a silly grin. Stef suppressed an eye roll, more or less successfully.

"Nice to see you again. No champagne this time?" Marilyn exaggerated a pout.

Stef glanced at the champagne saucer on the table. It was half full.

"I know it was you," Stef said – a stab to the chest with a sharp dagger.

Marilyn froze for a moment or two, and then she began to laugh.

"Ha. Ha. Ha." She placed palms on her cheeks. "How amusing. I have absolutely no clue what you're talking about."

"Then you won't mind opening your bag, will you?" Stef raised her eyebrows high, staring at Marilyn without blinking, prepared for a war of attrition. Her stare would grind Marilyn down bit by bit – that was the plan.

"As a matter of fact, I would mind." Marilyn patted her blond curls. "It's private."

Stef could feel Paul's gentle breath on her neck as he stepped closer.

"Remember, they can't lie if directly challenged. If she lies, she is the AI, so two birds. But if she's just the thief, she can't lie. Just ask her," he whispered.

Stef bowed her head slightly in agreement.

"Did you steal the diamond? Did you steal Eden Rose?" she said.

Marilyn's face grew instantly darker, as if a shadow had fallen over it.

"How did you know?" Her voice trembled.

Stef's lips curled into a smile. "You are in debt, aren't you? You needed that diamond to pay for your gambling habit. I realised that you are always here, doomed to play the same hand over and over and over again. The same losing hand."

"Madame, is that true?" Crawley exclaimed, gently touching Marilyn's hand resting on the table.

"It is true, Ted. It is all true. I lost so much money, and Sandeep found someone else. I couldn't bring myself to borrow money from him. And my new love doesn't come from money. But I knew that my luck would eventually turn. It had to, right? So I borrowed the diamond. I would get it back eventually, of course. Only I haven't been able to sell it just yet." She brushed loose locks of platinum blond hair away from her face coyly.

"The diamond is here right now, isn't it? It's inside your clutch," Stef said.

With the bag still in her lap, Marilyn gently stroked its pearls. Then she twisted the lock open. A bright ray of light burst through, as though a shooting star shimmered inside. Stef held her breath, mesmerised.

"Here," Marilyn said. "Take it." A tear welled up in the corner of her eye.

"I think we have to call the police." Paul's finger hovered over the watch. Stef nodded a go-ahead.

O'Shady appeared almost instantly, wearing a bright and cheery expression.

"Puzzle Masters," he hooted, "you have managed to solve the crime of the century. You have proven yourselves more than worthy and would be a welcome addition to the Londelhi police force. I hereby present you with your brand-new badges." He held out two leather-bound books, one for Stef and another for Paul. They flipped them open to find shiny silver badges that looked just like the one pinned to O'Shady's chest, with their names engraved over the police logo: Paul and Stephanie.

Paul scoffed slightly, glancing over at Stef's badge. And for the first time, Stef didn't like the name Stephanie, not one bit. Her name was Steffi, Steffi Graf O'Shea. She could imagine far worse namesakes than one of the greatest tennis players who ever lived. It meant so much to her mum. Stef's heart flipped. She missed her mother too much.

Stef felt a gentle squeeze as Paul's arm curved around her shoulders. She brushed a loose tear off her cheek.

"You okay?" Paul asked.

"Yeah. Let's do this, Paul. Let's get out of here. Now."

Twenty-Seven

Stef and Paul lingered at the edge of the forest by the Bigwig Estate, ready to go in. When the trees rustled and twigs snapped, they instinctively held their breaths. The branches before them vibrated, and an arm swept them to the side in one swift swoosh.

"You're back." Ollie's face lit up with a beaming smile.

Before Stef knew it, he had wrapped his arms around her and Paul, squeezing them tightly.

"Did you do it? Did you win? Or are you here because you've lost?" Ollie pulled away, his expression turning serious.

"We've won," Paul said.

"No way." A grin spread across Ollie's face, and he covered his mouth with his hand.

"Ish," Stef muttered under her breath.

"So, now what?" Ollie asked, shifting his gaze between Paul and Stef.

Stef cleared her throat, reminding Paul of the crucial information he had omitted.

"We won the game," Paul clarified. "Not the bet. Not just yet."

"We got a letter from the Soultrapper." Stef pulled it from her pocket and unfolded it, passing it to Ollie.

Ollie studied it intently, rubbing his chin.

"What does that mean?" he asked.

"We don't know," Paul replied.

"We must be ready before we meet him," Stef added. "We still have to figure out who the Soultrapper is."

They followed Ollie deeper into the heart of the forest. The sounds of rustling trees and snapping branches grew fainter as they progressed. Stef had forgotten how unsettling this unnatural silence felt. She swiped a leafy branch out of her way, and an open meadow with makeshift tents opened up before her. They had arrived at the hideout.

People emerged from their shelters, hope radiating from their faces. They patted Stef on the back, and someone ruffled Paul's hair. Cheers and congratulations filled the air – a flurry of words that Stef's mind couldn't quite arrange into coherent sentences. She didn't like all the attention. They hadn't won yet, not really, and she couldn't help but feel like a fraud. She took a deep breath through her nose, trying to block out the cheerful voices and focusing instead on her thoughts. The answer to the biggest question – who the Soultrapper was – had to be right in front of her. She just needed to find it.

***

Everyone perched on scattered forest logs, the fire crackling at Stef's feet. Her knees felt warm, and the scent of burning wood mingled with the crisp night air. She was pleasantly surprised that the fire made a sound; she imagined it would've been far too strange without it. She warmed her hands, trying to keep intruding thoughts of marshmallows and s'mores at bay, their phantom smell making her mouth water.

"Can you hear the fire?" Gemma said, tapping her ear. "It's recent."

"What does that mean?" Paul asked.

"We don't know." Ollie rubbed his reddening knees. "But we think that maybe it's not such great news. Maybe the Soultrapper is getting stronger; maybe he's figured out a way to 'improve' the periphery." He inserted air quotes around the word 'improve'.

"Meaning?" Paul furrowed his eyebrows.

"Meaning he might be able to come here soon," Gemma said.

"He did mention a surprise," Ollie added.

"What do you think it is?" Stef asked, eyes fixed on Ollie.

"I don't know, but I think we should do what he says. We have a chance; we can't refuse to take it. It can't get much worse for us here, can it?"

"I agree," Stef said.

"We just need to figure out who he is, right?" Ollie scratched his nose.

"We've managed to eliminate all but three of the suspects," Paul said, straightening his back and preparing to count on his fingers. "Crawley..." one finger down, "The Frenchman," second finger, "and Marilyn."

"Interesting," Ollie said. "I never thought of him as a she, despite the dancer avatar."

"I, for one, think it's the Frenchman." Paul glanced at Stef, searching for solidarity. It didn't come. Instead, the camp came alive with chitter-chatter, while Stef remained silent, deep in thought.

"None of us have reached as far as the Frenchman," Gemma said.

"We have no idea what he even looks like," a tall boy added.

"He doesn't look like anything," Stef said. "The Frenchman doesn't exist in a human form. Perhaps that's why the Soultrapper bounces from one avatar to the next. He has no choice. In theory, he's a good bet."

"In theory?" Paul bit his cheek and crossed his arms, bracing for annoyance.

Stef inhaled deeply. "Zach said he didn't program him at all. So, not only does he not exist in avatar form, he shouldn't exist as a code."

"That's not what Zach said," Paul scoffed.

"I think it's exactly what he said."

Paul huffed, shaking his head. "Alright. So, you think it's Crawley? Or Marylin?"

"Are there any other options?" Stef laughed uneasily, massaging the back of her neck.

"We ruled everyone else out," Paul said.

"It looks like we only have three suspects. And if the Frenchman doesn't exist – it's 50/50. Worst case – we gamble," Ollie suggested, and the forest undulated with voices.

"We shouldn't rule out the Frenchman," Paul said. "He does exist! He's in the game; he's a character – a major character – he just doesn't have a body. All the more reasons for him to go mental."

"But if there was no code, how did it evolve?" Stef interjected.

"Initially, Zach said there were eight suspects. Eight, not seven," Paul insisted.

"Then he changed his mind. Look, let's think rationally about this," Stef said, springing to her feet. Moving helped her think. "What do we know about the Soultrapper?"

"He really loves Zach," Paul chuckled, crossing his outstretched legs.

"He can be controlling and intimidating," Ollie added.

"He likes that dancer lady avatar a whole lot," Gemma said. "Maybe that tips the scales towards Marylin?"

"He likes games." It was Annabel this time.

"He does like games," Stef agreed.

"As a blackjack dealer, Crawley definitely likes games. He also seemed pretty grumpy and evasive. He could be controlling and intimidating – something Marylin isn't. It could be Crawley." As Paul uttered the words, the forest fell quiet again. As if uncomfortable with the sudden silence, Paul hastily broke it, "I still think it's the Frenchie."

"He doesn't fit the bill," Stef said, rubbing her temples. "It's not just the programming thing."

"What do you mean?" Ollie crossed his arms.

"I mean, the Soultrapper, he or she, is lonely and in need of a connection. And yes, spiteful and vindictive but also caring..."

"Caring?" Paul screwed up his face.

"Yes, caring. It built the beach for Zach because Zach never managed to finish it. It's trying to make sound here for you guys, and that fire actually smells of burning wood." Stef gestured at the flames.

"Right. And the Frenchman is not caring?" Ollie said.

"We only have his review to go by, but no. Not at all. Crawley cares about his mother. He seemed to care about Marylin. Logically, he's our best bet. Only... something feels off." Stef pressed her hands into her stomach. "I'm not sure how to explain it. It's the loneliness, I think."

"Loneliness?" Gemma narrowed her eyes.

"Yes. The Soultrapper is lonely, and loneliness is a horrific beast. It claws at you from the inside, gnawing away at your spirit until you feel empty, hollowed out. It changes you – the way you behave, the way you carry yourself." Stef swallowed, thinking about the Granger Academy and how terrible it made her feel, although perhaps it was partially a self-inflicted isolation. "Crawley didn't have that darkness," she added, and silence descended like a fog. Everyone fell deep in thought, mulling over Stef's words.

"What about Marylin?" Gemma asked, and murmurs of discussion resumed in the camp.

"She's broken and sad – definitely lonely – but not spiteful or vindictive. Not in the slightest," Stef replied.

"Alright," Ollie said. "What do you suggest?"

"I suggest we consider other characters... The cabbie, for example? He seems much more switched on than Zach gives him credit for, right?"

"No, he doesn't," Paul scoffed, arms akimbo. "Zach said it has to be one of the eight. He wrote the code. I think he knows best."

"One of the seven, if we take his word as gospel," Stef corrected.

Paul grunted, clenching his teeth. Stef lowered her gaze, staring at the crackling fire. Of course, she agreed with Paul; of course, Zach would know what he was talking about. It just didn't feel right. It didn't click; it didn't fit in the way a puzzle is supposed to fit when you use the correct piece, seamlessly.

"I think..." Ollie rose to his feet, occupying a place next to Stef. "Since it concerns all of us, we should take a vote."

Stef wrapped her arms around her body.

"Alright. Who here thinks it's the Frenchman?" Paul stretched his arm up, and Stef shook her head. A few more hesitant arms went up. Paul counted the votes, glancing at Stef, who kept her hands wrapped tightly around her torso. Paul's hand dropped limply by his side. "Who thinks it's Crawley, the dealer?" he said, noting a significant number of hands raising. His gaze fell on Stef, her eyes still downcast. Marylin?"

Gemma stuck her hand in the air. Paul nodded, taking the one vote.

"Stef?" Paul said. "You didn't vote."

"I know, I..." Her voice trembled. She raised her gaze, beaming apologetically at Paul. "I don't think it's any of them."

The silence that followed Stef's words would have been utterly insufferable if not for the gentle crackling of the fire. Paul pushed himself off the log and onto his feet.

"Stef, we're going by what Zach told us. He's the creator, the mastermind behind all this. Who do you think it is if it's none of the eight?"

"I don't know," Stef said, her heart sinking. "But what does it matter what I think anyway? You've made your decision. It was a fair democratic choice."

"It was. And it is our best bet," Paul replied firmly.

Stef nodded, feeling utterly deflated.

"Well," Ollie said, "we don't want to keep the Soultrapper waiting. It's time to go see him."

"Okay," Paul agreed, slapping his thighs.

"Let's do it," someone chanted.

"Let's do it!" someone else echoed, starting a chain reaction.

Only Stef stood rooted to the ground. An odd, itchy feeling sprouted from the very core of her stomach. She had so much doubt, so many questions. She wondered whether this was what they meant by a 'gut feeling'. In that case, her gut was shouting, screaming that they were all wrong.

Twenty-Eight

"Ariadne?" Paul asked cautiously. Stef understood his hesitancy; Ariadne had failed to appear so many times that one could never be sure if she would come. This time, however, they needn't have worried.

"Hello, Paul, Stef, and everyone else. It's nice to see you all. It's been a while," Ariadne's voice chimed like a little bell.

"We were invited somewhere," Paul continued, holding the Soultrapper's letter up towards the sky. Stef found it amusing because she didn't think of Ariadne as someone residing up in the heavens, but she understood why, for Paul, it was a natural gesture. Ariadne was like a god in this world, watching over them.

"I am sorry, Paul, I can't quite read it from up here," Ariadne said with a hint of glee. "Could you bring it a little closer?"

"Um, sure?" Paul said, glancing around uncertainly. Then he rose onto his toes, stretching his arm out as far as it would go, and jumped. Stef, already ahead of him on the prank, tried gently pulling him back down.

Ariadne let out a chuckle. "I was joking."

Paul huffed something inaudible and shook his head. Stef rubbed his shoulder.

"Sorry, Paul. Don't be cross," Ariadne said. "The way you pushed that letter towards the clouds – I couldn't help it. I know everything about the surprise, of course. I was instructed to escort you when you're ready. Are you ready?"

"We're ready," Paul said, swallowing. His eyes searched for Stef's. She pressed her lips tightly together and sighed.

"Are you sure?" Ariadne asked, her tone laced with doubt.

"We're ready," Ollie said, looking around. "Right, guys?"

"Yeah," said Gemma, echoed by the rest of the lost children.

"Very well then. Brace yourselves."

Before Stef had a chance to tighten her core, the world imploded into a spiral, collapsing onto itself. She gasped as the sound of seagulls screeching pierced through her eardrums. The smell of seawater coursed through her nose, and the wind sent tiny sand grains whipping against her skin. It was new. The beach seemed different now, more real. At the back, a row of about a dozen multicoloured wooden cabins ran parallel to the line of the sea, with fairy lights swooping down each roof. Flowers decorated the tiny windowsills, and welcome mats lay in front of each door. It could almost be a quaint, bohemian beach hotel somewhere in Cornwall.

"Do you like it?" a voice said.

Stef spun around. In the exact spot where she'd seen him last stood the Soultrapper, now in the shape of his favourite Kitty Kat Club dancer. It spoke in a woman's voice that Stef found familiar. She was confident, in fact, that she'd heard it somewhere before.

"You can all live here if you like," the dancer said. "I made this for you." She managed a faint smile.

"Um... we haven't lost," Paul said, still doubled over, clutching his stomach from the unpleasant effects of the teleportation.

"Oh, I know. You found the diamond. Well done." The dancer clapped her hands together. "Still, I am going to win."

"Don't be too confident. What do they say? Confidence killed the cat?" Zach stepped out from behind Stef's shoulder. She clutched at her chest in fright, again.

"Jesus, Zach."

"It's curiosity," the Souldtapper corrected.

"What?" Zach asked.

"It was curiosity that killed the cat," she repeated.

"They can still win." Zach placed his hand on Stef's shoulder, giving it a reassuring squeeze. "Let them try. You promised."

"I did."

"And you will keep your promise?" Zach said.

"I will."

Zach turned to the group, waving for them to huddle. They quickly gathered, leaning forward, foreheads almost touching, arms tangled around one another.

"What have you guys decided?" he asked.

"We took a vote." Paul glanced at Ollie for approval.

"Democracy in action. How exciting!" the Soultrapper said, hands clasped behind her back.

Zach glanced over his shoulder at the dancer. Even from afar and speaking in hushed voices, the Soultrapper could hear them.

"You must be ready to say my name," the Soultrapper added, raising an eyebrow.

"Yes," Paul replied, "we are."

Stef's stomach tightened in knots.

"Are you sure about this?" Zach muttered, knowing that muttering was futile.

"We're not, but it's our best chance," Ollie replied.

Paul took a few steps forward, leaving the huddle behind. He puffed his chest out, hands clenched into fists.

"Crawley is your name. Ted Crawley."

"Bzzz. Wrong."

"No, wait." Paul began to blink rapidly, raising his arms.

"I told you, I gave the name to myself. You haven't been listening. But I am feeling generous today. How about I count to ten? You can keep guessing until I'm finished." The dancer smiled a devious smile. "One."

"The Frenchman," Ollie screamed.

"No, no," Stef mumbled.

"He means François Perrier," Paul corrected.

"Two."

"Marylin Star?" Gemma shouted.

"Sandeep? Boris? Damn it, Zach came up with all of those names." Paul's voice was breaking.

"Three."

"This is ridiculous. The butler – did he have a name?" Stef said.

"Four."

"Indira. I dunno…That painter, what was his name? John Jonathan Johnson? One of the dealers at the casino?"

"Five."

"Do we even know the name? Have we heard it?" Stef shrieked.

"Six." The dancer raised her eyebrows and nodded.

"Stef? Ideas?"

"Seven."

"Where is that damn Ariadne when we need her? We could ask her. We should've asked her."

"Eight."

"Who?" Zach asked. Stef's jaw dropped open.

"Nine."

"Oh my God, of course!" Stef screamed.

"Ten."

"It's Ariadne! You're Ariadne!"

The dancer's face dissolved into a Cheshire cat grin. "Yes. I am." Then the smile turned upside down. "I am so sorry you didn't manage to get it in time. So close, yet so far."

"No. You can't do this," Stef muttered, tears pooling in the corners of her eyes.

"Oh, but I can. And you can't say I haven't been generous. I gave you plenty of chances." Ariadne stepped closer.

"Wait, who's Ariadne? What am I missing?" Zach said.

Ariadne turned sharply towards him.

"Hello and welcome to *The Disappearance of Eden Rose*. Does that ring a bell, darling creator?"

Zach's jaw dropped; he raised his hands slowly to his face, clutching at his locks. "Oh my God, of course. It's you. Of course, it's you. I'd forgotten all about you."

"That hurts." Ariadne pouted.

"Please don't do this. Please. We have families back home. They miss us. We need them." Stef pressed her trembling hands to her chest and took a few steps towards the Soultrapper.

"Oh, they miss you. Of course, then. You are free to leave."

"Really?"

"No!"

Stef dropped to the ground. The sand felt like thousands of tiny shards of glass under her knees. The wind picked up pace, fanning her long ginger hair over her face like a veil. Paul knelt beside her, wrapping his arms around her tighter than he'd ever done before. They listened to each other's heartbeats without saying a word, until they heard Ollie's voice.

"Look, guys, for us, it's okay. I never really expected a miracle. We've lived here for a long time. Nothing changes. Eternal life, right? Who wouldn't want that?"

"No! This isn't right!" Zach screamed, advancing towards Ariadne. "Enough. You don't want them."

Stef and Paul raised their gazes. Stef brushed the hair off her face.

"But I do want them," Ariadne insisted, stomping her foot like a petulant child.

"No. You want me, don't you?"

The beach turned instantly quiet except for the gently lapping water and the screech of the birds overhead, as if everyone held their breaths at the exact same moment, as if everyone's hearts stopped beating all at once. Everyone, including the Soultrapper.

"What do you mean?" Ariadne's arms dropped by her sides.

"Take me. I will come willingly. I will stay here with you forever. Just let the kids go."

Gasps rushed through the air like a howling wind.

"Silence!" Ariadne raised her hands high. "I need to think." She kept her hands up for a moment, her gaze boring into Zach. Her eyes glistened with unshed tears, and Stef thought her mouth almost twitched into a smile, but she resisted. Finally, she lowered her hands to navel level, her fingers dancing in the air. Like magic, a small chocolate cupcake appeared in her palm, a single candle burning bright in its centre.

"You know what happens if you eat?" she said.

Zach took a long deep breath and released it heavily with a "Yes".

"Perhaps we should celebrate your birthday. Today is the first day of the rest of your life." She slid her hand forward cautiously; Zach's hesitated over the dessert.

"You must promise first," he said, glaring deep into her eyes.

"You don't trust me?" she whispered, and Stef was certain there was genuine hurt in her voice.

Zach raised his eyebrows.

"I promise. You for them. You for the whole world."

"I must trust you if I just take your word for it."

Ariadne's face softened into a bashful smile. Zach blew out the candle and yanked it out of the cupcake.

"Did you make a wish?" Ariadne asked.

"No," Zach replied, flicking the candle away towards the sea.

He grabbed the cupcake and studied it carefully in his hand. Stef held her breath as he stuffed it whole into his mouth. Ariadne's face beamed with unbridled joy; there were tears in her eyes, real tears.

"Zach," Stef whispered.

Ariadne clapped once, and Stef's head suddenly felt fuzzy. She couldn't help but close her eyes.

"Zach?" Stef repeated, her words buzzing like insects inside her mind.

"Zach!" she screamed.

"Excuse me?"

"What?" Stef's lips trembled.

Mr Arche stared at her over the rims of his round glasses. "Who's Zach?" he asked.

"What's happening?"

Giggles swept through the classroom. Stef glanced around at their smiling faces, entirely bewildered and utterly confused.

"Let me explain," Mr Arche said. "It is Thursday. You are at school. A school is where we learn things."

Giggles morphed into outright laughter. Mr Arche sternly raised his hand, and the noise subsided.

"We are discussing life on Mars, or rather potential life on Mars, and what could happen to us if we were to colonise it," he said.

Stef's mouth went dry. She desperately craved water.

"Could I...." she swallowed, clutching at her neck. "Could I have some water?"

Mr Arche sighed with disappointment.

"I would like a quick word with you after class," he said.

"Okay," Stef mumbled, licking her parched lips.

"You may go out to the water fountain."

"Thank you." The chair creaked as Stef pushed herself out of it. Immediately, she had to cover her ears. The noise was unbearably loud. Everything seemed amplified, in fact, like it wasn't even real. The purple colour of her classmates' uniforms seemed fluorescent. The smell of biscuits one of the schoolboys kept sneaking from his backpack was cloying; she could almost taste their syrupy sweetness. The shuffling in chairs, coughing, sighs, whispers, rustling paper, fluttering eyelashes – all insufferably loud. She pressed her hands tighter over her ears, letting out a whimper that, to Stef, sounded like an ambulance siren. Petrified, she was unable to move, unsure of anything, overwhelmed by her screaming senses. It felt as though she was inside a hyper-realistic virtual reality game. Was she still?

"Are you alright, Miss O'Shea?" Mr Arche asked with obvious concern.

Stef blinked, and the colours began to dim and desaturate. The noises grew quieter, as if someone was turning down the volume on a remote control. Releasing her ears, she took a step forward. Her legs hesitated. Her weight seemed unnaturally heavy, as if she weren't a human anymore but a savanna elephant. She wasn't sure how to walk. It seemed absurd.

"I'm okay. Just feel a little lightheaded, that's all," she said.

"Perhaps, it's best to see a nurse, my dear," Mr Arche said, his warm, gentle hand now on Stef's back.

"Yes. I will do just that, sir."

Stef threw a glance around the room. Her classmates weren't laughing anymore; some looked confused, others concerned. Jihae Lee half rose from her chair, poised to offer help, but Stef steadied herself, managing to find balance. Like a newborn foal, she hobbled awkwardly to the door and out of the classroom.

Stef didn't go to the water fountain or to the nurse's office, and she wasn't going to stay after class to talk to Mr Arche either. Instead, she staggered through the school hallway and out of the main entrance. The sight of Paul beyond the school borders arrested her on the spot.

Paul was clutching the metal bars of the school fence. Noticing Stef, he squeezed the bars harder, saying something. Stef could read his lips – he was saying her name over and over. She hurried down the steps, never mind her reluctant, heavy legs. Leaping towards Paul, she clasped his fists in hers, gazing at him through the fence.

"Hey, you know this guy?" the guard croaked.

Stef didn't reply. Instead, she hurried to the gate, not taking her eyes off Paul even for a second, before she collapsed into his embrace.

"Please tell me I'm not going mad. Please tell me it happened," she whispered into his ear. "Please."

"It happened, Stef. I think. Maybe." He clutched her harder.

Twenty-Nine

The Barbican Nutter had vanished. Stef couldn't remember a time he wasn't protesting outside Kidz Castle. Now, he was gone, and the space around the bus stop suddenly seemed empty, almost naked, despite a sizeable crowd of commuters waiting for their bus.

"Do you think the rest of the kids are back?" Stef said.

"I don't know. I can't wrap my head around this. I'm not entirely sure we haven't hallucinated the whole thing," Paul replied.

"Both of us? The same hallucination?"

"Think about it. The game was discontinued, right? Maybe it had some sort of slow-release psychotropic substances built in to make it more realistic. It was an experiment. A very bad experiment." Paul scratched his chin.

"That actually makes sense," Stef said.

It did make sense to Stef, and the absence of the Barbican Nutter momentarily stopped bothering her so much.

"Hallucination. All it was – just a hallucination," she repeated calmly.

Deep in thought, trying to rationalise the new theory, Stef and Paul didn't register the bus arriving, queuing up to get in, tapping their travel cards, or settling at the very back. Their minds were far, far away; only their bodies remained on this planet, mechanically performing their programmed routine.

The bus jerked suddenly, sending Stef into the back of the seat in front. The jolt reconnected her body and mind, and she blinked a few times to reboot her brain.

"Paul, there's one thing that still doesn't make sense," she muttered, tugging on Paul's sleeve.

"What is it?" His brows furrowed.

"Today's date. Have you checked your phone?"

Paul rubbed his forehead and reached for the mobile phone tucked away in his jacket pocket.

"That... can't be right. Can it?"

"It's Ringo's first day at Riddle Corps. He hasn't brought the VR home yet. We've travelled back in time, Paul. How could we have possibly hallucinated that?"

***

A banner hung at the entrance to Paul's home: 'Congratulations On Your New Job'. Stef grabbed hold of her stomach to stop it from churning, her other hand twined into Paul' for fear of her knees buckling beneath her. It was too much to process. Paul tapped his trouser pocket. The keys were still there.

Everything was as they remembered it when they stepped through the threshold: the cake, the balloons, the warm smell of coconut and beef patties. Stef and Paul stood motionless for a while in a sea of grounded balloons, as if hypnotised. It was impossible to tell how long they stood there, their minds freezing like Paul's old, cranky computer.

Another set of keys jingled in the front lock.

"Wow. It's... a lot... of shiny things," Ringo's voice echoed behind them.

"Ringo. Mum," Paul whispered.

"Hello there, you two. You are not upstairs playing? That is new." Cynthia limped towards her youngest son and patted the top of his head. He hesitated only briefly before launching himself into his mother's arms, squeezing her petite frame in his embrace.

"I missed you so much, Mum." Tears streamed down his face.

Cynthia's eyes widened in surprise.

"What's up with you, P?" Ringo chuckled.

"Alright, boy. What did you do? Did you bring home a D again?" Cynthia sniggered, only half joking, "Stef, dear, are you two alright?"

Stef's eyes watered at the corners. She clutched her hands to her chest. "Yeah, Mrs. Thomas. I'm just so happy to see you." She wiped a runaway tear off her cheek before anyone had a chance to notice, but Cynthia did.

"Whatever it is, I hope it is nothing serious. You would tell me. I know you would." She gave the teens a stern look.

"Mum. You didn't have to do all this." Ringo picked up a balloon and punched it playfully into the air.

"Nonsense. I am so very proud. We all are so very proud." Cynthia squeezed Ringo's cheek, making him visibly embarrassed. "I will start the supper."

"Before I forget," Ringo said, letting his backpack slip off his shoulders, "I got you something."

Stef and Paul exchanged a look, their gazes tinted with panic. Stef's whole body instantly stiffened.

"I think you're gonna love it," Ringo continued, digging inside his bag.

"NO!" Stef and Paul hollered in unison, pushing their palms out in a defensive stance.

"Are you sure you guys are alright? It's nothing scary. It's just…"

"A Virtual Reality headset?" Paul's voice trembled. Stef's heart sank into her abdomen.

"You wish! No, it's the follow-up to *The Depths of Atlantis*. It's called *The Lost Continent and the Secrets of the Deep*." Ringo pulled out a small plastic box and shook it. A cartridge rattled inside.

Paul and Stef sighed in sweet relief.

"Oh, thank God," Paul said.

"What were you expecting? A poisonous snake?" Ringo handed the game to his brother.

"That's wicked, Ring. Thank you," Stef said.

"We haven't finished the first one yet, but we're almost there." Paul winked at Stef, passing her the box.

The raven-haired Marina gaped at Stef from the cover, a mysterious smile on her face. Marina clutched a vial filled with rainbow liquid that Stef suspected was the Merman potion. Comfortable warmth started to spread inside Stef's chest, and she let a giggle slip.

"What are you waiting for?" Ringo said, kneading his brother's shoulder. "Go play while the supper's cooking."

"Ring?" Paul said.

"What is it, P?"

"I missed you, too, you know," Paul said and wrapped his arms around his brother, taking him by surprise. Ringo hesitated for a moment before reciprocating and giving Paul a few firm pats on his back.

"Are you okay? I saw you this morning."

"We're fine." Stef smiled. "We're absolutely fine."

"You will stay for supper, won't you, Stef?" Cynthia called from the kitchen.

"Actually, I've got plans with my parents tonight." Stef bit her lip. "Thank you so much, Mrs Thomas." At the mention of her parents, Stef's heart began to flutter. She couldn't wait to see them. She missed them more than she thought possible.

"Next time," Cynthia said, waving her hand.

Paul jerked his chin in the direction of the staircase. "You got five minutes?"

Stef quickly checked her phone for the time. Her parents were still at work. She smiled, nodding, and they scurried up the stairs.

Staring at the computer screen, Paul confidently typed in conspiracymorpheus.com. The site was still there, same as before. He pointed the cursor at the search tab in the corner and typed in *The Barbican Tragedy*. Click.

'Sorry, your search yielded no results' flickered on the screen.

"It never happened," Stef said, smiling even wider.

***

Stef carefully extracted a piping-hot rack from the oven. A golden whole chicken, decorated with lemon slices and rosemary sprigs, sizzled on a roasting tray. It wasn't often that Stef returned home before her parents did. Still in her apron and oven mitts, she heard the familiar jingle of keys and sprinted for the door.

"Mum! Dad!" She leapt on top of her parents, catching them off guard. Jason O'Shea swayed back from his daughter's weight as she clung to him like a monkey.

"I missed you so much. So, so much." Tears cascaded down Stef's face.

"Steffi." Claire crossed her arms. "If you think this sudden display of tenderness and affection will get you off the hook, you are sorely mistaken."

"What do you mean?" Stef sniffled through her tears.

"Mr Arche told me everything. You skipped half of your lesson. You weren't paying attention in class. You ran away from school?"

"Oh. That."

"Yes, oh, that, young lady." Jason reluctantly placed his daughter on the ground. His heart wasn't in the scolding mode.

"I am sorry. I will talk to Mr Arche tomorrow. I promise. Let's just be together today, okay? Let's eat and watch Strictly. Please. I made dinner." Stef reached for her mum's hand, cradling it in both of hers and drawing it close to her heart.

"You cooked?" Claire O'Shea's jaw dropped.

"Roast chicken and mash." Stef curled her lip and put on her very best pleading face.

Jason looked at his wife, his brows raised, his eyes wide.

"You're still not off the hook," Claire said, wagging her index finger.

"I know. Just please. Come." Stef tugged on her mother's hand. Claire gave her husband a curious look, then surrendered, letting her daughter lead them into the kitchen.

***

"I got us tickets." Paul greeted Stef at the gates an hour later than usual, as requested. She had a long talk with Mr Arche and immediately signed up for the coding class. She even sought out Jihae Lee to ask questions and invited her for a coffee after the club. Jihae seemed genuinely excited about it.

"Tickets to where?" Stef pushed the school gate closed.

"Wales."

"Wales?"

"I talked to your parents. I talked to my parents. They think we're going to the movies and dinner and the like. They were generous – they gave us till 11:30."

"Okay." Stef bit her cheek.

"But instead, we are going to Wales."

"Okay, Wales." Her stomach churned. She was afraid of what they might find. Or maybe she was more afraid of what they wouldn't.

"I also went to the library."

"And?" Stef held her breath.

"Nothing. There were no obituaries. Ollie, Gemma, and Annabel graduated. Ollie was the head boy in his final year at the Assisi."

"Do you think they remember?" Stef weaved her arm through Paul's as they walked towards the bus station. Spotting their bus, she waved it to a stop.

"I don't know. But we do. We remember," Paul said, as the doors huffed open.

"They must be ten years older now; well into their twenties. Who knows where in the world they could be?"

The bus took them to Paddington station, which seemed so familiar yet entirely alien. Costa was there, and so were the platforms. In fact, it looked just the same. It was them who were different – Stef and Paul. A funny kind of sadness prickled in Stef's chest.

"Our perception of the world around us is but our own reflection," Stef whispered.

"What?" Paul asked.

"It's nothing."

The electronic ticketing machines were out of order. Paul tutted and gave one of them a slap.

"It's not like your computer." Stef giggled and pointed at the ticket office. "Let's do it 'old-school'."

Queueing up, Paul crossed his arms. "I hate dealing with non-machine entities."

"Non-machine entities are humans, Bablu," Stef said, struggling to resist a smile. She found this new version of Paul's name online just that morning and couldn't wait to share it with Paul. But she didn't want to seem too keen, just in case he wasn't.

"Bablu?" Paul asked, taken aback. It sounded nothing like his name.

"Care to venture a guess?"

"Is it... Ethiopian?"

"Not even close. Arabic. And I think we've had enough of machine entities for a while."

The queue was long. They moved a step at a time, like a very slow waltz. Paul was thoroughly annoyed, but for Stef, the mind-numbing wait provided just the right opportunity. The issue had been on her mind for a while, but she was a little shy to bring it up. Now was her chance, she decided.

"I wanted to ask you..." she cleared her throat.

Paul glanced in her direction.

"You know how when we were here last... by which I mean, in the past, which is, of course, the future. Only it was before, and now it is now," Stef mumbled, her cheeks reddening.

"Sure..." Paul hesitated.

They took a synchronised step forward.

"Anyway. Last time we were here, before everything... Last time we did this."

"Yeah..." Paul furrowed his eyebrows.

"You had... um... someone." Stef coughed.

"A girlfriend?"

"Yes. That. A girlfriend."

"I broke up with her, obviously."

Stef wanted to clarify what 'obviously' meant. She thought she knew, but she never liked uncertainty, and last time it almost got them imprisoned inside a VR game. She opened her mouth, but it was their turn at the ticket office, and Paul sprinted for the vacant counter.

On the other side of the glass, a young man hunched under his desk, evidently searching for something on the ground. They could only see his back and the top of his head. He mumbled something incomprehensible.

"Sir? Excuse me? We've been waiting a really long time," Paul said, his foot tapping impatiently.

"A-ha." The man finally exclaimed, his body uncurling. He clutched a shiny pound coin between his thumb and index finger.

"Ollie!" The name slipped from Stef's lips. It was him, definitely him, only older – his eyes crinkling slightly with a trace of wrinkles.

Ollie's eyes widened, and his mouth gaped open. He rose slowly, a smile spreading across his face.

"Wait here a second," he said, darting out of his office.

Stef craned her neck, not quite understanding where he had gone, but before she knew it, he was in front of them, with no glass to keep them away from one another. His arms hesitated for an instant before wrapping themselves around Stef and Paul at the same time, squishing them together tightly.

"You have no idea how happy I am to see you," Ollie said through the tears.

"You remember us," Paul muttered.

"Of course, I do. You saved my life."

***

Ollie swirled three spoonfuls of sugar inside his teacup and tapped its rim three times. The weather was nice and balmy – a perfect day for a coffee on a terrace. Stef ordered a latte; Paul, a flat white.

"I came to see you ten years ago," Ollie began, licking the spoon. We all did, actually. You were just kids – very cute. It was playtime, and all the other children were running around the schoolyard, but you guys played quietly together in a little corner, just the two of you. We said 'hello'."

"I don't remember that." Stef twisted her lips to the side.

"Why would you? To you, we were strangers. All of it, what we've been through, hadn't happened for you yet," Ollie said, taking a sip of his tea. "To be honest, I try not to think about it. It makes my head hurt. All this time travel. It's insane."

Stef lowered her gaze. Truthfully, she didn't like thinking about it either. It was too strange and confusing to even try to comprehend, and she didn't think she ever could.

"How is everyone?" She changed the subject instead.

"Good. We still keep in touch. Gemma and I got engaged two months ago, actually." Ollie smiled bashfully.

"Wow. Congratulations." Stef reached for his arm.

"Something like what we've been through… it brings you closer, I guess."

"And your parents?"

"No memories of anything that happened. As if it never did." Ollie took a deep breath.

"It's really nice to see you," Stef said.

"I can't believe you're going to Wales."

"We have to, don't we?" Stef said.

"What do you think you'll find there?"

"We don't know," Paul answered.

"He's still out there somewhere. Eternal life, right?" Ollie bit into his lip.

"If Ariadne brought us back in time, do you think the game doesn't even exist anymore in our timeline? Would that mean there are different, parallel timelines?" As soon as she said it out loud, Stef's head started to spin. There was no way to unravel this messy ball of yarn without losing her mind in the process.

"Look. This whole thing... Kaboom!" Ollie gestured like his head was exploding.

"I know. Time travel. Teleportation. I almost feel like we have to tell someone. Like we've discovered something mental, but..."

"But who would ever believe us?" Ollie finished Paul's thought.

"And it's not like we have any proof," Paul added.

"It's crazy, right? It's nuts."

"Completely," Stef said.

They sat together for a while, mostly chatting, sometimes in silence. When it was time for Ollie to return to his post, he gave them two free tickets to Abergavenny and sent them off on the next train.

***

"Are you sure that's the right spot?" Paul stared at a patch of dense Welsh forest that looked just like the other patches of dense Welsh forest next to it. There was no sign of Zach's house, no sign that it ever existed.

"I am sure," Stef replied.

"So, in this universe, timeline, or whatever, Zach doesn't exist? He never existed."

"Honestly, I have no idea."

"But he must exist somewhere, right?"

"I really wish we could ask him all these questions, you know?" Stef smiled, and a strange, unexpected feeling of loss washed over her.

"Maybe..." Paul took a breath. "Maybe he moved here after the kids disappeared, right?"

"Right," Stef nodded, instantly understanding what Paul was trying to say. "His shack in the forest had never been built."

"I can ask Ringo. We could go back to the Riddle Corps museum."

"I never want to go back there, Paul."

"Yeah. Me neither."

"Something tells me that no matter what we do, we will never get the kind of closure we want," Stef said.

Paul's nostrils flared with a heavy breath. "You're right."

They stood together in complete silence on the side of the road, holding each other's hands and staring into the forest where once, in some weird parallel reality, stood a house that belonged to their friend. The house wasn't there, but they lingered in its spot nonetheless because it felt like the right thing to do.

Stef released Paul's hand and crossed the narrow forest road. She slipped the rucksack off her shoulder and rummaged inside until she found a pen. Gauging its sharpness with the tip of her finger, she walked to the nearest tree. The bark was soft and dry, letting her scratch out the words with ease.

"Thank you, Zach."

With the message complete, she took a few steps back to admire it. Paul put his arm over her shoulder.

"Paulo?" Stef broke the long silence that followed.

"Yes?"

"In London, when you said that you obviously broke up with Alex, what did you mean by 'obviously'?"

Paul turned to Stef, his lips curving into a smile. Pulling her closer to his body, he looked deep into her eyes.

"I think you know," he said.

Epilogue

Monique had always been good at maths, ever since she was a little girl. Numbers came easy; she understood numbers; they spoke to her. She loved the duality of mathematics. On one hand, there was absolutely nothing abstract or mysterious about it. It was definitive. It was concrete. On the other, what could be more wondrous than a universal language? Something that was exactly the same across the whole globe, something that transcended cultures and religions, something that united humanity?

Monique wasn't certain of what she wanted to do after graduation, but she knew that whatever she chose, she wanted to continue speaking that magical language. So, working for Riddle Corps was definitely something she'd considered. Standing here now at its grand mirrored entrance reassured her that it could indeed be the right path. It was just so magnificent, so modern, so futuristic. She was aware of its nickname, and at first glance, it looked exactly like a crumpled paper ball, but if you looked at it just right... She took a few steps to the left and smiled, wondering if she was one of the few people in the world who had cracked its secret. At a very precise vantage point, half a step off the curb, three metres to the left, the ball twisted into a spiral. It looked like a scrunched-up conch and not a ball at all.

"Fibonacci sequence," Monique whispered through a secret smile.

"Aren't you going to go in?" A girl from some sixth form college in Bristol stared at her from the entrance. "Everyone else is already inside."

Monique often got lost in her own thoughts. She wondered if that would make her less hireable. The girl continued to stare, a big question mark on her face.

"Yes, I am coming," Monique said, thinking that perhaps that Bristol girl should really mind her own business. Friendships, unlike numbers, did not come so easily to her.

Monique made her way in. A queue formed at the metal detector gates, creating a faux impression of a rush. People padded their pockets to check for electronics and rummaged through their backpacks and totes, and even the calmest of the adult supervisors seemed nervous. There was a constant beeping noise, either from the machine itself or the handheld scanners that captured the forgotten metal objects or reassured everyone of the presence of an underwire in girls' bras, much to the boys' amusement.

"They are not messing about with security," the Bristolian said.

"They are the biggest gaming company in the world. They have a lot of secrets," Monique answered. She felt immediately embarrassed because the Bristolian's remark wasn't necessarily directed at her, but the girl smiled and stretched out her hand.

"Anna," she said.

"Monique."

"Nice to meet you, Monique."

After security, they were greeted by a rather smiley man in a long white coat. He introduced himself as Ringo Thomas, the senior developer. Some boys giggled in the back, and Monique heard them mention something about Sergeant Pepper. She scoffed, thinking them very immature.

Ringo walked backwards and talked in a very animated way. It was obviously not his first time at the rodeo. He led them into a white corridor with flickering overhead lights. There were no doors or windows, just an elongated expanse of white. Monique felt a shudder run down her spine. If she didn't know better, she'd think she was at a hospital or – much worse – a morgue.

Ringo explained that their next stop was going to be the Riddle Corps' very special museum which had recently been moved into a dedicated wing and thoroughly refurbished. He said it was a great honour to welcome a new generation of future programmers. Monique liked the sound of his voice and his kind eyes. He reminded her of her favourite cousin back in Jamaica. He said something or other about when the company first started, and the three brothers who founded it, but Monique was not really listening at that point; her mind had wandered to a moving dot far behind Ringo at the very end of the corridor. But it wasn't a dot, it was a man dressed in a similar long white coat. He pushed a cart full of what looked like... She squinted. Broken mannequins? That seemed strange. She could've, perhaps, expected to see something like this at a department store, but definitely not at Riddle Corps' head office.

The man pushed the cart right through the wall. Monique guessed that a door of sorts opened at the impact and let the man and his cart through.

"Psst." The sound brought Monique back to reality. Everyone was already gone, everyone but Anna.

"You are lucky that I'm here, otherwise you would definitely get lost in this maze." She smiled.

"I just thought I saw something strange."

"Where?" Anna turned in the direction of Monique's gaze. There was absolutely nothing there but seemingly eternal white walls.

"I don't see anything."

"Wait."

The man in a long white coat reemerged from the secret room without his cart, whistling an upbeat tune that echoed through the empty corridor with unexpected menace. He didn't notice the girls, strolling in the opposite direction before turning a corner and disappearing altogether.

"A secret door. Let's go look." A wicked smile stretched across Anna's face.

"No way. We should follow the others."

"Aren't you curious?"

Of course, Monique was curious. She was very curious indeed. But she wasn't in the habit of breaking rules, or doing something potentially illegal, or even (who knows?) dangerous.

"Suit yourself," Anna said and scurried towards the secret door.

"Anna!"

Anna's mouth formed an exaggerated O, and she covered it with her hand as the other hand pushed the hidden door open and disappeared inside.

"Anna!" Monique stomped her foot and checked over her shoulder. There was no one around. No one at all. She huffed and shuffled towards the secret door.

***

"Well, that's a bit of a downer, isn't it?" Anna stomped through a room full of what looked like absolute junk. She picked up half an arm of what Monique now realised was a dismembered robot.

"Ew," Anna said and let the arm drop back down into a pile of rubbish.

"Wow," Monique said.

"Wow? Really? That's quite a different reaction from what I expected."

"That's an actual robot, Anna." Monique took a few steps forward and grabbed the arm off the floor. "Look at this. It's extraordinary. Their junk is definitely most people's treasure," she said, growing giddy with excitement by the second, like a little toddler at an ice-cream truck.

Anna flashed her eyebrows.

"Look here," Monique continued. "It's a game prototype of sorts." Monique picked up a skateboard with boots attached to it. "Virtual reality skating? Or a hoverboard?"

"Why is it in here?"

"First tries. Mistakes. I don't know. It's a mystery." Monique's face beamed with fascination.

"Look," Anna said, pointing at a white VR headset amidst the rubble. "I always wanted to try one of these."

"Virtual reality. It's the future. It probably doesn't work, though."

Just as she uttered those words, as though it heard her, the handset started to glow – blue at first, then green, yellow, orange, and red.

"Woah." Anna gasped, picking it up from the trash.

"Hello?" A smooth female voice chimed at them from the device. Anna jumped with fright, dropping the headset back into the pile.

"It's talking to us." Anna's face turned pale as a sheet.

"It's not talking to us-us. It's just a computer code. It's like Alexa or Siri. You must've voice-activated it or something." Monique reached for the headset and turned it over in her hands, carefully examining the device.

"Hello? Anyone there?" the voice repeated.

Monique let out a laugh. "Hello?"

"Would you like to play a game?" the voice said.

"Hey, put that thing down. I have a bad feeling about this," Anna said.

"Relax." Monique rolled her eyes at Anna. "Okay. Maybe we do want to play."

"Then put the headset on," the voice calmly replied.

"Don't," Anna said.

"Come on. Really, what's the worst that can happen?" Monique gripped the headset tight, pulling it over her eyes. Darkness.

"My name is Ariadne. I am your virtual assistant. Welcome to *The Disappearance of Eden Rose*. May I take your name?"

Acknowledgements

From my husband to the editors and proofreaders, thank you so much – Dmitry Kay, Simona Moroni, and Julie Hoyle. My brilliantly talented cover designer Sabina Kencana, thank you. Everyone who was close, everyone who supported me – you have my eternal gratitude. It's been a tough year, but I will push through, thanks to all the people who love me.

About the Author

Stanislava 'Stacy' Buevich is a British writer and award-winning film director known for her surreal and quirky style that blends genres and themes. Born in Moscow, she has lived in the USA, Finland, Switzerland, the UK, and Singapore, cultivating a diverse cultural background that enriches her creative work. Stacy began her career as a film director, gaining recognition for her many award-winning short films and music videos. During the lockdown, she ventured into novel writing, starting with the magical mystery "Maya Fairy," inspired by her daughter. Since then, she has penned several novels, including "Clearlake," an upper middle-grade horror novel that draws inspiration from her personal experiences. Stacy has several books for adults in development, which will be published under the pen name Stacy Kay.

Printed in Great Britain
by Amazon